I hope you enjoy reading it as much as I enjoyed writing it.

Andy Johnson

Top of the Mountain

A Story of Love and Success

by

Andrew Johnson

authorHOUSE™

1663 LIBERTY DRIVE, SUITE 200
BLOOMINGTON, INDIANA 47403
(800) 839-8640
WWW.AUTHORHOUSE.COM

This book is a work of fiction. People, places, events, and situations are the product of the author's imagination. Any resemblance to actual persons, living or dead, or historical events, is purely coincidental.

© 2008 Andrew Johnson. All Rights Reserved.

No part of this book may be reproduced, stored in a retrieval system, or transmitted by any means without the written permission of the author.

First published by AuthorHouse 08/25/08

ISBN: 978-1-4208-5493-0 (sc)

Library of Congress Control Number: 2005904019

Printed in the United States of America
Bloomington, Indiana

This book is printed on acid-free paper.

Contents

Foreword vii

ONE: The Story Begins 1
TWO: Getting Acquainted 21
THREE: New Horizons 31
FOUR: Pueblo 47
FIVE: Mileposts 53
SIX: Time Passes 59
SEVEN: Holidays and Family 71
EIGHT: Family Time 85
NINE: Birthday and Church 93
TEN: Wedding Bells 97
ELEVEN: Edith Stays 107
TWELVE: Marriage and Family 111
THIRTEEN: Live on the Oxbow 115

FOURTEEN:	*Family Matters*	123
FIFTEEN:	*New Assignment*	129
SIXTEEN:	*The Axe Falls*	145
SEVENTEEN:	*Rebuilding*	153
EIGHTEEN:	*Marty, Charley and Lulu*	163
NINETEEN:	*Projects*	179
TWENTY:	*Motherhood*	183
TWENTY-ONE:	*Carmelita and Boots*	191
TWENTY-TWO:	*Tom Houghton Retires*	201
TWENTY-THREE:	*Changes*	209
TWENTY-FOUR:	*The Changeover*	219
TWENTY-FIVE:	*Onward and Upward*	225
TWENTY-SIX:	*A New Home*	233
TWENTY-SEVEN:	*School and Home*	239
TWENTY-EIGHT:	*Top of the Mountain*	243

Foreword

Sometimes strange results come from ordinary chains of events. Such is the pattern of this story. George Toland was an ordinary person in many ways, but had made some choices in his early life that threatened to derail his personal future. He'd always wanted, to be in charge of a ranch, the bigger the better. He'd been a member of Future Fanners of America in high school and had gone on to agricultural school in college. His ambitions had driven him to the top third of his class and he'd graduated Magna Cum Laude in Agricultural Management from the University of California at Davis. His rise had begun almost immediately.

An opening for an assistant manager had been available at a corporate owned ranch in Colorado and he'd applied. His academic record had stood him in a favorable light and he'd been hired. A year later, he married the daughter of one of the prominent families of a large corporation in California, a girl he'd dated frequently in college. He settled her on the ranch with high hopes of the beginning of a beautiful life.

Unfortunately, he'd not gotten to know the inner attitudes of Lois Marie Hardesty before he married her and things began to deteriorate almost as soon as they moved into the housing the ranch provided.

The ranch, called the Oxbow, was located in a foothill area west of Pueblo, Colorado and was over twenty miles from any settlement of any size. The ranch took in over thirty thousand acres and was dedicated to raising beef cattle. Lois's initial problem was that she was used to social activities involving parties, ski excursions and other exciting activities that were based on large numbers of people. Ranch life was just the opposite and she didn't like it at all. It wasn't long before she regarded herself as "dying or the vine".

Lois discovered that she was expecting a child after five months of married life and she nearly panicked. What was going to happen to her girlish figure? She pictured herself as soon to be "fat and thirty" and surrounded by a herd, of 'snot nosed' kids that she didn't want anyway. She'd mentioned abortion to George, but he'd managed to talk her out of it. But she'd become more and more dissatisfied with her situation as the date for her delivery approached. Finally;, the day came when she went into labor and after a difficult delivery she viewed the red and wrinkled little form the nurse presented to her. She was not pleased and she told George so.

Arriving home after the birth and days in the hospital, she discovered that she was expected to take care of this new little member of her turbulent family. As time went on, she became more and more unhappy and contributed to George's already unstable life with quarrels and spats over anything and everything. Finally, Lois decided that she would do something to end the whole affair.

The story develops from there!

CHAPTER ONE

The Story Begins

    It was in the early spring of the year 1969 when George Toland, as the assistant manager and financial officer of the Oxbow Ranch was sent to San Francisco to negotiate some of the ranch's financial affairs and he persuaded his wife, Lois to go along. It would give her a chance to see her parents and enjoy some of the social life she had complained that she was missing. He promised that he'd arrange for care of the baby, now three months old. He called an agency in San Francisco that specialized in baby care in hotels for couples in the same situation that he was in. Arrangements were made for a baby sitter to come in whenever he and Lois wished to be gone for any length of time.

    This done, the couple and baby flew in the ranch's airplane up to Denver and caught a United Airlines flight to San Francisco. They picked up a reserved rental car and drove to the hotel where they had reservations. Everything was going smoothly according to the plans George had made. Lois didn't say much in the way of complaints during the trip. Unbeknownst to George, there were two plans unfolding at the same time. His and hers.

    They arrived at the hotel, checked in and were settled into a suite of rooms on the fourteenth floor. George ordered dinner from room service and the couple retired for the night shortly after dinner. George had an early morning meeting with the finance committee and needed his rest.

The next morning, George gathered up his briefcase and started to kiss Lois "good bye". She stopped him with "What am I supposed to do all day?" He said, "Why don't you call the baby sitting service and have one of their people come and stay with Junior. You can go shopping or sight seeing, whatever suits your fancy. I'll call and reserve tickets to one of the shows or a concert here in town and we can have a gala evening of it. OK?" Lois grumped. "I guess." "Love you Sweetheart!" and he was out the door and gone.

Late that afternoon, he called Lois at the hotel to tell her that he'd made the arrangements for the evening and that he'd be back at the hotel within the hour. He got the baby sitter. She said, "Mrs. Toland isn't here. There's a problem and I think you'd better get over here as quick as you can." George exclaimed, "What?" She said, "That's all I can tell you over the phone. Please come, now." She hung up.

Within minutes, George was at the door to his room and, using his room key, unlocked and rushed inside. He met the babysitter in the sitting room and she handed him an envelope. "Your wife's gone." She said. "She left this letter and told me to see that you got it as soon as you came in."

George was stunned. He glanced at the letter and noted that it was addressed to him and sent from a prominent San Francisco attorney. He also noticed a note attached to the envelope. It was from Lois. "Dear George. I've gone home to Mother and I'm filing for divorce, here. I've had enough of living out in the middle of nowhere and I'm through with that. Further, if I never see you again it'll be too soon. I'm not coming back, ever.

I never wanted the baby and you'll notice that custody is given to you in the divorce papers. If you wish to contest any part of this action, feel free, that is if you have that much money you want to spend." The note was signed, "Lois." There was a post script. "Don't try to call me. The servants have instructions to hang up on you. L."

George was devastated. He'd no idea that Lois had planned and carried out such a break. What was he to do? He had business that had to be completed tomorrow. Who was going to take care of Baby George? How was he going to handle everything Lois had left him with? The baby sitter had gathered up her coat and purse. "Mr. Toland, my hours are up and I've got to go. I'm sorry that this has happened, but our service doesn't cover such things and I couldn't stay even if I wanted to. There's formula for the baby in the refrigerator. If you need more, call room service and they'll send up what you need. The baby is asleep and will probably sleep for another hour or so." With that, she disappeared out the door and it closed with a final click. Now, what to do?

The badly shattered husband and father sat down. He got up again, quickly and raided the refrigerator for a soft drink. He needed to think things out. Sipping the drink, he began to do what he was trained to do, sort out the problems and look for answers.

"First, Junior was taken care of for the moment. On second thought, I'd better look at the formula supply." He got up and went to the refrigerator again and found a half dozen bottles of formula in it. He checked the kitchenette and found a small pot and a hot plate he could use to heat the milk. "Good!"

"Now, what about diapers. Check the supply. Ah, yes, here they are. OK, we got plenty for now. I can get more from room service, I guess. I'll ask in the morning. Now, what about clothes?" He checked the baby's suitcase and found an ample supply of everything needed.

"OK, What about tomorrow? I've got that final meeting in the morning and I'm done there. I'd better find a lawyer and arrange for him to answer this divorce filing. I'd better call in the morning and arrange to see one in the afternoon, I guess. Then what?"

'Then what' consisted of a couple of hours of TV and fixing up George Jr. for the rest of the night. The little heir apparent was reasonably easy to deal with and got changed, fed and put back down for the night. That didn't work too well. George Jr. wanted to play! Finally, an exhausted dad got the little boy to close his eyes about midnight and Dad undressed and laid down to do the same. That didn't work out the way he expected and he tossed and turned until at 2:00 AM, he finally dropped off.

Wake-up call came at about 6:30 with a squall from Jr. which said, "I'm hungry, feed me, and oh, yes, I'm wet, too. How about a change?" Dad got up and took care of the immediate problems and fed the little one some baby food on top of the bottle. Things were going pretty well. George put the boy down in the crib with a couple of toys he could rattle and went off to get a shower and dress.

Finished with that, he ordered a breakfast and called the baby sitting service, asking for a sitter at 8:30. He had to be at his last meeting at 9:00, so that should give him plenty of time. Breakfast came and was consumed. The baby was having a good time in the crib, so George left him there for the time being. Finally, the baby sitter came and George briefed her on diapers, formula and everything else she'd need. With that, he left the phone numbers where he would be and departed for his meeting.

The meeting consisted of several decisions that were needed on several projects the ranch had been contemplating for some months. Each was laboriously dissected and taken apart for the managers to look at and make decisions on. Finally, the last one was approved and George was done. He could go on about his business.

He made several phone calls to attorneys he knew of in the city and finally found one that could see him that afternoon at 1:30. He grabbed a sandwich at a local deli and caught a cab to the attorney's office. Finally, he was ushered into the lawyer's inner office and sat down to explain his problem.

The attorney looked at the notice of filing and remarked, "Alright, Mr. Toland, what do you want to do with this? Do you want to just get a divorce, contest, make some kind of settlement or what? I notice that you wife isn't asking for much of anything but out. She hasn't even been definite about the baby except that she doesn't seem to want anything to do with it. However, I don't think the court will accept that and I'd suggest that you decide just what you want to do about his custody and sue for that."

George thought for several minutes. He realized that he was in a serious fix. First, someone would have to take care of the little one night and day, he was too little and too young to fend for himself. There was no one at the ranch that could do that although several of the men had wives that lived there permanently. Unfortunately, they had kids of their own and would be overloaded taking care of another. His mother had suffered a heart attack two years ago and that was no option. Finally, he decided that he had to find a 'live-in' baby sitter somewhere, one that would consent to living on the ranch. His thoughts covered that, too. His job was important, he couldn't very well abandon that. He wanted to keep the little tyke. He was attached to him He was dad's son after all.

George turned to the attorney and said, "I want to sue for permanent and sole custody. I noticed that Mrs. Toland asked for some kind of visitation rights, but I don't think she's serious about it and they wouldn't be in the boy's best interests anyway. See what kind of a deal could be made to get her to let go of that. She hates the ranch, apparently. See if you can specify that all visitation must be conducted at the ranch. Either that, or see how much it would take to buy her out of the idea."

The attorney agreed to look into that and let him know if his presence would be needed at any time during the action. He said it would depend on what Mrs. Toland demanded. George wrote out a check as a retainer and, shaking hands with Mr. Hardin, the attorney, George departed.

George decided that it was time for some concentrated thinking. He'd taken care of the financial problems the company paid him to look after and he'd made arrangements for an attorney to negotiate with his wife, now, he had to solve the big problem. What to do about George Jr.

George dropped into a fast food lunch counter and purchasing a sandwich and a cold drink, he settled at a table in the back of the room. He began sorting through the whole difficulty. First, the solution had to be good enough to satisfy a judge. Judges could be sticklers for children's welfare, especially when the child's residence was out of state. Second, he, George couldn't take care of the baby twenty four hours a day either. He had a job to do at the ranch and he could be anywhere and everywhere during a typical day. The only solution was to hire a live-in baby sitter. Of course, the arrangements would have to be satisfactory to a judge and George thought that could be worked out at the ranch. There were several cabins that were vacant most of the time and the live-in could be put up there. More thought! He could advertise, but that would take time and he didn't have time. He had to have someone he could get right away, even if she were only temporary. Suddenly, he had an idea.

George went back to the hotel and gathered up George Jr. He took the bag of supplies, loaded it with a couple of bottles of formula and several diapers including a disposal bag with them. He put George Jr. in his car seat and went down to the garage where he put everything into the rental car. With Jr. in the back, he started the car down the street. He needed to ponder and think about the problem. After a few minutes, he had a thought and pulled the car into the curb and parked. Just ahead of him, a girl had just slammed the door on a sporty looking Ford Mustang. Her "Get lost, Creep." could be heard clear down the block. She turned and started to walk away.

Suddenly the door of the Mustang flew open and a man in a wild colored jacket jumped out and started after the girl. She heard the door open and started to run. She reached George's sedan and jerked his door open. She slid onto the seat, slammed the door shut and locked it as she cried, "Please, mister drive away, he'll hurt me if he catches me." George looked surprised, but pulled out and sped past the Mustang. The Mustang started to pull out in pursuit, but stopped to pick up the man who'd jumped out. By this time, George had reached the street corner and the girl exclaimed, "Turn here, turn here!" George didn't hesitate; he turned sharply and sped down the block to the next intersection where the girl pointed left. Again, "Turn here!" He turned left and sped down the cross street, then left again. This brought him back to the street he'd been on originally, so he turned right and followed it. The girl kept looking back and finally said, "Good, we lost him," Just, then, the baby started to howl. She looked in the back of the sedan. "What the?" Was all she could say for a moment, then, "Mr. you've got a hungry, wet baby there. Why don't you take me up to Golden Gate Park so I can fix him up?" George said, "How do I get there and why up there?" She told him it was quiet up there and she could take care of the baby where it was secluded and they wouldn't be bothered. She directed him onto the streets he needed to take and they made their way into the park. She said, "I'm Angel. Who are you and where's your wife?" George decided to be a bit cautious. "I'm George and my wife took a hike as of yesterday. Now, I'm left with my son and a job in Colorado." Angel hesitated, then said, "That's tough. How are you going to take care of this baby?" George turned into the park and found a place to stop the car. He said, "Why don't we take care of Junior, now, and I'll explain." "Fair enough." Angel said.

Angel got out of the car, opened the rear door and laid Little George out on the seat. She found the diaper bag and went to work. Little George quieted right down as soon as Angel went to work on him. In a few minutes, he started gurgling and laughing as she changed him and cleaned him up. George watched her deft hands do the necessary ministrations one has to do when a baby is wet, dirty and hungry. He could see that she'd had lots of practice in baby care and that she was enjoying the chance to do it. She cooed and laughed with him. In a few minutes, she'd tucked the dirty diaper in the disposal bag and cleaning her hands, picked him up and brought him up to the front seat. She cradled him in her arms and gave him a bottle from the baby bag. Once she got him started on the bottle, he did just what most hungry babies do. He proceeded to fill his tummy. "Now," she said, "What's this job you mentioned?" George thought about what he should say and decided that he'd be better off by leveling with her. He started at the beginning.

He told of his failed marriage, his job in Colorado and what had happened during the last few days. He said, simply, "I've got to find a live-in baby sitter for him. My wife, now my ex, I guess; she doesn't want anything to do with the baby. He's mine and I'm going to do all I can to keep him. But, if I want to keep him I'll have to show a judge or the child protection people that I have the means to take care of him. Where I am, that means a live-in baby sitter. I make enough to pay a reasonable salary to the right person. Would you be interested?" Angel turned and stared at George. "Was he serious?" She turned to Little George, her vision centered on the feeding baby. Her mind turned to the narrow escape she'd just made. She thought about the times she'd been robbed and of the beatings she'd survived. She flinched when she thought about several incidents where her life had hung in the balance. Then her thoughts picked up on what the father of this tiny babe had said about being from Colorado and having a job there. Was this an opportunity to get out of the frightening environment she lived in every day? Angel asked, "Mister, are you really serious?" George assured her that he was. She said, "It a lot better than what I'm doing, now. You saw what happened to me awhile ago. That happens too often. I'm tired of getting beat up by creep's like that one. That's not the first time something like that's happened." George's interest increased markedly. "Now, let me say from the start, so you'll understand. I'm offering a legitimate job. There'll be no hanky-panky involved with this. Do you want the job?" She said, "How much does it pay?" George thought a minute, "I don't know for sure. I guess I'd have to ask how much you'd want." They were stuck.

Finally, George said, "This gets a bit complicated, I suppose. You, see, I'd be willing to pay you a salary, supply your groceries and a place to stay as part of the deal." He hesitated a moment, then said, "How would you feel about $50.00 a day?" She asked, "You'd provide a place to live?" "Yes, you'd have the baby with you all the time, so you'd have to live there at the ranch. I'd have to put you in the house I live in now and I'd have to move into one of the three room cabins. That would put me close to the baby where I could come in and see him every day." This was beginning to be realistic. Again a question, "And you'd furnish my food too?" "Well, you'd probably have to cook for yourself, but I'd supply the groceries, whatever you want within reason." Angel had heard enough. It was worth a try. She exclaimed in a joyful voice, "Mr., you've got yourself a deal! I'm tired of being pawed by drunken customers and a lot of other things. What I've been doing is pure hell and I'm tired of it. What do you want me to do?" "Right now, tonight?" he asked. He thought for a moment, then said, "If you're coming with me, shouldn't we gather up your belongings and things?" She thought for a long moment. "I don't have much and I don't have anybody to tell, except my Mom and she's in Sacramento, so I can write to her. Now, look, George, what I've been doing is purely a hand to mouth existence. I haven't much and most of it is junk anyway. These clothes I have on aren't what you'd want me to be seen around the ranch in and I hate them. Do you suppose we could do a little shopping before we leave here?"

George thought the whole matter over for a couple of minutes then said. "Look, suppose we do this, suppose we agree that as of this minute, you're hired. I'll buy whatever you need as a down payment on your salary. As of now, you are George Jr's baby sitter or caregiver, whichever you want to call it. As his baby sitter, you'll stay in my rooms for tonight. I have a suite at my hotel and there are separate bedrooms in it. You can lock the door on yours. I'm in San Francisco on business for the ranch where I work and I just finished the business I had to do. First thing tomorrow, we'll fly to Colorado Springs and we'll be picked up and flown to the ranch.

Now, if you are serious about doing this, I have a couple of requests that you may not like. First, I know what you've been doing and there are diseases that happen to people in that business. I want you to take a test and make sure you don't have any of those you might have picked up. I can't afford to risk Little George's life. I hope you don't mind and I'm willing to pay the cost of the tests. Is that OK with you?" Angel never hesitated "George, I'm with you on that one. It's not too late to have the tests started right now. Do you have time? I know where there's a doctor's office that does that." George started the car. "Tell me where."

They left the park and ten minutes later, they were in the doctor's office. George explained to the receptionist what they wanted. She told Angel to follow her and turned her over to the doctor with an explanation of Angel's being there. The doctor said, "Good thought, Angel. Just follow the nurse. It'll only take a minute to get the needed samples and you be all through. It takes about a month to get the results back, but they're accurate." Within fifteen minutes, the test samples were collected and the paperwork was done. George paid the fees and they were out in the car again.

George said, "Let's get you some clothes, now and then we can go out for dinner if you like. I think we can find a restaurant that will tolerate little Junior, here. Are you hungry?" Angel said. "Just lead me to it." George went on, "Do you like Italian?" "Yes" "Good, let's see if we can find one downtown someplace." "George, you're alright. Look, forget this 'Angel' stuff. That's a name that I use so people think I'm somebody. My name is Sarah Elizabeth Mills. You can call me Sarah or Liz, or even Elizabeth if you like." George promptly said. "I like Sarah. Is that OK.?" Sarah nodded. "That's fine with me."

George found one of the large clothing stores and a parking lot to put the car in. They took little George with them and went into the ladies department. A half hour and several fittings later, Sarah had a complete new wardrobe. As she left the store, everything she wore was new including a traveling outfit and two house dresses. She also had a couple of pairs of Levi's for wear around the ranch along with the necessary shoes and stockings. While she was getting the clothing, George had visited the luggage department and collected a suitcase and a traveling bag. Finally, they packed everything but the clothes Sarah had been wearing into the suitcase and the traveling bag. These were stowed in the car. The clothes George had found her in were carefully folded up and chucked into a convenient trash can.

George found the Italian restaurant he'd been looking for and they sat down to a delicious pasta feast. Sarah hadn't said so, but it became obvious that she'd not eaten that day and possibly the day before. Finally, George asked her, "Sarah, why did you decide to accept my job offer?" Sarah took her time about answering. "George, that baby did it. He looked so helpless. When I heard him cry I knew he was hungry and wet. I can tell just by the way a baby cries what its problem is and I couldn't resist. I was so fed up with what I've been doing that a little boy like him just melted me. I've had a lot of experience with little ones his age. I used to baby sit a lot when my father left my mom and we had to take care of ourselves. I hope you're never sorry you asked me." Sarah's eyes got shiny with tears as her emotions came to the surface. George was a little embarrassed. He said, "Sarah, sorry I made you cry. Just let me say this, I'll keep my side of the bargain if you'll keep yours. Promise?" She reached her hand across the table. "Promise!"

The meal finished, Sarah picked up the baby and George paid the bill. In a few minutes they were on their way to the hotel. Between them, they got everything upstairs and into the suite. Junior was ready for attention again. He'd not been fed since they'd been in Golden Gate Park. Sarah took him into the bathroom and gave him a bath, then dressed him for bed. George heated some formula and got a can of fruit for him. Once he was dressed, Sarah fed him, burped him and laid him down for sleep. It only took a minute and he was out for the night.

George noticed something significant. Little George was often fussy when his mother had worked with him. She had nervous ways of doing things with him and he didn't like it. In contrast, Sarah was relaxed around the baby boy and he enjoyed her being there. It took George a little while to notice the difference, but he could see that Sarah liked what she was doing and that the baby was comfortable with her.

Finally, with Junior in the crib and sound asleep, Sarah and George sat down to unravel from what had happened to them that afternoon. Sarah said simply, "I can't believe what's happening to me. When I started out this morning, I never dreamed I would wind up here like this. And with a baby! What's happened almost seems like a miracle" George just laughed. "You think you're the lucky one? I lost my wife and then I had a baby that I couldn't take care of by myself. Now, I've got a baby sitter that loves babies. And that's the best thing that's happened all day. Wait 'til you get to the ranch, I hope you'll like it, there. I do. It's got space and all kinds of things to do and see. I hope you don't mind being twenty miles from anywhere, 'cause that's what you'll be." Sarah laughed. "I'm tired of crowds. I can use some wide open space for a change."

George changed the subject. "Sarah, do you mind talking about yourself?" "Well," she answered, "just so it doesn't get too personal." George started in, "Well, I'll tell you about me if you'll tell me about you. I know what you've been doing up to now, but I'd like to know how you got into it. Do you mind?" "George, that is kind of personal, but I dropped out of high school when my dad disappeared and I didn't know what to do with myself. I had no skills and no job other than baby sitting. That doesn't pay a lot around here. Mom got me into this. She showed me how and men liked a young face. I did alright for awhile, but I hated it. You saw what happened when that Mustang bunch tried to get me to go with them. They wanted something I won't tell you about, it's too filthy.

I'm glad you came along. My Mom got into the business because my father split one day. He just walked out like he was going to work and never came back. That left Mom with herself and me to support and no skills. She hit the streets and kept us alive. I can't blame her, even though I hate what she and I were doing." That's about it, although I want to say that I never got into drugs or liquor. Mom helped me stay out of that. She wouldn't tolerate either one. I have to admit, though, I'm a lot short on formal education. I'd like to go back and finish my high school diploma and learn a skill. I always liked arithmetic and figures. Maybe I could learn bookkeeping." She stopped, then asked, "Now, what do you do?"

George leaned back in his chair and debated where to start. Finally, he said, "Well, I've always liked animals and I liked raising them. I was in the Future Farmers of America in high school and I made good grades all the way through that. I raised several cows and made money off of them, too. Then, I went to the University of California at Davis and graduated with a degree in ranch and farm management. I got lucky and got this job at the Oxbow Ranch two years ago. I married Lois just before I got the job. I met her and dated her in college. She's from an upper crust family. I thought that she was a regular girl when I was in school with her. Boy, was I wrong. She hated the ranch. She wanted parties and lots of people around her. I never did figure out why she went to an agricultural school like UC Davis. She never wanted the baby and she hated the ranch. She left yesterday and went home to her mother. She filed for divorce even before she left town. She left me with Little George to take care of.. Boy, I never figured she'd be like that.

My job on the ranch is about everything, although my official title is financial manager. I keep track of where the money comes from and where it goes. They tell me that I'm good at what I do and I like what I do. The ranch is big enough that we are constantly trying new things to see if we can do what we do better. To me, it's pure fun. I hope you'll like it when you get used to it. Anything else you want to know?"

She said, cautiously, "Well, we're far apart on our education. I hope you won't think I'm a dummy." George responded almost instantly, "Don't worry about that. We've got all kinds of people on the ranch, some that are short on education, but they are sharp at what they do and I've learned to appreciate that in each one of them."

George glanced at his watch and then spoke again. "I tell you what. We've got reservations on a United flight to Denver at eleven, tomorrow. Lois left her return ticket here, so you'll be able to use that. Now, I'm starting your pay as of today. I'm going to pay you for a full week in advance, that's three hundred and fifty dollars. That'll give you some money so you won't be broke." He'd gotten his checkbook out, then he said, "No, wait, I'll go down and cash a check for you. Be right back." He went out the door and hurried down to the lobby, where he wrote out a check for three hundred fifty dollars and cashed it. He tucked the money into his trousers and grabbed the first elevator up. Once in the room, he counted out the money and told her to stash it in her new purse. "Thank you, George, I haven't seen money like this in months."

He said, then, "Why don't you get off to bed. I think Little George is down for the night. He'll wake up about six in the morning and I'll get him if you don't hear him. We'll have to move right along, to make that eleven o'clock flight what with the rental car and all. Oh, yes, remind me to change your ticket, too. I'll have to go to the United counter to do that. It's made out to Lois and I'll have to explain why the name change. Never mind about that, I'll take care of it. Good night, Sarah."

The next morning, right on schedule, Little George let go with a blast precisely at six. George was just getting ready to rise when Sarah appeared. She had on a robe that George recognized as one that belonged to Lois. She'd forgotten it in her rush to be gone. Sarah reached into the crib and picked up the baby and kissed him. He simmered down and squealed with delight. Sarah spoke to him. "C'mon, Little George, let's get you put together and fed. We've got lot's to do and you're first in line. I'm going to give you a bath and feed you right now, so here we go." With that, the two disappeared into the bathroom. George went to the kitchenette and got a bottle warming for his son, then laid out his traveling suit for later.

It wasn't but five minutes later when Sarah appeared at the bathroom door and laid Little George out to get him changed and dressed. She turned to George and said, "Your turn, get in there." George responded. "Thanks, I won't be long and his bottle and a jar of fruit are ready for him." "Thanks, Dad, That's going to be a great help." George smiled and went into the bathroom and took care of his morning routine, including shower and shave. Dressed in fresh underwear with his robe over, he reappeared and grabbed up his shirt and suit along with shoes and fresh socks. Back into the bathroom and five minutes later, he came out dressed for the day. He moved over and took the spoon Sarah was feeding with and told her that she could go get ready, too. He finished feeding Little George and gave him his bottle. Once that was accomplished, he set about cleaning out the closet and packing his suitcase. Finally, Sarah ducked into the room she'd used the night before and got dressed for travel. She then completed her own packing, using the new suitcase George had bought for her the day before. The only case left to pack was Little George's and they decided to wait until after breakfast to pack that.

George called down and had breakfast sent up along with a supply of bottles of formula for the little one. These would have to last until they got back to the ranch, which wouldn't be until after sundown tonight.

Breakfast appeared and George invited Sarah to take time out from packing the baby things to eat breakfast. Within twenty minutes, that was done and George called to have the suitcases taken down. He asked Sarah to take Little George down and to wait by the luggage while he brought the rental car around.

In a few minutes, he'd gotten the car and loaded the luggage in the rear. Sarah climbed into the seat and George handed Little George to her and turning, tipped the bellboys.

He got in and started the engine, then drove out into traffic It took them over a half hour to maneuver through traffic and to reach the terminal for United Airlines. George then turned the car in to the rental agency and paid the charges. He and Sarah got the luggage to the check-in counter and George took care of changing the ticket to Sarah's name. Finally, they were checked in and ready to depart.

George picked up the carryon bag and started off for the departure lounge. Sarah followed carrying Little George They made their way down to the United departure lounge and sat down to wait for the flight to be called.. Within a few minutes, the flight was ready and they finally were allowed to board. They'd held back two bottles of formula and felt confident in being able to feed the baby if he got hungry. Four hours later, the DC-6 landed in Colorado Springs and they were able to deplane and claim their luggage.

George put in a call to the ranch and advised them that they had arrived. The ranch told George that the airplane was waiting at the executive terminal and to catch a cab over there. Within minutes, they'd loaded their luggage into a cab and made the transfer to the executive terminal. Their luggage was loaded onto the ranch's utility plane and they were soon airborne for the Oxbow. An hour later, the airplane touched down on the ranch airstrip and George announced, "We're home."

As soon as the airplane came to a stop in front of the hangar, everyone clambered out and George started unloading luggage. Just then a station wagon drove up and the driver picked up the luggage and began loading it in the back. Sarah picked up the baby and got into the back seat. George slid into the right seat and told the driver, "Bill, this is Sarah Mills. She's going to be Little George's baby sitter. Lois isn't coming back, so let's take Sarah and the baby to my house and unload her luggage there. Then you can put my suitcase in the little cabin next to the house. I've got some moving to do and I'll be sleeping in the cabin." Bill had a mystified look on his face, so George explained. "Lois filed for divorce day before yesterday and abandoned the baby. She decided that life on a ranch just isn't her style." Bill exclaimed, "She did what?" "That's right, she's gone!"

"I hired Sarah to take care of Little George and she's agreed to live here and do that. She'll need room to do that, so I'm going to put her in my house and I'll move into the cabin next door. That way I can see my son and be a father to him and Sarah can still have her privacy. Sarah can have the run of the ranch the same as your wife and the others do. I want her to be happy here and that's the best way I can see for her to be comfortable with this 'lonely place' as Lois so aptly described it."

"Things are going to be a bit mixed up for the next little while as long as the divorce suit is going on and while Sarah is getting used to being here and putting up with the way we do things. I plan to take her around so she can see the ranch and get acquainted. I hope you can persuade your wife and the other wives to be friendly so Sarah can feel at home, here."

The station wagon pulled up to a rambling dwelling set among some trees. A white picket fence surrounded the house and flowers and shrubs completed the setting. Sarah spent a minute or two looking at the house and commented. "Is this where I'm going to be?" George smiled and asked, "Like it?" Sarah said, simply, "I'm going to love it. I never had it so good, not since I was a little girl. Can I see the inside?" George just laughed. "Sure you can. Just go right on in. It was a little disorganized when we left, but I'll clear out what Lois left and get it out of your way. Little George's stuff is all there except for formula. There may be some of that in the fridge, but I'd make some fresh instead. The formula's instructions are on the refrigerator."

Sarah hadn't been listening. She was in a dreamy state. She couldn't believe such a house was going to be hers as long as she wanted.. She picked up Little George off the car seat and walked up to the gate and opened it. She stood a moment gazing at the house, then her voice broke. All she said was, "Home." She moved forward and opened the front door and disappeared inside.

George picked up her luggage and the baby's bag and followed her in. He found her standing in the living room with an awestruck look on her face. "I can't believe I'm going to be living in a place like this. This is heaven. I'm sure of it. With that, she wiped the tears from her eyes and moved on to put Little George down in his crib. It was time to get on with the needs of this baby that would be a part of her life for more years than she could imagine.

George set the luggage down and went into the kitchen. He found the bottles and makings of Little George's formula and made up several bottles of it. In the meantime, Sarah had changed the baby and was ready to feed him. She sat down in a rocking chair and tempted him with the bottle George handed her. The baby needed no coaxing. He went after it with his usual gusto. Sarah looked up at George with a contented look. "George, this is wonderful. I'm going to like it here!" George just smiled. "I'll be back over in a few minutes and help clean this place up. Lois wasn't much for housekeeping."

With that, he went over to the cabin that would be his quarters for the foreseeable future and started setting up housekeeping for himself. He emptied his suitcase and hung up and put away as best he could. He'd have to bring bedding over from the house, but he could do that later.

Back to the house, George started picking up the loose items he found in the living room and put them away. He then went into the kitchen and started clearing up the mess that Lois had left when they departed for San Francisco. He gathered up the dishes from the table and put them in the sink. He ran hot water and dashed in some soap, then began the job of washing the dishes, rinsing them and putting them in the drainer.

That done, he picked up and put up; leaving the room a lot neater than it had been. Just then, Sarah came in and told him she'd take care of the rest. George said that he was sorry the house was in such a mess. Sarah just smiled. "George, don't worry about it. I've seen worse and I'll have it cleaned up by tomorrow. Let's get your cabin set up so you can sleep there tonight and we can get things in order tomorrow. I'll take care of the baby tonight and worry about the house when things start to settle down. Don't worry about me. I'm happy to have such a nice house for a change. You wouldn't believe the dumps I've had to live in for the last six years."

George suddenly thought of something he'd not asked Sarah about. "How old are you, Sarah?" Sarah gave him a quizzical look and said, "I just turned twenty one last month. I feel like I've lived half my life already, though. I hope the second half will be better than the first one." George smiled and said quietly, "It will be, Sarah. I'll see to it."

With that, he turned to a closet and began taking out bedding to move over to the cabin. Sarah followed him into the cabin and, taking the sheets from him, started making up the bed. She checked the bathroom and made sure he had soap and towels. She went back to the house and did the same for the bedroom she was going to use. This took nearly a half hour as Lois had left it in the same condition as she'd left everything else.

Finally, the closet was cleared and the bed made. Stray clothing had been carried out to the living room and stacked on the couch temporarily. "At least," Sarah thought, "I won't have to sleep in a mess." She turned to George and bid him good night and ushered him out the front door. It had been a long day.

CHAPTER TWO

Getting Acquainted

The next morning came in a burst of sunshine and a loud wail from Little George. Sarah roused out of a sound sleep, wondering where she was. Everything was strange. For a second, she wondered how she'd gotten there. Suddenly it all came back with a rush. She rose up, put her feet over the edge of the bed, then went over and picked the baby up. She gently rocked him in her arms for a moment, then slung him over her shoulder. "There, there, Baby, it's alright. I'm here. C'mon. I'll get you cleaned up and fed; then we'll see what's going on around here."

She laid him back down, changed him and got a bottle ready to satisfy his hunger cravings. That done, she took care of her own needs and started putting breakfast together. Once she'd eaten, she got a shower and got dressed for the day. Rough clothes were the best for what she envisioned her activities would be, so she got out the new Levi's and a flannel shirt and put them on. Next, Little George got her undivided attention. She fed him a jar of cereal and then got him ready for his bath. She smiled to herself as she went about her ministrations with the tiny little fellow. "You're getting to be a regular little mother, aren't you." she said to herself. "Not only that;

you're liking it a lot, huh!" She admitted to herself that she'd not been this satisfied with herself for a long, long time.

Finished with feeding she put the baby back in the crib and gave him a pacifier she found on the table in the room that had been his before his mother had left. Sarah thought about that and decided that the crib was going to be moved into her room 'til the little tyke got bigger. She liked having him close and he liked her being around. She watched as she moved around and noticed that his eyes followed her everywhere she went. "Isn't that something?" She thought, "I took care of a lot of babies, but I don't remember one that liked me as much as this one does. I'd better see if I can get a book of what a baby does as they get older. There's a lot I don't know about them except that I sure like this one. If I'm going to take care of him, I'd better know how. I wonder if any of the mothers here on the ranch would have a book like that. I'll ask George."

Just then, a knock sounded on the front door. She opened it and met George's eyes face to face. "Good morning Sarah. How's my son this morning?" She smiled, "Come in. Why don't you ask him?" He grinned, "I'll just do that." He went in and picked up the baby and started talking to him. Little George reacted to his dad's attention by waving his arms and kicking his feet. It was obvious that he welcomed his dad's interest. George turned to Sarah, "What's for breakfast?" She got a surprised look on her face. "I didn't know that was part of the deal. You never said." He got a sheepish look on his face. "Yeah, I didn't, did I? Maybe we ought to talk about that."

Sarah moved over to the kitchen table and sat down. George followed and seated himself with the baby cradled in his right arm. "I guess I should explain how things work around here. Our hands are hired at a salary per month and 'found'. That means that we pay them so much a month and furnish meals and housing. For most of them, that means a common meal three times a day. Everybody comes in for breakfast, lunch and dinner. Most of the hands are housed in a common building called the bunkhouse; that is except the foremen and married couples. They have private housing like this and like the cabin I moved into." He went on to explain where that left him since his wife had departed.

"I have a choice as far as meals are concerned. I'm a manager and I can either eat at my house or I can eat at the common dinner table at the cook shack. My problem is this. Little George is my kid and he needs to know that I'm his dad. That's the way it should be and that's the way I want it. I love that little boy and I want him to know that I'm always there for him if he wants me. He's awful little now, but as he grows, he'll be sitting up to the table and I want to be where he can see me and talk to me if he wants to. See what I mean?" Sarah just nodded. George went on. "Now, again I have a choice. I can cook my own meals here if I have time, which most of the time, I don't, or I can get you to do it if you want to. The trouble is, that makes you sort of a housekeeper instead of just a baby sitter. I don't know if you want to do that or not. In the press of things during the last few days, I didn't even think about it."

Sarah thought for a time, mulling the thing over in her mind. Finally, she said, "Well, it looks like you're giving me the choice of being a housewife of sorts or not. I'd have to think about that. You see, I've never been one and I don't know if I want to be or not. See what I mean? First, off, I'm not much of a cook. Doing what I did before, I never had to be. I just haven't done that kind of thing before. Do I want to be? I don't know. Why don't I try it for a few days and if you don't die of food poisoning or something, I can decide if I want to keep on. Now, as far as being a dad to Little George, you're welcome to come in any time. Just don't forget to knock before you come in, so I can make sure I'm ready for you."

"Deal!" George hastened to say. "Now, have you ever made pancakes before?" Sarah shook her head. "OK, I'll show you. It's easy." George got out everything, mixed up the batter, explaining as he went. He heated the griddle and pointed out that the griddle needed to be oiled or greased before pouring on the batter. Otherwise, the pancake would stick to it.

Then, he poured on a little batter, letting it spread and told her to wait long enough to cook on one side, then turning it over, repeated the process on the other side. "Now, you try it," he said.

Sarah moved in and copied George's moves. Suddenly, smoke began to curl up from the pancake. "Quick, turn it over," George cried. She did so, but it was too late. The first side had burned and the cake had splattered over the entire griddle because she'd flipped it too hard. She muttered, "Darn! OK, what did I do wrong?" George just laughed. "You aren't the first one to do something like that. Never mind, that one isn't ruined, a little extra syrup will make it taste alright." He used the turner to remove it from the griddle, handed Sarah the batter again and said, "Here, try again." She did and this time got the pancake turned before it burned. She turned it gingerly so it didn't spatter. She exclaimed, "I did it. Look at that!" George just laughed. "OK, now, how about frying a couple of eggs to go on top of the pancakes." Within thirty minutes, they'd put together a passable breakfast with coffee and hot chocolate. George patted Sarah on the back and said, "Good Job."

Breakfast done, George started off for the ranch office to explain the results of his conferences in San Francisco. Sarah stopped him as he reached the front door. "George, what do you want me to do with all of this stuff Lois left?" George thought for a moment, then said, "I'll have a bunch of boxes sent over. I want you to sort out everything that belongs to the baby and set it aside. Then, if you have time, gather up everything of Lois's and pack it in the boxes. I want to get everything of hers cleared out of this house. It's yours to live in and I don't want anything of hers around." Sarah just said, "Alright, George, I'll take care of it. I haven't much right now, but I suppose that'll change." George just nodded and said, "See you later." and headed for the office..

Sarah settled down to cleaning up the breakfast mess. That done, she looked around and found that there was a baby swing in the nursery. She got the baby out of his crib and put him in it to keep him busy and where he could see her as she went about doing the needed housework.

An hour's work and most of the mess Lois had left was taken care of. There was a knock at the front door and when she answered, there was a man there with a number of cardboard boxes. "George sent these over for you, ma'am. Where do you want 'em?" "Just put them here in the living room. I'll take care of them later. Thanks for bringing them." She finished the house cleaning and remarked to herself. "Now, the house looked more presentable. I feel better about it at least." She gathered up some notepaper she'd found and sat down to write to her mother.

"Mom," she wrote, "you'll never guess what happened to me or where I am. I've got this job on a ranch in Colorado. I'm taking care of a three month old baby that got deserted by his mom. It's a sad story, but I'm his baby sitter. It's so beautiful here, there's mountains and hills everywhere." She went on, describing how she'd gotten into the whole thing and how glad she was to have gotten away from San Francisco. She ended with "I love you, Mom." She addressed an envelope and sealed the letter in it, put a stamp on it and set it aside.

Just then, a knock on the front door interrupted her thoughts. Opening the door, she found herself confronted by a stout woman dressed in slacks proclaiming, "I'm Barbara. Bill's my husband and he told me about you, so I thought I'd come over and get acquainted. Welcome to the ranch. Is everything alright?" Sarah wasn't used to this kind of introduction, but she smiled and said, "Hello, I'm Sarah. Won't you come in?" She stood aside and Barbara walked in, glancing around the room as she came. "My, you got things cleaned up in a hurry. I hope you'll excuse me for saying so, but Lois wasn't the best housekeeper around here."

Sarah remembered her manners and asked Barbara to sit down and "Would you like a cup of coffee or tea?" "Tea for me if you don't mind." It took a minute to put water on to heat and set out cups with the tea bags. Sarah sat and asked Barbara to tell her about the ranch and the people on it.

Barbara started off with, "Well, there're four families living here. I've got four kids, Marney Sowles has two and Laura Williams has three. Mine are the oldest, all in school. Marney's are all under three and Marie has one in school, the other two are under school age." She went on to describe some of the social activities that went on, then turned to the inevitable subject; Lois's departure.

"Lois always was quick to let everyone know that she didn't like the ranch. It was too lonely for her. She constantly reminded us of that. She was a party animal and wanted excitement. She didn't like kids at all and the feeling was mutual. My kids thought she was mean. They wouldn't even talk to her if she asked them a question or asked them to do something. I think that George didn't spend enough time getting to know her before he married her. I think she sank pretty low to desert the baby the way she did. I hope you get along with Little George OK. He's actually such a sweet baby."

That struck a responsive chord with Sarah. She said, "Listen, that's the nicest baby. I just fell in love with him the moment I first saw him. I'm really lucky with him. He's so easy to get along with, almost never cries about anything and so easy to please." The conversation went on for a time and finally, Barbara rose and said, "Well, I've got to get back to the house. Is there anything I can do for you?" Sarah thought for a moment, then said, "No, not now, but I'm sure there will be. I've got so much to learn. I'll let you know if something comes up. Oh, by the way, where do you go shopping when you need things, groceries, clothing, etc.". Barbara said, "Well, we usually go into Pueblo or Colorado Springs. That isn't too often, they're so far. If you go, you want to be prepared to spend the day. That's what we do. Well, gotta go. See you later. Thanks for the tea." With that, she walked off toward her own house on the other side of the ranch compound.

With Barbara's departure, Sarah got busy packing Lois's belongings. With a break for lunch and tending to the baby, she got done putting everything in the boxes that had been brought by 2:30. Busy morning and busy afternoon. She decided to take a rest. She put Little George in his bassinet next to the couch where he promptly fell asleep again. She got a pillow and propped her head up on the couch. Within minutes, she was sound asleep. Little George was close by, so if he woke and needed her attention, she would be aware of him.

A firm knock at the door woke her up an hour later. It was George. He said, "Just thought I'd check and see how you're doing. Little George giving you any trouble?" Sarah responded, "Not a bit. I don't understand Lois at all. He's such a good baby. I'm almost against letting him grow up, he's so good." George just chuckled. "Never mind, you'll find out all about him before long. I remember my aunt's baby. He was a good little guy until he got to be two. That's when the fireworks started. She said she thought she had a different little boy for a little over a year. Just stick around, you'll see." All Sarah could say was, "I don't believe it."

George looked around the room and said, "I see you got all of Lois's stuff packed. I'll have a couple of guys come over and take it up to the warehouse for storage. Oh, you know what? I better have somebody inventory all of it. That way, when this divorce comes up, we can deliver all of this with the inventory and she can't say we've kept any of her stuff for ourselves." He started out the door with, "I'll send the fellows over to pick up the boxes and get them out of the house." Then, he turned back. "Oh, by the way, I want you to make up a list of everything you think you'll need. Bedding, dishes, cooking utensils, and anything else. All those items that are here now, belong to Lois. As soon as we can replace them, I want them packed along with everything you've already boxed up. I don't want anything of hers left here. It all goes back to her and she can do whatever she wants with it. Don't worry about the furniture. That belongs to the ranch. It's not hers."

With that said, he disappeared out the door again, leaving her to rub the sleep out of her eyes and wondering when all of this confusion over the departed Lois would end. Sarah's eyes swung around the room and came to rest on the tiny form just beginning to stir in the bassinet. Suddenly, she had a strange emotion rise within her being. She decided she was glad that Lois had abandoned Little George. Sarah suddenly felt very possessive. Little George was hers. He was her responsibility and she embraced the reality of it. This was something she'd never experienced before. It was new to her, but she liked the feel of it. She wondered how she'd feel as he grew older.

The baby woke and needed attention. Sarah got him up and changed him, fed him a bottle and some fruit. She looked out the window and realized that the afternoon wasn't over yet and dinner time was a couple of hours away. Why not put Little George in his stroller and go for a walk. She'd seen little of the ranch complex so far. If she was going to live here, she'd feel better if she had some idea of what was here. She found a three wheeled stroller parked outside the door; put the baby in it and away she went.

Sarah got no further than the horse barns. There were several men working with a small bunch of horses, training them for use as saddle horses. She became so interested in what was going on, the sun went down and the horses were turned into the adjoining pasture before she realized the day was over.. Sarah said, "Little George, we'd better go back to the house and get some dinner and get ready for the night. What do you say?" Little George didn't say anything. He'd fallen asleep again and was dreaming baby dreams. No help from him.

Sarah found enough in the cupboards to make a meal for herself. She put the baby in the baby swing and proceeded to feed the baby the rest of the fruit she'd started to feed him earlier. Finally, she changed him, dressed him in his sleeper suit and put him down in his crib. She gave him his bottle and when he'd had enough, burped him, then gave him a pacifier and turned him on his tummy. He promptly did what he usually did. He went to sleep.

The evening was a bit early for going to bed, so Sarah sat down in the rocking chair and began to think about what life was going to be like doing what she was hired to do. From the day's experience she could see that taking care of Little George wasn't going to tax her available time. Keeping the house wouldn't either. She was determined to keep the house spic and span, but it wasn't big enough to be overly demanding. She'd work out a schedule for doing all of the household chores along with cleaning and washing. She still could see the probability of a lot of spare time. In other words, it would be easy for her to become bored. What to do about that? Suddenly, she thought of something she'd considered several months ago in San Francisco. She'd been attracted to computers. She'd been in a computer store and had played with the keyboard for a bit. Then a clerk had showed her how to do different things, use the internet and other things. She'd had to put her ambitions aside after a time, though. She'd not had enough money or a place to even think of having her own computer. She remembered her disappointment over that. Now, she wondered; "Can I afford one on my babysitting salary?" She decided to ask George about it.

CHAPTER THREE

New Horizons

The next morning, George came in for breakfast and Sarah dived right into the subject of the previous morning. "George," she said, "I've decided that I'm going to try to cook your meals for you. It will probably be awhile before I'm very good at it, but I'll get Barbara and maybe one of the other wives to help me learn. That is if you are willing to put up with what I cook. What do you think?" George was taken aback by this declaration. He remembered that he'd mentioned it the day before, but he'd put it aside because Sarah hadn't seemed too interested. He asked, "What changed your mind?" Sarah put it simply, "I got to thinking about time and I realized that I've got more time than I need to keep busy, so I decided that I'd try to cook your meals. Think about it and let me know if you want me to try it." Sarah turned the conversation to another subject. "George, I've been thinking of something else, too. Especially since Little George isn't very active, yet. Even with cooking and housekeeping, I'm going to have quite a bit of time on my hands, so I thought I'd like to get a computer and learn to use it. I want to learn book keeping, too, and I thought I might combine the two."

George thought about that for several minutes, then said. "Look, you'll have earned enough by the time you've been here a month or so, that you can buy a new computer if you want. I know there are all kinds of learning programs available. All you have to do is find them. They're in the internet, lots of them. Now, another subject. Have you made up a shopping list for the things you'll need for the house, yet?" Sarah admitted that she hadn't. "Well, the reason I ask, we're planning a trip to Pueblo for supplies day after tomorrow and that would be a good time to get a lot of the things you need., especially groceries, dishes, utensils, etc. Why don't you ask Barbara to help you with it? Or Marney. Both of them would be glad to help." Sarah agreed to get organized on that activity later that day and vowed she'd be ready. "Oh, yes, one more thing, Little George has a doctor's appointment that day, too. So, can you be ready to take him for that? Marney knows the doctor and where the office is. She'll show you.

"One last thing. I got hold of my attorney in San Francisco and he told me that the judge that's been assigned to the case has asked that we submit a report from the Colorado State Welfare Services, children's division. The judge wants to know the circumstances of Little George's care. Who you are, what kind of care is he getting etc. We can submit pictures and statements from others living here, but they will probably send a social worker to interview you. I don't want you to be scared of this, but I do want you to be careful. The less they know of your background, the better. If they ask specific questions answer them as briefly as you can, but answer them honestly. We will have an attorney present if they decide to ask you any questions. You have rights and he'll see that they aren't violated. Remember this! I want you to take care of my son. You're doing a better job than his mother ever did and I don't want to have any trouble with the courts over this."

What George told her scared her more than a little. She was afraid of what would happen if the authorities pried into her past and branded her as being unfit to care for the baby. Finally, she determined to give out no more information than was asked for and she remembered that the only arrest she'd had was when she was fifteen and would be protected from scrutiny since she'd been a juvenile at the time. Further, she'd not been convicted of the charge. She also remembered that she'd made much of the money she'd earned by watching the young school aged children of a friend of her mother's while the mother was out on the streets. That had been when she and her mother had lived in Los Angeles. Maybe, her activities were obscure enough that her past wouldn't be a problem. She crossed her fingers and hoped.

Finally, she got into bed and put the lights out. Sleep didn't come easy, there was too much on her mind. "What am I going to do tomorrow? Well, Marney was going to Pueblo with the excursion for supplies. Maybe I should go and meet her and get acquainted." She'd only got as far as the horse barns in her explorations the day before. Why not explore some more. She thought some more about the computer. "As soon as I can afford it, I'm going to get one." She thought, "That's definite., I'm tired of being a dummy! It's time I learned some things." With that, she dropped off to sleep and didn't wake until Little George decided that she should.

She reviewed her plans for the morning in her mind and laid out a schedule. The baby came first. Always! Bath, change, dress and feed. She'd found that he responded to that regimen best. Once clean, dressed and fed, he was happy for awhile. That gave her time for her own morning preparations. Then she could go ahead with George's breakfast, house cleaning and other necessary chores. She'd have to wash today. She was about out of clean things herself and Little George went through clothes like a cyclone. Well, she could get that started as soon as George was out the door after breakfast. Breakfast! Good heavens, what am I going to fix for him this morning? Bacon and eggs with buttered toast. She'd seen that numerous times in restaurants. Appealing and nourishing. Maybe some jam for the toast if he wanted it. "Good. Now, let's get started."

George came in dressed for the day and sat down to a mug of hot chocolate. Sarah put two pieces of bread in the toaster and went on to frying the eggs and bacon. The trouble was that there were lots of ways to fry eggs and different people wanted them fixed different ways. She'd not thought to ask George how he liked his.

Sarah suddenly realized that her eggs were getting hard, so she scooped them out of the pan and put them on a plate. Just then, the toast popped up and she buttered it and stuck it on the plate, too. Oh, oh. Forgot the bacon. She put that in the pan and turned it once before putting it on the plate with the eggs. George never said a word, but slowly ate what he had before him. Once done, he cleared his throat and said. "Sarah, could I talk about breakfast for a minute?" "Sure, George, what is it?" "Please, I don't want to hurt your feelings, but there are some things you need to know. First, you should always ask how people want their eggs cooked. Some like them soft, some like them hard or well cooked and others like them somewhere in between. Mine were hard and I like them over easy. That means that when they are partly cooked, you flip them over and cook them a little more. OK? Next, always warm the plate before you put eggs on the plate. Otherwise they get cold and there's nothing worse than cold fried eggs. They get greasy that way. Now, about the toast. I like my eggs on top of the toast, so what you do is to start the toast a little ahead so it pops up before the eggs are done and gives you a little time to butter the toast. Finally, you should put the bacon in to fry with the eggs. That way it gets done about the same time as the eggs and it's hot, same as the eggs. Think you can do that?" Sarah felt badly that she'd not done very well and said so. "Na, na, na, na, na. Don't worry about it." George said. "You gotta learn sometime and you didn't poison me." He just laughed. "Sarah, you are doing just fine. Keep trying. It'll get better, I assure you." He rose and grabbed his coat. "Well, I gotta go. See you for lunch. Why don't we have a tuna salad or something like that? It's gonna be too warm for anything cooked." He picked up Little George and kissed him. "Bye Pumpkin. See you all later." With that, he was out the door and gone.

Sarah got out two more eggs and asked herself. "How do I like my eggs? Soft and straight up!' She put a plate in the toaster oven and turned it to "Warm". She put two pieces of bread in the toaster and pushed the handle down. Finally, she broke the two eggs into the pan and added the bacon. As soon as the toast popped up, she buttered it. She got the warmed plate out of the toaster and put the toast on it. She scooped the eggs and bacon out of the frying pan and plopped them onto the toast. Her eyes got a little moist. She said to herself. "Why didn't I think of all this the first time? Well, better luck next time."

She gathered up the dishes, washed and dried and put away. She gathered up the soiled clothes and started the wash, taking care to read the instructions on the machine and adjusting the water temperature and level. She thought about that after the problems she'd had with breakfast. Think first, then go ahead.! Finally she attacked the house and put it in order. The baby was awake by this time so she decided to go and visit Marney Sowles and get acquainted with her.

Sarah loaded the baby in the three wheeled stroller and walked around the residential street to another house that had a small sign on the fence that said. "Sowles". She let herself through the front gate and knocked on the door. In a moment, it opened to reveal a young pleasant faced woman dressed in a house dress and holding a broom in her hand. "Hi. Can I help you?" Sarah laughed and introduced herself, giving her title as "Little George's baby sitter". The lady replied "I'm Marney Sowles. Won't you come in? I was going to come over yesterday but I had a sick baby and I couldn't leave. She just had an upset stomach, nothing catching."

Sarah liked Marney within the instant. She came across as a cheerful relaxed, easy going mother who was delighted to have company. She put Sarah at her ease immediately. "Won't you come and sit. I was just sweeping up a mess my two year old made out of breakfast. I'll be right back." She disappeared for a moment and came back without the broom. Sarah had taken Little George out of the stroller and parked him in her lap as she sat down on the couch.

Marney remarked, "I think he is the cutest baby I've ever seen other than my little one. I never could understand why Lois had such a hard time with him. He's really a good baby, I thought. How are you getting along with him?" Sarah agreed with Marney's statement. She said. "I'm not very experienced with tiny ones like him, but I just love the little guy. He's easy to keep."

Sarah went on. "Marney, I don't know how much has happened with George and this little one. I don't want to say too much, but I think you should know why I'm here and Lois is gone." Marney responded. "Well, I know that she didn't come back with George, but I don't know why or if she's coming back at all. Whatever you tell me is safe with me. I don't gossip, but I'd like to know what to expect and what has happened in case someone else asks. If I know, I'll know what not to say."

Sarah said simply, "Well, apparently, what happened was that Lois has never liked the ranch and she didn't want a baby in the first place, but went ahead and had it. When she got to San Francisco, she went to a lawyer and had him file for divorce, then gathered up her stuff and went home to her folks. What I can't understand is why she left the baby. Mothers just don't usually do that."

Sarah changed the subject slightly. "Marney, I took this job on the spur of the moment, but I'll tell you this. I wouldn't trade the job for anything right now. Little George is such a sweet baby, I almost wish he were mine. Sorry, I can't help it. That's the way I feel."

Marney put her hand on Sarah's knee and patted it. "Sarah, I am a mother and I know just how you feel. You'll do just fine with him. George came by this morning and told me that you are going in to Pueblo with us tomorrow for the baby's three months check-up and would I show you where the doctor's office is. His appointment is for 2:00 PM tomorrow afternoon. I've got an appointment for Peggy Ann at 1:30, so we can go in together. This trip is to get supplies. We'll leave here about 9:00 AM, so be ready. My husband, Fred, will take us in. We make these supply trips twice a month. We have about thirty thousand acres in the ranch and it's divided up into six different divisions with a crew running each division. Because we are divided up that way, we supply each division individually, but we buy supplies for all of them and then Fred takes the supplies out to each one the day after we get them back here at the home ranch. That's one of the main jobs that Fred does. He also sees to the welfare of the rolling stock, pick-ups, trucks, company cars, tractors and other odds and ends. He oversees the shop and schedules the needed maintenance. Ranch work is hard on equipment and Fred's on the go all the time."

Sarah was a bit overwhelmed with Marney's explanation of the ranch organization. She made a mental note to ask George more about it when he had a little time. She glanced at her watch. Time to get ready for lunch. She got up and made her excuses to Marney and promised to be ready for the trip the next morning. Marney said, "Glad you came over. I'll see you tomorrow." Sarah put Little George in the stroller and headed for her house.

As soon as she got in the door, she took care of the baby. She fed him a jar of fruit and gave him a bottle. He took half and quit, so she burped him and put him down for a nap. Next she went through the refrigerator looking for sandwich materials. Finally, she was able to make up a couple of tuna salad sandwiches and a small pot of soup from a ready mix she found in the cupboard. She heard George come in and set out the sandwiches along with glasses of milk.

George washed up and sat down, eyeing the sandwiches, then started in. Sarah joined him and the soup and sandwiches were gone in minutes. She then began with, "What do you like for lunch as a rule? I put the sandwiches together from what was here, but I'd like to know what you like, so I can get a supply of it tomorrow in Pueblo." George looked at her in surprise. Lois had never bothered to ask him his preferences for his meals. She'd just put it on the table and he ate what was there or went without. George took time to help Sarah make up a list of groceries that Fred Sowles would pick up tomorrow for her. He remarked to himself that things were improving. He'd not had it so good since he'd been married two years before.

As George got ready to go back to work, Sarah told him that she'd have a list made up of the things she wanted for the house. She told him she wanted to get good things, but not extravagant ones. She'd been put off with the things that she'd packed the day before. She wondered why some of them were so obviously expensive when lesser would be just as useful and wiser with a little one in the house. George said, "I'll take a look at the list when I come in for dinner tonight."

He went on, asking, "What did you do this morning.?" She told him of her visit with Marney Sowles and remarked that she seemed to be a very nice person. She said, "I think I could become very good friends with her. She seems to be an easy person to be around." George told Sarah that Marney was just what Sarah said she was and that her description of her was 'right on target.' With that, he started to bid her 'good night', then stopped. "By the way, do you suppose we could arrange meal schedules so that I can have a little time with Little George before he goes to bed at night?" Sarah stopped, then said, "You're right. Sorry, I forgot. Tell you what, you come just a little earlier and you can play with him while I fix dinner. How'd that be?" George replies, "Sounds good. Let's try it." With that, he disappeared out the door and was gone.

Dishes done, Sarah concentrated on the dry clothes that she'd washed that morning. She folded them carefully and put them in different dressers, Little George's in a brightly decorated one in the nursery and hers in the dresser in her bedroom. She thought about that for a moment, realizing that her life was becoming organized better than it had been since she was a little girl. In spite of the fact that life had taken a different turn for her, she was pleased with it, so far. It was beginning to have a feeling of security to it.

Top of the Mountain

Once the clothes were folded and put away, Sarah sat down and started on the list she'd promised George she would work up. She started with the kitchen and dining area. She'd looked at the dining table and realized that the fancy linen table cloth was Lois's and had been packed. She started with an order for a table cloth. Nothing fancy, just a serviceable table cloth. Next, she listed a set of dishes. Plates, bowls, cups, saucers etc. were put on the list. She made a note to consult with Marney on these items. She realized that she knew very little about what to look for. She'd missed so much of routine day to day life when she was growing up. Hopefully, Marney could help. She thought about serving dishes and cooking utensils, next. Then she thought about cutlery. There again, "Help, Marney, help!" This was getting monotonous.

That area covered as best she could, she took her thinking into the bedroom. All the bed had was a set of sheets and a couple of blankets. She'd need quilts and a pillow. Better get two of each. Finally, she needed a bedspread. She thought she could manage to pick good quality and attractive things for this part of the house.

Next, was the living room. There was enough furniture in the room, but she decided that it needed a stereo with a record player and a collection of soft music. She'd never gotten excited about the modern music that had gotten popular. She decided that the baby wouldn't appreciate that kind of music either. She debated about a TV, but decided to ask George what he thought about that.

Finally, she put the list down and brought her pillow from the bedroom. She laid it on the couch and popped her shoes off. She stretched out and in five minutes was sound asleep. An hour and a half later, she was aroused by a knock on the door. She quickly slipped on her shoes and answered. A lady she hadn't met stood on the porch.

Sarah spoke first. "Hello, can I help you?" "Hi. I'm Laura Williams. I'm one of your neighbors. I just came over to get acquainted and let you know that I'm going to Pueblo with you tomorrow." Sarah brightened up, "Please come on in. I talked to Marney Sowles this morning. She is going, too. We both have doctor's appointments for the babies tomorrow afternoon. Also, I've got to buy a bunch of things to replace the things that belonged to Lois. George is packing that stuff up and sending it back to her, so I've got to buy everything I need to replace it." Laura just nodded her head, "Yes, I knew about that. Silly female. She never did get her head on straight. She had the best deal in the world and a beautiful baby and she takes a hike. I heard about it and I still can't see what in the world she's thinking of. George is a prince of a guy and gets along with everybody. He's really a sharp business man and he'll go places, too. She couldn't see it and she complained every hour of every day she was here! Well, I hope she's happy. She sure never made any points around here." Laura stopped suddenly, "I better shut up. I should feel sorry for her. She had a good thing and I think she's throwing it away." With that, she sat down and said, "Don't mind me, I get diarrhea of the mouth sometimes and I talk too much." Sarah just laughed. "Never mind, I won't say anything. I happen to feel the same way about Lois. I just don't want to say anything around George about it. He's got troubles enough over her." Sarah went on, taking a different tack. She said, "Laura, I'm dumb. I've never had to buy house stuff before. Would you help me pick out good stuff for the kitchen and the bed linen I'll need. I hope we can find all that tomorrow in Pueblo. Is that possible?"

Laura laughed, "Sure, Marney and I'll help you. In fact, it ought to be fun. Lois never tried to be friends with us. Lord knows we tried. She snubbed us so many times, we gave up trying. No, don't worry. Let us help. We'll make this place so comfortable you won't know it. George will think you are a genius." Sarah suddenly realized that she had something she'd never had before. People were trying to be sincere friends. She'd always had to be careful of so called 'friends' before. They were always looking out for themselves first. She hesitated to trust in these three women that had befriended her here on the ranch, but she was willing to accept their friendship if that's how they felt.

She opened the door a little further by saying, "Laura, I appreciate that. If there's anything I can do for you, just let me know." Laura replied. "Well, yes you can. Sometimes I have to do errands for my husband. Would you be willing to watch my two little ones when I have to do that? It's usually not more than an hour or two. I'd be happy to do the same for you if something comes up." Sarah grinned and grabbed Laura's hand and shook it. "Deal! I've been worried that I'd have something like that come up and I didn't know what I was going to do with Little George. That solves the problem." Laura asked another question. "Sarah, do you like to ride horses?" Sarah said, "I don't know, I never rode one. Why?" Laura smiled and explained. "I do. The trouble is, everyone else here, either doesn't or they don't have time. I hate to go by myself. I like to talk with people and being by myself is no fun." Sarah thought, "Well, why not?" She said, "Tell you what. If you'll teach me how to ride, I'll give it a try." Laura was overjoyed. "I know that Marney would watch the baby for an hour or so if we asked her. She doesn't like horses that well and I can never coax her to go except once in a great while. Besides, Barbara is always busy and I can never get her to baby sit. Oh, I'm so glad you've come here." Sarah's feelings were glad ones. Things were working out better every day! She decided there and then that she was going to be happier than she'd ever been. So many new things to see, learn about and people she hoped she could lean on and trust.

Laura rose and said, "Well, I've got to get back. I've got kids coming home from school in a minute and I gotta be there when they show up or I won't have any cookies left." She reached out and gathered Sarah into her arms in a bear hug. "See you later. She turned and out the door she went. "Bye" Sarah wiped her eyes. No one had ever treated her that way before. It took several minutes for her to accept the feelings she had. Finally, she turned and started getting ready for George.

The baby was awake, so she changed him and played with him for a few minutes. He was old enough, now, that he was learning new movements. He'd begun to discover his hands and to kick his legs. She encouraged him by kissing him and tickling him to which he responded by laughing at her and smiling. She admired his big blue eyes. She'd not noticed them before, but now, she did. She realized that he was a pretty baby, usually good natured and likeable. She felt a great gladness rise within her. She was beginning to realize how fortunate she was. Only a few days ago, she'd been on the streets that she had to regard as a battlefield. No one was her friend. She could trust no one. Sarah was becoming a different person and she liked the prospect.

George knocked once and came in. "Ah, there you are, you little scamp!" He picked Little George up and kissed him. The baby just laughed. He liked his dad. George sat down in the rocking chair and continued his play with his son. Sarah couldn't help notice the joy this little boy gave his dad. She tucked the thoughts away in her being and vowed that she'd try to have the baby in a good mood for his dad whenever she could. George deserved that and she would try to see that he got it. She said, "Now, don't get him too excited. I'll never get him calmed down to feed him." George just laughed. "Don't worry, he'll eat if he's hungry. I know that much about him."

Sarah started into the kitchen and then turned back. "I hope you like meatloaf. I found a recipe for it and I made you one. George smiled and replied, "You say you made it from a recipe?" "Yes. I tasted it and it wasn't too bad." He smile, then continued, "Well, good, it's worth a try. What are we having with it?" Silence, then, "Oh, what do you mean?" George grinned, "Well, we usually have a salad or a green vegetable with any main course like a meat loaf. He explained. Sarah gasped, "I'm so dumb. I didn't even think of that. Omigosh, now what am I going to do?" George put the baby down on the floor and came into the kitchen. "Here, I'll show you." He went to the cupboard and found a can of green beans, got a can opener and opened it. He got a small pot, dumped in the can's contents and added a pat of butter, then put the pot on the stove to heat. "Now," he said, "just bring it to a boil and turn down the heat so it'll simmer for, oh, five minutes or so. Put it in a bowl and you're all set. Easy!"

Five minutes later, they were seated at the table with Little George in his swing set to watch. "Meat loaf and green beans weren't bad for a first try." George remarked. "Next time, why don't you ask me what I'd like and we can work out a menu for the meal? Then, if you don't know how to make some part of it, I can help you or you can ask Marney or Laura. They're both pretty good cooks and they can tell you the best way to do something you don't know about."

He turned to Sarah with a serious face. "Sarah, I know where you came from. I know there are a lot of things you don't know about, but, to me, the important thing is that you're trying. Not only that, but you keep trying. That means a lot to me. I'm the one that asked you to do this job and I accepted you as you were. All I want from you is for you to keep on trying and not give up. You're different than Lois was. She wouldn't even try." Sarah wanted to cry, but she felt she shouldn't. She gritted her teeth and asked herself how anyone could be so patient. "Well if he could stand it, she'd keep on learning." She wanted desperately to succeed. And she found that she wanted desperately to please him. Everyone was being so nice to her. She wanted that more than anything.

George picked up the baby, gave him a fatherly hug and said, "Good night, Junior. I'll see you tomorrow. That goes for you, too, Sarah." With that, he picked up his hat and headed out the door. Sarah gathered up the dishes and washed up. Done with that, she picked up a book and started to read, couldn't get interested, put it down and went to put Little George to bed. Having finished that, she got ready herself and put the light out. Sleep came slowly, she'd had an exciting day and it took awhile to clear her mind.

Six o'clock and the baby's wake-up call came just as the sun came up in the east. Sarah then did something she hadn't done before. She got up, changed Little George so he'd be comfortable again and took him back to bed with her. She cuddled him in her arm and talked to him for awhile. His reaction was one of delight. He liked her and he liked the attention he was getting from her. He could sense the love she was communicating to him. Finally, she kissed him and got up to begin her day. Showered and dressed, she took the baby into the kitchen and set him up in his swing where he could see her. She fed him and then set the automatic swing into action so she could get breakfast ready. She'd asked George what he wanted for breakfast and she got out the oatmeal, and boiled enough for both of them. She heard him come in, so she set out the bowls and milk along with sugar, then made up some hot chocolate.

George sat down and stopped the swing. He picked up the baby and held him up high above his head, laughing at him. Little George laughed and squealed as his dad tossed him up and down in his hands. Finally, he set him back down in the swing and started it swinging again.

Breakfast was on and George remarked that the oatmeal was just right, which brought a smile and 'thank you' from Sarah. George went on to outline the events that would take place throughout the day. He said, "Marney told me that she and Laura Williams will be going with you, so you should be in good hands with them. Now, I want you to pick out the things you want for the house. Don't let them push you into something you don't want, like dish patterns and bed clothes. Choose what you like. OK?" Sarah responded with, "Alright, I'll be careful. Now, one other thing, I'd like to buy a stereo and some soft music recordings. I want to get a record player with it and I don't want anything big or fancy, but I like music and I want soft music that Little George will feel comfortable with. I don't like this cheap modern music and I'm only into country western a little bit. What do you think? Can you afford it?" George thought for a moment. "Well, I don't see why not. Here, again, talk to Laura and Marney and see what they recommend for a stereo. Marney just bought one for their house, so she should be up on what's best right now. Well, I've got to get going, so I'll see you when you get back."

With that, he picked up the baby and kissed him good bye, set him back in the swing and was gone.

Little George started fussing and Sarah stopped and warmed a baby jar of fruit and fixed some baby pablum. She picked him up, cradled him in her arm and began feeding him. She'd given him a bottle while she'd gotten dressed and he was getting to a point where that wasn't enough. He wanted solid foods as well. She'd only known him a few days, but she was quickly getting onto his wants and needs. Not only that, but she was getting attached to this little boy more and more.

Finished feeding him, she cleaned him up with a soft damp cloth and burped him. Burping saved 'spit ups' later. She changed him and put him back down in his crib. She had to clean up the house and she wouldn't get him ready for travel to Pueblo until later. In the meantime, he could get a nap.

CHAPTER FOUR

Pueblo

Dishes done, house swept, and dusted, she got herself dressed for the trip and packed baby supplies for the day. Two bottles of formula and some solid foods went into the 'diaper bag'. Sarah was learning to look ahead when traveling with a baby. Finally, 9:00 came and she put Little George in his baby seat for the trip to Pueblo. The truck was there finally and everyone climbed in. The truck was a 'crew cab' model with doors and seats in the rear part of the cab. Sarah settled the baby into the rear seat next to Peggy Ann and climbed in with him. Laura moved in on the other side with a cheery "good morning", leaving the front seats for Marney and Fred Sowles.

Fred turned and bade Sarah "Good morning. We're going to be on rough roads for awhile, so hang on tight. I'll try to take it slow. OK?" Sarah nodded and they rolled out of the yard. Fred was right about the road. Thirty miles an hour was tops because of washboard and chuckholes. Laura just laughed when Sarah asked, "Is the road always like this?" She shook her head. "No, we're coming out of wintertime and the county hasn't got around to grading our road yet. Actually, it's pretty good in the summer time once they grade it. It's gonna take us about 45 minutes to get to paved road, then we'll go on down through Canon City and then about forty five miles on into Pueblo."

Marney joined the conversation, then. "Sarah, Pueblo was known as Fort Pueblo during the war with Mexico. There is still an army depot there, but it's used for a storage point for army equipment. Nowadays, Pueblo serves the ranches and other agricultural interests here about. We go there because we can get more of what we need without traveling all over town to get it. Saves us money that way."

The conversation went on over a variety of subjects including gossip and comments on the scenery as they passed through it. It was nearly eleven o'clock when they slowed for the outskirts of Pueblo. Sarah was awestruck. This city wasn't anything like she was used to. Laura remarked. "There's only about a hundred thousand people living here, so it's one of the larger cities in Colorado, actually third in size below Denver and Colorado Springs." This awed Sarah as she was used to cities the size of San Francisco and Los Angeles, California.

Fred had turned off in the meantime and pulled into a wholesale grocery warehouse. He turned and backed up to a loading platform on the side of the building. He turned to Sarah and informed her that they'd pick up their grocery order here, then, they'd go have some lunch. After that, he'd drop Marney and Sarah off at the doctor's office and go make the other stops he had on his schedule. He promised to be back by two thirty and would wait for them. Marney said, "We do this all the time. It makes it easy for us to do all of these things in one trip and saves us a lot of time and money." Sarah asked, "What do you do if someone needs medical help right away?" Laura chimed in, "We go to Canon City, then. They have a good emergency facility there, but the best doctors are here, so we work our problems that way. Canon City is closer, but the best facilities for check-ups and major medical problems are here."

A bump and a jar of the truck signaled the loading of the groceries and Fred was back. "OK, girls, where are we going for lunch?" Marney and Laura said together, "Turnip Gardens." Sarah got a question mark on her face. "Turnip Gardens? What's that?" Marney just laughed "Don't ask. Just get ready for good food. Our treat this time, OK?"

In no time at all, they were parked at a restaurant and had a table that would accommodate all four of them and the two babies. Marney and Sarah grabbed their baby carriers and headed for the Ladies Room. Changes had to be made and Little George didn't want to wait. Back again, food jars came out and two little ones got their nourishment while the adults pored over their menu's. Finally a waitress took their orders and the chatter began. Sarah wanted to know how they were going to sort out all the groceries they had in the back of the truck. Fred explained that they'd taken orders from all of the divisions including the home ranch. "That includes all of the groceries you ordered, Sarah. George and I went over that and added a number of things you probably overlooked. Don't worry about that. You're new at this and some things you wouldn't know. Now, we keep a separate list of the different orders but we make up a combined list from those lists so that we know how much of this and how many of that to order. Once the order is complete, we phone it to the wholesale place where we got this load. Then, they make up the order and all I have to do is sign for it and pick it up."

Sarah asked the next logical question, "OK, what happens when we get this back to the ranch. How do the divisions get what they ordered.?" Fred smiled. "That's the next step. We take the individual order sheets and pick out each box of items. Let's say that we want to sort out the canned corn. We just make seven piles and if Division five ordered ten cans of corn, we put ten cans of corn in their pile, etc. When the corn is distributed, we go on to the next item and do the same thing again. This goes on until each order is filled. Next, each pile is packaged in boxes and marked for the division it belongs to and I load them up and deliver them. And, there you are. We usually do this twice a month except during round-up time when we have extra men working in each division. Then we sometimes have to make three deliveries." All Sarah could say was, "Wow. You're organized. I never dreamed--"

Food interrupted the conversation and it got quiet at their table for awhile. Finally, Marney put her fork down. "I gotta quit or I'll have to go on a diet. 'sides, its after one. We'd better get over to Doctor March's office. He sometimes starts a little early. Come on Fred, let's get moving. We've got things yet to do." It took only minutes to settle the bill and load the truck again. The doctor's office was across town, but they were early and Laura followed them in to keep them company. Fred took off to accomplish his errands with the promise to, "be back in an hour."

In due time, the two babies had been poked and prodded and pronounced in good health. Little Jenny got a small bottle of medicine for her stomach disorder with instructions to Marney for its dosage. Little George surprised and embarrassed Sarah by wetting all over the examining table, but Doctor March just laughed and said, "Happens all the time, especially boys. It's normal." Doctor March gave the baby his DPT shot and pronounced him good for the next three months.

That done, they loaded back into the truck and discussed what they should do next. Laura said, "I don't have anything special, so let's go get Sarah's shopping done." Marney agreed and they headed for a hardware store Fred knew about. It took the ladies a full hour to decide the dish issue, find and collect enough pots and pans to equip Sarah's kitchen and get them packed and loaded.

The stereo was easy. They stopped at a stereo shop and found a popular brand that offered a compact stereo for a reasonable price. It would play tapes and records both, so it was added to the load along with a collection of country and classical records and tapes. Then, Sarah mentioned computers. Laura told her, "You need to look into one offered by a company in Oklahoma City. They are very reliable, easy to use and the company stands behind their products better than any company we've seen so far. The ranch has several. Why don't you have a look at those and see what you think? Tell you what. I've got one. Come over and I'll let you play with it and you can make up your mind. You aren't in a hurry with this are you?" Sarah hesitated, then said, "Gee, thanks Laura, I'd be glad to look at yours. No, I'm not in a hurry. I've got to earn enough to pay for it first, so that's going to take a couple of months I suppose. Alright, all I have left to get are bedding items. Where do we go for that?" Fred said, "I know just the place."

Ten minutes later Marney accompanied Sarah into a large department store and they made their way to the 'Sleep Shop'. Sarah looked at blankets, quilts and bed spreads. The more she looked, the more confused she got. Finally she turned to Laura and asked, "What do I need, here. It's warmer in summer and colder in winter than California, isn't it.? What should I get? Right now, I've only got a couple of blankets and a spread. That's OK for right now, but that won't do for winter, will it.?" Marney chipped in with, "No, it won't. I'd get two quilts and at least one more blanket. That's a cute bedspread, there, why don't you get that one and pick out a different one just for change. What do you think, Laura?" Laura slowly nodded her head. "I think that'll work. Why don't you pick that blue quilt and a soft brown one? They'll match your bedspreads. Other than that, I think you're pretty well fixed, here. Now, lets go over to the bath dept. and get you some towels and other bath fixin's. Then, let's go home. I'm tired."

With that, the shopping expedition was complete and Fred headed for home. Two hours later, the truck was backed up to the warehouse unloading platform and everything was deposited inside. Fred told Sarah that her dishes, stereo and other items would be brought down to the house in the morning. She thanked him for helping out with everything and, carrying Little George who'd conveniently gone to sleep; walked the short distance to the house.

She arrived home to find George in the kitchen fixing dinner. He'd stuffed a chicken and roasted it, made gravy and fixed a green vegetable and a fruit salad. Sarah gasped at the feast. "My gosh, George, how'd you do all of that?" He grinned and explained, "I used to have to do this all the time. Lois didn't want to cook and about all she would put on the table was stuff she'd heated out of a can. Not for me. I've got to have more. I fixed all this for you because of two things. First, you've tried to do the best you could with everything you've done for me and Little George. Second, you don't cook too well, just yet, but you keep trying and you're getting better. Besides, you must be pretty tired from everything you've done today. You deserve a rest. Come on, sit down and eat."

CHAPTER FIVE

Mileposts

She did what she'd gotten in the habit of doing, now. She put the baby in the swing and sat down. George smiled and asked her. "How'd you day go?" Sarah was vastly pleased that he asked her. In between bites, she described the day from beginning to end. She took pains to tell him how helpful Laura and Marney had been and she told about all the things she'd gotten. She got George to laugh at what had happened in the doctor's office when his son wet all over the examining table. Sarah stopped and thought for a moment, then asked him a question.

"George," she said, "Who's paying for all this stuff I bought? I must have spent nearly a thousand dollars in goods and equipment for this house." George said simply, "I am. Now, don't get excited, but understand why it's that way. Why are you here? Answer, you are here because I hired you to take care of my son. That little bundle in the swing is worth a hundred times what you spent today. If it makes your job easier, its money well spent. If it pleases you so you like your job better, its money well spent. I love my son and I think you are doing a great job with him. Now, do you understand? Sarah choked as her emotions got away from her. "George, don't do that. I've only been here five days as of today. I've gotten so attached to this little guy-- I never thought such a thing would happen." She used a napkin to dry the tears. George was a bit embarrassed as was Sarah. Finally, he said, "I never dreamed this would work out this way, but I'm glad it is. I remember asking myself when I brought you back to the hotel if that was what I really wanted to do. It was a crazy thing to do. Do you know what decided me, Sarah?" Sarah said, "No, what?" "I kept seeing you when you turned around and kept looking at Little George and telling me that he needed care. You'd forgotten all about those people trying to chase us down. You forgot everything but the baby. That's what decided me. You cared!" All Sarah could say was, "Thanks, George."

George gathered up the plates and dishes. He put the leftover chicken in the refrigerator and cleared off the table. Finally, he picked up the baby, gently bobbed him up and down, then kissed him and put him back in the swing. "Well, I've got some work I have to get done tonight. See you in the morning." With that, he headed out the door to his cabin. Sarah got out food for the baby and fed him, changed him and dressed him for bed. She sat down in the rocking chair with him in her arms and fed him a bottle while she rocked him gently. He was asleep in moments. She would have burped him, but she didn't want to wake him so she put him down in his crib.

Sarah sat in the rocking chair for nearly an hour, going over the things that had been done, had been said and the things that George had told her. She found it hard to believe that she had done so well so quickly. She wondered where it would all lead. She reminded herself that she'd never been where she was now. She'd never even dreamed of how her life could change the way it had. Her final thoughts were on what she could expect in the days to be come.

There were mile posts that would have to be passed. George's divorce was one. That has to come to pass, that has to be settled. Second, as George had told her, she would have to win approval from the Colorado Welfare Services as Little

George's baby care giver. Once those were passed, the structure of the baby's care should smooth out and she could concentrate on helping him to grow up in a normal world. She'd gotten ready for bed as her thoughts rambled on. She moved on to another subject. George. She realized that her work with Little George was keeping her in close contact with the baby's father. She wondered how close she should let that get. She didn't have an answer to that problem either. She finally decided to leave things as they were for the time being and look at it later. Now was not a good time for that. Sleep finally came.

Sarah awoke to a fussy baby's distress. He definitely didn't feel good at all and he let the world know it. She felt his brow and decided he had a slight fever. She confirmed it with a thermometer the doctor had shown her how to use. Two degrees. Doctor March had said that Little George would probably react to the DPT shot he got and that it would be about two degrees for a day or two. She got him up and changed him as she did every morning. She cooled a damp cloth and gently wiped him down to try to lower his temperature. Finally, she dressed him and fed him a bottle, which didn't interest him much.

Quickly, she got her own morning routine done with a shower and brushing her hair. Dressed for the day, she started breakfast. George had called for pancakes and she mixed the batter and set it aside for when he came in. She was determined that she'd do better than the first time. She went back and got the baby and set him in the swing where he could see her. Then she went on with breakfast preparations. This time, she'd set out orange juice and was ready to fry eggs to go with the pancakes.

George came in and picked the baby up. Then he noticed Little George wasn't very happy to see him. He turned and asked Sarah what was the matter and she told him about the baby's shot and what the doctor had said. George's reaction was just, "Oh." He laid Little George over his shoulder and gently patted him on the back. Little George turned his head and laid it against his father's neck. He wasn't in a good mood at all. George just said, "Well, this will probably pass within a day or two, but you keep a close eye on him. If he has any problems, call me or come get me right away. We can always fly him to Canon City if we have to. We've done it before

Sarah just nodded her head. She turned and started the first pancake. Her thoughts were on the baby, but she managed to produce a plateful of reasonably good pancakes in spite of the distraction. She followed with the eggs and put two of them with George's pancakes and set the syrup next to his plate. Holding the baby and using his left hand, he managed to clean up the plateful of pancakes she'd fixed for him.

Finally, he said, "Well, I have to go. I hate leaving him for you to take care of, but that's about all I can do. I think he'll be alright. Sarah nodded and said, "I hope so." George left, then, saying as he went out the door, "I'll be back for lunch."

She picked the baby up and rocked him before laying him down in his crib. She managed two pancakes and an egg, then had an idea. She called Marney on the phone and asked her to come over. She just explained with, "The baby's sick." Marney was just as brief. "I'll be right over." Five minutes later, she came in the door and Sarah explained what had happened and what the doctor had said and done. She explained that Doctor Marsh had warned her that the DPT shot would probably make him a little feverish, but not to worry. Marney took the baby's temperature again and said, "Still two degrees high. Doctor Marsh is probably right. I'd say, just watch him and leave him alone unless his temperature comes up from what it is now."

And, so it went through the day. Finally, about the time the sun was going down behind the Sangre de Cristo Mountains, Little George's temperature began going down. All of the things Sarah had bought the day before were stacked in boxes on the living room floor, ignored while she kept watch on Little George. She'd held him, rocked him and cooled him with cool cloths all day long. George had come in several times, he spent some time rocking the baby and giving Sarah a chance to rest. Finally, the baby began to perk up. He was fed some fruit and given a bottle. He took most of the fruit and some of the bottle, then was laid down in his crib. The crisis was past. Sarah hadn't been so tired and drawn out for a long time.

Sarah did something she'd not considered before. She set her alarm clock for two AM and got up to check on Little George. She found him sleeping soundly and she was relieved to note that his breathing was smooth and regular. She went back to bed feeling better than she had all the previous day.

CHAPTER SIX

Time Passes

As Little George returned to normal health, Sarah began taking more time to care for the house. She sorted her new dishes and got them into the cupboards where they belonged. The pots and pans went into other cupboards. And the knives, forks and spoons went into the proper drawers. She took pride in keeping her kitchen spic and span and she was beginning to feel confident about her cooking as well. In her mind, the house was becoming hers!

Sarah completely redid the bedroom, moving the bed so she could see out the window in the mornings when she awoke. She pulled off all of the old bedding and rebuilt the entire bed with a blanket and a quilt on top, covered with a colorful bedspread.

A month passed, then two. Suddenly, the divorce hearing was there. It was in California, but her qualifications were being investigated by a worker of the Colorado Welfare Services agency. One day, a strange car drove up to the ranch, then another with a State of Colorado logo on the side followed. A man came to Sarah's door and identified himself as an attorney for George Toland. The other car disgorged a lady with a briefcase who said she was from the Colorado Welfare. Could she talk with a Miss Sarah Mills? Sarah invited them both in and seated them

The attorney told Sarah that he was there to monitor the questioning to see that her rights and privacy were not improperly invaded. The welfare worker assured her that she would avoid questions that were improper. The questioning began. She was asked where she got her experience in baby care. She answered, "In Los Angeles, California."

"What did you do?" "I cared for a three year old and a five year old for a lady who worked at night." The questioning went on. The answers were given. Finally, a question came that caught the attention of the attorney. "Have you ever been arrested?" The answer was, "Yes" The next question, "What was the charge?" The attorney interrupted. "Improper question." He turned to Sarah, "How old were you when this happened?" Sarah said quietly, "I was fifteen." The attorney turned to the welfare worker, "Strike the last question. You can't ask it, she was under aged and her privacy is protected as a juvenile in this state and in California." The welfare worker got a 'prune face' and asked, "Have you ever been arrested after you turned eighteen?" Answer, "No." The attorney turned to the welfare worker and asked her to see that he got a copy of all questions asked and the answers that were given before the report was sent to the California court. The welfare lady reluctantly agreed. He further warned the welfare worker that any reference to an under aged arrest must be stricken from the report. She agreed. The interview was over.

George left for California and the divorce hearing on a Monday. He was back with a smile on his face on Friday evening. He wasted no time seeking out Sarah and told her the news. The divorce had been uncontested and granted. The custody of Little George was solely in George's hands. His ex wife had no visitation rights. It had cost him a bit, but, as he said, it was worth it. He picked up Little George and hugged him tightly. "Mine, all mine you little monkey." He turned to Sarah and hugged her, as well. "Oh Sarah, I'm so happy.". She just smiled. He didn't realize that Little George was half hers. All he had to do was ask Little George, if he could have talked he would have told his dad that. If he's asked Sarah how she felt at that moment, she would have blushed even deeper than she did. A new feeling nearly surfaced that she'd not recognized before.

In the midst of the divorce hearing and the interview by the Colorado State Welfare agency, Sarah got a letter from the doctor in San Francisco about her medical tests. She was informed that she had tested negative on all of the tests! One more milestone passed.

During the previous two months, Sarah had developed a routine to her days. Care of Little George was the center of it, but she'd expanded her horizons. She had collected a supply of recipes and was now able to put a variety of dishes on the table without repetition. Further, she continued to expand and store her library of recipes every chance she got. Laura had introduced her to horseback riding and she got considerable pleasure from being out in the fresh air away from the house. It gave her a chance to enjoy the older woman's company and to see something of the surrounding country around the ranch headquarters. Along with her association with Laura Williams, she'd developed a closeness with Marney Sowles. She liked her open forthrightness and drew on her knowledge of children constantly in her efforts to understand Little George's growth.

Two months time brought large changes in the baby's development. He'd gained weight, size and capabilities that changed almost from day to day. Where he'd been content to lay in his crib or sit with his back supported in the swing, now he could hold his head up and move about. Sarah was surprised one day to see him turn himself over so that, instead of being on his back, he was now on his tummy and trying to push up with his arms. Once he'd mastered the technique, she couldn't leave him by himself on a bed or table. He could move about and that had its hazards. She delighted in just watching him grow and develop. To her it was a miracle.

To George, his son's growth was his joy. He came every day to play with him in the brief time he could spare from his work as assistant manager. He'd come to enjoy being with

Sarah at mealtimes and their conversations were easy and covered the activities going on around them. Little George, the ranch, events in the community. All came up and were part of their times together. Sarah learned early that Little George enjoyed the music she played on her new stereo. What delighted her more was that George enjoyed it, too. She often had something playing softly when he came in for meals. He remarked one day that he liked country western which she often played, but that he'd developed a liking for classical things, too. The next time she had a chance to got to Pueblo, she gathered up a collection of Mozart, Handel and others on 45 records and surprised him by playing one when he came in for lunch.. He was delighted and she gained an appreciation for classics at the same time. Her world was expanding as never before.

One day, George came in and asked, "Would you like to see what this ranch looks like? You've been around the headquarters with Laura quite a bit, but you haven't seen the whole ranch yet." Sarah was a bit surprised at his asking, but she'd been curious about it and nodded her head. Yes, she would like to see it. "Well, do you mind going up in a small airplane?" was the next question. She shook her head, "I've never done that, but I guess so." George explained. "I've got to do a survey of the cattle and I've got to cover the whole ranch. We'll use the Super Cub, so we can see better. I'll be flying the airplane, so I'll be careful not to do anything scary. Do you want to give it a try?" Sarah just smiled. She'd decided that she'd do just about anything George asked of her. He'd been so kind and helpful in her new life, that she'd come to trust him. Sarah said, "I'll give it a try. When do you want to go?" George's answer was quick. "I'd like to go in about an hour. It'll take at least a couple of hours to do the survey. Why don't you see if Marney can keep Little George until we get back? She's done it before when Lois had to go to Canon City or Pueblo."

Sarah picked up the phone, made the request and got a positive answer. "I'll go get the baby ready right now. I'll be ready in a few minutes." George smiled and told her to come down to the hangar when she was ready and they'd go.

Twenty minutes later, she met George in front of the hangar and was helped into the cabin of the utility airplane. George explained about seat belts and noise, so she wouldn't be startled or fall out of the seat. He told her that they'd be doing a lot of turning and going up and down as they covered the territory of the ranch, but they'd be perfectly safe. He finished with, "OK. Are you ready?" She smiled and nodded her head. She wasn't sure, but she wasn't going to back out now.

The engine started and began warming up. George turned and put a set of head phones over Sarah's head, explaining that she could hear what he said better over the noise of the engine with the phones on. She adjusted them so they were comfortable and nodded again. George released the brakes and the airplane started moving towards the runway. George stopped and spoke, "I'm going to test the engine before we go up, so it's going to get noisy. Nothing to worry about." Sarah discovered that the little bar in front of her face was a microphone and that she could talk back to George. She told him to go ahead, that she was fine.

Finished with his engine testing, he spoke again and explained what was about to happen as they took off and climbed up. She just smiled again and nodded her head. The airplane turned onto the runway and the engine noise rose to a soft roar as the airplane leaped forward and ran down the runway. After a short run, it lifted into the air and climbed up. In a minute it leveled off and turned toward the west. George explained that he was going to cover Division Five and Division Six first.

As they hummed along, George handed Sarah a note pad with a pen and asked her if she could take notes. She looked at the pad and saw that he'd marked the first page as 'Section Six'. She asked him. "Just what do you want me to put down?" He explained. "I'm going to try to see where the cattle are out on the range. I'll tell you the name of the area and whether there are lots of cattle there or smaller amounts or what. What you can put down is the name of the area and I'll say 'lots, maybe 100' or I might say 'not many, maybe 40' etc. Can you do that?" Sarah nodded her head. "That sounds easy enough." George continued. "When we finish section six, I'll tell you. Just write down 'end' and turn the page. The next section will be Section Five. Just do the same thing on that page and we'll go on and do each one in order. I'll tell you when to change sections. Got all of that?" Sarah said, "I think I can do that, OK." George nodded. "Alright, here we go. First spot, Pine Canyon. 'some, maybe 50. Now put a line under that and write, 'Little Creek'" As he said that, he banked around and headed to a new area. Again, he turned, looked down and called out, "'lots' maybe 150. New line."

This routine went on for twenty minutes or so and George finally banked one last time, and headed toward the north. "Alright, that takes care of Section Six. Now, we'll do Section Five. Soon, he started calling out areas and numbers as he had before. Finished with that one they went on, completing each section in turn. Finally, George turned to Sarah and asked. "Alright, would you like to see how this ranch is laid out?" She nodded and he turned the airplane around and pointed down. "See where the creek crosses the road down there?" She said, "I see it." George explained. "That's the northeast corner of Oxbow Ranch. Now, I'm going to fly west to the northwest corner. It's where Rocky Creek flows into Chatter Creek." He turned the airplane so she could see through the left windows and pointed. "You can just see it over that next rise just before you get to that little peak out there." She looked carefully and suddenly everything came into focus. "There it is, I see it." George turned back toward the west again. "Alright, see the buildings off to our left. That's Section Five headquarters." She saw that and nodded. "Yes, I see them."

On and on they went, identifying each section, its headquarters and its layout. Finally, George pointed down to a large group of buildings close to the side of the airplane. "Sarah, can you guess what those building are?" She thought for a moment. Suddenly, she realized she was looking down on the Oxbow itself. He'd taken them almost directly over her new home. She recognized the house she was living in, the cabins, Marney's and Laura's houses, the warehouse and all the other buildings she'd gotten familiar with during the time she'd been there. It looked different from up here, she thought. Still, now that she knew what she was looking at, it was familiar.

Finally, George asked her, "Would you like to fly the airplane?" She drew in a sharp breath. Was he joking? She asked, "Are you sure you want me to?" He nodded. "Only of you want to." He replied. She hesitated, then breathed, "I'd like to try." He said, "OK. We'll do something simple to start with. First, I want you to put your feet on the pedals just ahead of your feet. Don't push hard, just rest them there. Now, take hold of that lever just in front of you, the one that keeps moving around. Just hold it lightly, just feel it move when I move it from up here. Now, I want you to keep the airplane pointed at that little cloud straight in front of us. Do you see it?" She nodded her head, "Yes" He then told her to push the left pedal a little bit and watch what happens to the cloud. She did so and the nose of the airplanes swung to the left and the cloud moved to the right. Then, he told her to push the right pedal gently until the cloud came back to where it was before."

This exercise went on as she learned that the lever would lower one wing or the other depending on which way she pushed it to the side. She found that if she pushed it forward, the nose went down and if she pulled it back, the nose came up. A little at a time she became familiar with controlling the airplane by moving the controls one way or another. She learned to turn, using the lever or stick and the rudder pedal on the side she wanted to turn towards. She learned to use the stick to hold the airplane level or to climb or descend. She learned that the engine was controlled by using a small lever called the throttle on the left sidewall of the airplane.

Finally, she spoke to George through the interphone and told him that she liked what she was doing but that it was hard work. He laughed and told her it was time to quit. Flying was supposed to be fun, not hard work "Let's go home. We've done enough for today. I think I could teach you to fly without any trouble." He remarked. "Would you like to learn?" She replied. "I think so." George said, "Fine, we'll do this again one day soon. Is that alright with you?" She grinned, "I'd love it!" George took control and started down toward the Oxbow airport. He had Sarah keep her hands and feet lightly on the controls so she could feel what he was doing as he made his approach and set the airplane down on the runway. They taxied up to the hangar and George explained what he was doing as he shut down the airplane and made it safe to get out.

They rolled the Cub into the hangar and shut the doors, then Sarah said, "Thanks for the ride. I enjoyed it immensely. Oh, here's the note pad, too." George thanked her for keeping notes and told her he'd be over for dinner as usual. She said, "I'll go get Little George and start dinner. I'll see you when you get there." She remarked to herself, "Life is sure full of surprises."

One of the responsibilities of her new life was handling money. On her second trip to Pueblo, she'd opened a bank account in her name and had deposited the money she had earned for her work with Little George. The bank suggested that she should take out a credit card so that she could pay for purchases without carrying large amounts of cash. Later that day, she remarked to George, "Guess what I did today?" His "What's that?" was answered when she told him about her bank account. "You, know, I never used to have to worry about carrying large amounts of cash, I never had any. I remember I had a hundred dollars one time. I only had it two days before a customer robbed me and I didn't have it any more. I remember that he beat me up, too." George reminded her that she could still be robbed in a dozen different ways, but at least she could protect her assets if she was careful.

Sarah hadn't forgotten her curiosity about computers. One day, shortly after her first trip to Pueblo, she showed up at Laura Williams' house and asked if she could try Laura's computer. Laura showed her how to get it started and how to get on the internet. It was slow work at first, because she didn't know how to type. Laura showed her how the keyboard was laid out and how to set her hands and fingers to use it. As beginning typists do, she made many mistakes, but she began to get the hang of it after an hour or so. Laura gave her several exercises that taught her how to write things and to correct mistakes. At the end of an hour, Sarah was exhausted, but ecstatic with what she'd learned. She was hooked.

Sarah went home and started looking at advertisements for the various computer manufacturers. To start with, she didn't know a bit from a bite, or what floppy discs and hard drives were all about. She asked everybody and gradually amassed a comfortable body of knowledge. She talked to George and asked him what he'd recommend for a computer. It took several days of asking and writing down information, but finally she'd put together the specifications that she thought would serve her ambition. She showed it to Laura and to George. They both suggested changes and told her why. Those were added. She was ready to order.

Sarah had decided to take Laura's advice and purchase from the computer company in Oklahoma. She called them and went over her specifications. More changes were suggested, most of which she accepted. Finally, she asked the sales person how much and when she could get the computer. He named a figure and asked how she'd like to pay for it. She mentioned her credit card, remembering that she had more than the cost of the computer in the bank She gave him her card number and made arrangements for the computer to be delivered to the ranch's agent in Pueblo. She then phoned the agent and told him that the computer would be delivered to him, that it was paid for and that Fred would pick it up on his next supply run to Pueblo. She waited in anticipation.

Within a couple of weeks, the computer was delivered to her door and she asked George how to set it up. He just laughed and told her that was out of his capability but suggested that Laura's husband knew a lot more on that subject than he did. Sarah promptly called Laura. "Laura, do you suppose that Bob would mind setting up my new computer for me?" Laura laughed and said, "I just knew that was what you were going to do. I've already told him. I'll bring him over this evening. It shouldn't take long to set it up. Oh, by the way, do you have a table to put everything on?" Sarah gasped, "Oh, I didn't think about that. Where can I get a table?" Laura answered. "Never mind, they have several small tables at the warehouse. I'll have Bob bring one when we come. You'd better have Fred get a regular computer desk for you at that computer store when he goes to Pueblo next time, though. A flat table is kind of unhandy for everything you're going to have on it. We'll be over tonight."

Sarah got her computer set up and started learning to use it in earnest. She got a book on typing and practiced exercises on a daily basis. She discovered that her fingers were quite nimble and it wasn't long before she could type thirty words a minute without a lot of mistakes. She'd gotten a number of programs including a word processor with the computer and she started using the computer for all her letters and recipes. One of the programs she'd not received with the computer was a book keeping program. She asked Marney and Laura about that and they recommended a popular one they both used. She sent off for a copy of it and enlisted Laura's expertise to show her how to use it. Together, they set up her finances on it as soon as it arrived.

Sarah wasn't into sophisticated accounting so she got a book and got started learning the mysteries of this activity. It was easy at first, as she used what she was learning to keep her own finances worked out. However, things got harder when she started running into terms such as 'credits' and 'debits'. She had to learn the language and she pestered the Oxbow book keeper constantly for explanations of this discipline. He was helpful at first, but finally put her off as teaching her was cutting into his work time. Sarah turned to George. She'd found out that part of his course of study at UC Davis, had been basic accounting. He learned to set aside a little time each evening for answering her questions.

Time was passing, Sarah soon realize that Little George was starting to crawl. He was everywhere. He got into everything. Sarah made Fred get her special locks for her floor level cupboards, so the little explorer couldn't get into them. That happened one day when she found him in the kitchen surrounded by every pot and pan she had. This would never do! In spite of the increased workload of watching out for the little tyke, she loved him more and more each day. He was her life, now, he wasn't the inert being she'd cleaned up and fed in a San Francisco park any more. He was a real live little boy, soon about to walk and talk. The thought thrilled her and alarmed her.

Sarah had come to Oxbow in the spring, now, summer was passed and fall had come. She'd never seen such a riot of color as she now saw on the trees. The aspens were a brilliant yellow and other trees were passing from summer green to their own special colors. She often went riding into the hills with Laura and gained a love for the country she'd moved into six months before. It was an exciting time for her. Her only regret was that she couldn't bring Little George out to see all this, too. Because of his age and size, she had to leave him with Marney for the hour that she and Laura spent riding.

CHAPTER SEVEN

Holidays and Family

Suddenly, one November day, Sarah realized a couple of things. Thanksgiving was a week away, Christmas was coming and Little George's first birthday wasn't too far away. She consulted with George. Was he planning to visit his family for Thanksgiving and what about Christmas? George decided to sit down and work out their agenda for all this. He started reviewing the whole situation to see whether to stay at the Oxbow or go home for the holidays. Next, he had to consider Sarah and her mother. He felt that he owed her some consideration at least. He said, "Let me think about this and we'll talk about it tonight." "OK, anything you come up with is alright with me."

George did think about it. He thought a lot. The problem was his mother. She'd had a heart attack about three years ago and she wasn't in the best of health. Going home would put a heavy load on her, preparing for Thanksgiving or Christmas, either one. His dad wasn't a problem, his health was good and he was still running the ranch as he always had. But! And it was a big 'but'. Could he be away from his ranch in Idaho for very long? He'd phone tonight and ask. George looked at the possibilities again and decided that they hinged on whether his dad could be away from the home ranch for very long.

The next problem was, of course, Sarah. If he went home, he'd have to take her to care for Junior. He couldn't ask that of his mother. And, what about her mother? Sarah had said that she was in Sacramento and he knew that she'd gotten several letters from her since Sarah had come to the Oxbow. If they stayed at Oxbow for Thanksgiving, could the mother be brought here? He'd better ask Sarah about that. He decided that he'd better go back to Sarah and see what her thoughts were on all this.

That night after dinner was cleared away, he sat Sarah down in her favorite chair, the rocker and said, "I pawed over this holiday agenda thing all day and all I get are questions, not answers. Here're the problems." He then recited everything he'd thought about through the day. Sarah promptly said, "Look, that's an easy one. Why can't you bring your mom and dad here for Thanksgiving and Christmas? It would give your dad a chance to see what and how you are doing. You can move into this house while they're here and I'll move in where you are. I can move Little George in there just for night time care and your folks will have plenty of room. You can sleep in the nursery, there's a single bed in there." George broke in. "What about your mother? You ought to be able to see her. I don't think it's fair to ignore her, at least not for Christmas." Sarah responded. "I know, that's a tough one. I can't go to Sacramento. I've got to be here for Little George. I don't want to put that load on your mother and the other families have their own holidays to think about. How would you feel if I brought Mother here and put her up in the small cabin with me? There's an extra room there and I can put a single bed in there for her. She probably wouldn't want to stay more that a few days around Christmas, anyway." George said, "I think we need to make some phone calls right now. Can you call your mother? Sarah thought. "No, not tonight, but I can get her in the morning, I think." George pulled out a pocket phone list and reached for the phone. Shortly he had his mother on the line.

After exchanging pleasantries, he said, "Mom, I want you and Dad to come down here for Thanksgiving and Christmas.

Is Dad there? Good. Let me talk to him." A moment's pause, then, "Dad, how are things? Great. Now, I have a couple of questions for you. First, how's the weather up your way? Cold? You aren't doing much, are you? I see. Well here's the second question. Could you and Mom come down here to Oxbow for Thanksgiving and stay for Christmas? Could Walter take care of your place for a month while you're gone? Sure, we've got plenty of room here. I'd like to show you this place and talk to you about what we're doing. And I know Mom will want to spend time with Little George. He's almost ready to walk and I'll bet she'd like to see that. Yes, I have a young lady who is his caregiver and she's doing a wonderful job with him. No, Lois is completely out of his life. Dad, she abandoned him. If I live to be a hundred, I'll never understand why she did that. Well, that's another story and best forgotten. Now, do you think you can come? Good. When? Next Wednesday? OK I'll meet you in Colorado Springs. Just let me know what time you're going to be there. Goodnight Dad, give Mom a kiss for me." He hung up with a grin on his face.

George turned to Sarah and explained what was going to happen with his parents, then he went on to ask her if she wanted to call her mother tomorrow morning and see if she would come and visit with her daughter at least during Christmas. She said, "I'll call and see what she wants to do first thing in the morning." Sarah went on to ask about getting a turkey and the other fixings she'd need for Thanksgiving dinner. George told her, "Go see Laura and ask her what all she's going to be fixing. She can tell you what to order. Fred is going to Pueblo on Monday, so you'll have plenty of time to get recipes and the other things you need all organized. Mom can give you all kind of advice if you need it. She's a veteran on Thanksgiving dinners."

George went on to another subject. Little George's birthday. "That's on the 12th of January, so it's off a ways, yet." He felt that should be kept simple this first year. Christmas would get him about all the toys he'd need for the next year, so toys weren't a big item. "I'm going to suggest a snow suit and cap. He'll be walking by then, so a snow suit will probably be a good item, preferably a red one." George changed the subject again. "Sarah, let's plan Christmas now, so we can get things set up without a lot of fuss when we get to that stage of the holidays. Why don't you and Marney or Laura plan to go into Pueblo about the first week of December. We'll need a small tree , but we'll get that up in the hills. We'll only need a small one, that we can set up on a table out of Junior's reach but we'll need all kind of decorations for it. Lights, streamers, an angel or a star for the top and anything else that you see or that Marney thinks you should have. We don't have any of that. Lois threw it all out after last Christmas. I want everything to be nice for Mom and Dad and this way, they can be a part of it. I want them to get the chance to know Little George. They've never seen him, yet. I want them to meet you, too. They're regular folks and I think you'll like them. Anyway, let's find ways to decorate the house and make it reflect Christmas."

George had never talked about his family before, but now he explained about them and told how he'd grown up on a ranch in Idaho. He was part of a family of six children. There were three boys and three girls. He'd mentioned that he'd had an older brother, but the brother had died in a swimming accident while on a scout activity when George was only nine years old. His sister, Mina was the next one and then Walter and finally the two youngest girls, Joyce and Emily. Sarah asked what had happened to his older brother. George hesitated, then said that he'd gone on a summer scout outing in the mountains with his scout troop. One of the other boys had fallen into a rushing stream and his brother, Russell, had jumped in to help him. He'd managed to get hold of the boy and had pushed him to the bank where other boys and the Scout Master had pulled him out. However, the stream was so swift that Russell had been swept down into a whirlpool and had been held under for several minutes before the current had released him. It was too late. Russell had been the victim of his heroic rescue.

George said that he'd followed in Russell's footsteps and gone all the way to the top as a Scout. He'd won his Eagle badge when he'd turned sixteen years of age. He'd always looked up to his older brother and he remembered that he'd been a good example to George, always standing up for him and teaching him things that boys liked to do.

Sarah remembered Christmases when she'd been a little girl, but that all stopped when her family broke up. Her mother didn't have the time or the money to do much for the holidays and they had been largely ignored until now. Sarah had missed it. Now, with George's help maybe it could mean something again. She hoped so.

Sarah spent the next few days consulting with her friends, Marney and Laura. "What did you do to make Thanksgiving a special day?" This question and others were discussed and worked out. Recipes were looked at and ingredients listed. On Monday, Fred made a special trip to Pueblo. Every division of the Oxbow had sent in special requests for supplies needed for the holiday and these had been consolidated into a large, complete order which Fred phoned to the Oxbow suppliers. The three ladies climbed into the truck with the two babies and off they went.

It was an easy matter to pick up the prepared orders, but that was not why the girls had gone. Christmas was in a month and they wanted to get decorations and gifts so that they could spend the next month getting ready for the special holiday that Christmas always was. Each one had a list of thing she had in mind to get and this would mean running around to different stores to look, choose and buy. Usually, Fred began these trips around nine, allowing time to travel and arrive before noon in Pueblo. This time, however, they left at seven. They all knew that this would be a long day. The mood of the travelers was a jolly one, though. This event didn't happen but once a year and they were determined to make the most of it.

Arrival in Pueblo started the process. The supply orders were picked up and the real activity began. First to one store, and then another. "Well, that's not exactly what I had in mind, let's try----." Off they would go, again. Slowly, but surely, items got crossed off. Decorations and wrapping paper joined the stacks, along with Christmas cards and other goodies. Finally, Laura sighed a long sigh. "Well, that takes care of everything on my list. How about you ladies?" "Done." Said one. "Finished." Said the other. "Fred, it's time to go home. We're all set." Fred let out a "Yippee. It's about time. I think we're taking home over half of Pueblo!" Marney just laughed. "Never mind girls, he says that every year."

Home was a welcome place and each unloaded their treasures carefully. All were wrapped so that secrecy was maintained. "After all, what's the fun of Christmas if the receivers weren't surprised?" Sarah carried everything she'd bought into the house and stored them in a closet. She'd deal with them when she had time later. Little George was getting extremely fussy. He and Marney's little Peggy Ann had been somewhat neglected through the day. As the mothers and Sarah went from store to store, Fred had been left in charge of the little ones and they weren't used to his ministrations. They got fed and changed as time would permit, but it wasn't like home. Both babies were more than a little out of sorts by the time they got back to the Oxbow.

Finally, Sarah picked up Little George and, stripping him to the skin, gave him a bath and got him ready for bed. She put on some soft music and put him in a high chair that she'd got for him when he got big enough to sit up to eat. She fed him solids and a glass of milk, then cleaned his face and sat down to rock him. This kind of treatment was his favorite, and he soon softly dropped off to sleep. Putting him in his crib, she spent a few moments just looking at him and thinking. "Baby, you're almost through your first year. I'm glad I'm the one taking care of you. I wouldn't miss this for all the money in the world!"

Sarah blinked back some of the tears that had sprung to her eyes. "Oh, I'm so lucky. Why am I feeling this way? What have I done to deserve this?" No answer entered her thinking, but she reveled in her feelings. Was this what being a mother was all about? She pondered on the thought.

George came in just then and interrupted her train of thought. "Oh, I'm late. Come on and sit down while I get you some dinner." She bustled off to the kitchen and got out some leftovers that she'd set aside from the night before. She made up a green salad and added that to the meat loaf, she'd warmed for him. Sitting down with her meal, she started telling George what she and her two friends had done that day. She had to be careful, though, when describing the things she'd bought. There was a special sweater in the gifts and it was for George. She almost gave it away, but caught herself just in time. It had to be a surprise and she had to be careful.

George had seated himself in an easy chair and asked Sarah to sit down when she walked in to announce that his dinner was ready. "Please Sarah, sit down. I've had some very disturbing news and I need to tell you about it." Sarah sat down on the couch. "Yes, George, what is it?" George sat for a moment, then explained. "I got a phone call from the attorney in San Francisco this afternoon. It's about Little George's mother. He said that she had been killed in a car smash-up three nights ago. He said he had an investigator look into it and had him try to get the results of any autopsy. He was successful and it showed that she was over double the limit of intoxication. In other words, she had been intoxicated when the accident had occurred. Worse yet, she had two others with her and they were all killed. She would have been charged with vehicular manslaughter except that she hadn't survived the crash. The bad part of it is that the families of the ones that were with her will probably sue her estate and they may try to involve me. I told the attorney to keep me informed. I don't think they can get anywhere because our divorce was final and she made it plain that she didn't want anything more to do with me. I'm telling you all of this, because you will probably see letters, hear phone calls and maybe even be asked what you know about our relationship." Sarah was visibly upset by this time. "What can they do? I didn't even know you before she took off and I've only been taking care of the baby, I haven't been living with you or anything like that." George nodded. "I know, and our relationship can be proven. My attorney will try to protect you completely. We'll try to keep your name out of the whole thing and I think we can do that. Please, please, don't worry about it. Just know that something could come of all this. I'm sorry that the possibility of anything bad could come up. Try not to worry, OK?" Sarah nodded. "George, I'm glad you told me. Now, come on and eat your dinner. Its meatloaf, but it's a new recipe I got from Marney. It's really very good." George smiled. "Sarah, I appreciate you. You are always thinking of others. Thanks." With that, he arose and went into the kitchen.

After sitting down, he brought up another subject he wanted to talk about. "I got a phone call from Mom after you left this morning. She said that they'd be landing in Colorado Springs at three thirty Wednesday. I'll meet them at the airport and bring them back. I've been thinking about how I want to do that, so here's what I had in mind. See if you think it's a good idea or not.

I'd like them to see Little George when they get here. I'd like you to go with me to pick them up if it's alright with you. I want them to meet you. I know they have questions about who's taking care of their grandchild. Is this alright with you?" Sarah was just a little startled at this. She'd not really thought about it, she just thought they'd show up at the house somehow and she'd be introduced. She thought about George's plan. "Well, why not?" She put down her apprehension. After all, his parents were part of the family. She'd be as nice as possible. Maybe everything would be alright. "Well, what time do we have to leave here?" George set the time and the subject was dropped. "Sorry you can't play with Junior tonight. He was worn out when we got home and I gave him a bath, fed him and when I rocked him, he was gone in minutes." George just grinned and remarked. 'That's alright, I've got some work to do, yet, anyway. And speaking of that, I'd better get at it." He rose, picked up his coat and said, "Good night, see you in the morning."

Wednesday morning came and Sarah got ready. She waited until nearly departure time and then dressed Little George. She'd learned the best way to keep a kid looking his best was to wait to the last minute to finish dressing him. This ploy minimized accidents and spit-ups. George was just about past the burping stage but still had a lot of trouble with things in his hands. Sarah had bought him a new outfit the week before in anticipation of this event. To say the least, the little boy was 'dressed to the nines'.

Little George's father took one look at him and whistled at him. "By golly, you're a sharp looker there, kid. Your Grandma is going to be proud of you." To Sarah he said, "You sure have him looking like a movie star. He is a handsome dude. C'mon, Little George. Let's go get Grandma and Grandpa." With that, they started off for Colorado Springs.

Two hours and eighty miles later, they arrived at the airport. George parked in the arrivals parking lot and ushered Sarah and Little George into the terminal. They found that the flight was a few minutes late, so they settled down in the arrivals lounge to wait. Finally, the flight arrived and passengers came bustling into the baggage claim area. George arose and spotted his Mom coming toward him, followed by a rugged looking tall man with white hair.

George hugged and kissed his Mom and grabbed his Dad's hand and gave it a vigorous shake. Sarah had stood up by then and George introduced her to his parents. He announced that she was, "The best baby sitter in all of Colorado, bar none." His mother looked her up and down momentarily and then gave her a hug. "Pleased to meet you, Sarah. George has good things to say about you." She proclaimed. "Now, I want to meet my grandson" Sarah picked Little George up and held him up for his Grandma. Little George took one look at his grandmother and threw his arms around Sarah's neck, simultaneously hiding his head behind hers. Sarah said,

"Just give him a minute to get used to you. He's usually that way with strangers, but he's not bashful like some babies." Sure enough, after a couple of minutes, his head came into view and he started looking Grandma over again,

Within minutes, Grandma Toland held her hands out and he leaned toward her. Sarah handed him over and he settled in Grandma's arms. His first move was to grab for her glasses. Curiosity had got the better of his caution. Grandpa Toland spoke up then and remarked, "Well, I never." George told his dad, "He really likes people, but he's still a little cautious with people he doesn't know."

George told his dad, "Let me get a luggage cart and we'll get on out to the car. We've still got a two hour drive to get out to the Oxbow, so we'd better get started" With his dad in the front seat and his mother and Sarah in back with Little George, they headed for the ranch.

The back seat was filled with conversation. "How do you like it here, Sarah?" "I like it, it's wonderful. It's so beautiful." "Where did you come from?" I was born in Los Angeles, but I came here from San Francisco." "How are you getting along with Little George?" "Oh, that's easy, he's such a good baby. I've taken care of him since April and it's been one of the best times of my life." "Well, what do you think of Colorado and all of this empty space? It's different from San Francisco, isn't it?" "Oh, yes. I wouldn't trade it for anything, now. Laura Williams, she's my neighbor, we go horseback riding sometimes and it's so beautiful, especially this fall when the aspen trees turn the mountain sides all yellow. I wish you could have seen it." "Oh, I have, I have. We've got aspens up where we live, too. I know what you mean, though." This exchange went on for the whole trip back to the Oxbow and Sarah gradually became at ease with Mildred (Millie to you) Toland. She found that Millie had grown up on a ranch a lot smaller than the Oxbow, but much like it. She married a rancher, George's dad, and had raised five children, two boys and three girls on the ranch they still operated in Idaho. Albert (Bert to you) Toland was slowing down a bit, now," she said, but George's brother, Walter has been taking over some of the work and things were still humming along just as they always had.

As they turned off the county road and approached the Oxbow Ranch complex. Bert commented on the scene that lay before them. "Say, that's quite a spread you've got here. How big is this place, anyway?" George responded. "Well, Dad, this is just the home ranch. We've got roughly thirty thousand acres in the Oxbow, all told. There are six divisions in the whole thing. Each one is an independent ranch in itself. Each division has a separate crew and we do different things on each one. Originally, there were six different ranches, here. Oxbow Corporation came in about twenty years ago and bought up all of these ranches and put them together. They kept them separated so that they're manageable, but they're all part of the ranching complex. I'll show you later how we do all this and you can see how we operate. It's fascinating, really."

Bert was a little awed by the arrangement of the scene in front of them. He remarked, "It looks a lot like an old frontier cow town." He could see houses, warehouses, barns corrals and there was what looked like an old time schoolhouse, sitting back in one corner of the group. George just laughed. "Dad, this was a cow town at one time. When the corporation came in here, it had been abandoned, but many of the buildings were still standing. They just refurbished what they wanted to use, built some new ones, like several of the houses, etc. The warehouses are mostly new. One of them was the old mercantile. We've remodeled that and it's the office complex. I work in there, along with Tom Houghton. He's the ranch's general manager,. I'll take you on a tour in a day or two, when you get settled in."

"One of the things that the corporation did that makes this place so attractive is that they planted trees and kept most of those that were already here. It has given the place a pastoral look that says that it's been here a long time. It's permanent." "You're right, Son, it does look permanent. How many people live here, now?" George thought for a moment. "Well, counting kids and all, there must be about twenty five. We've hired mostly married folks to work here. It keeps our staff a lot more stable."

By this time, they'd entered the main street of the Oxbow and turned down to George's house. The car drew up in front and stopped. Millie took one look at the house and spoke, "I like this. It's nice." George said, "Mother, this is one of the new ones. The cabin you see next door and most of the other ones are old houses that were here when the corporation moved in. They've been remodeled, but, as you can see, they're smaller than the newer houses. Come on in, I'll show you the inside."

Grandpa and Grandma Toland followed George into the house with Sarah trailing behind, carrying Little George. Millie looked around as she went in. Finally, she said, "George, this place is nice. I like it." George just grinned. "Well, it was kind of a dump when Lois was here." Millie got a pained look on her face. "I don't even want to think about that. I never could understand her way of looking at things. I'm glad she's gone." With that, she turned toward the kitchen, the subject closed as far as she was concerned. Bert said nothing. He'd had his own opinions of George's ex wife and decided long before that enough had been said about that subject.

George remarked, "What you see here, now, is Sarah's doing. She started with what Lois left and cleaned it up, then did all the rest. She's a whiz at that sort of thing." Sarah blushed in embarrassment. She'd not dreamed that George had even noticed. She'd just done what she thought was needed to make the house a pleasant place to live. Her thoughts picked up the fact that she'd wondered if George would like what she'd done as she cleaned, painted and added the various things that the house now had. Pleasant curtains, stereo, clean everything!

George hadn't said much at the time she was doing it, but she was now aware that he'd been pleased. That made her feel good inside. She put the baby down in his swing and then turned to Millie. "Are you hungry? I've got dinner in the fridge. All I have to do is warm it up." Millie smiled. "Here, give me the baby and, yes, I'd like something. Why don't you go ahead and I'll talk to Little George while you're getting things ready. I'm sure he's got lots to say to me."

Dinner was on the table in a few minutes and as she called the guests in, she went to the stereo and put on a soft long playing classical record. Millie moved Little George's swing over next to the chair she'd chosen and sat him back in it as she seated herself. "I'll just sit here. Maybe Junior can have a bite or two while we talk."

Dinner went off well and ended up with George and his parents talking about things that they'd not discussed for a long time. They were catching up. As this went on, Sarah cleared the table and put the dishes in the sink. Finally, she put the baby in his high chair and finished feeding him. Done with that, she told Millie, "I hope you'll excuse us. I'm going to give him his bath and get him ready for bed. We'll be back in a bit." Millie rose. "Mind if I watch? I haven't had a chance to put a baby to bed for years. My girls haven't gotten married yet and Walter's wife is expecting, but it's a couple of months away.. Little George is our first grand baby." Sarah smiled, "Sure, come on along. This baby loves his bath. I give him one everyday just because he has so much fun." They headed for the bathroom where Sarah had set up a bathinette for him.

Twenty minutes later, they reappeared with a little tyke in pajamas, a shiny face and the smell of baby powder around him. He was in his grandmother's arms, now. "Look at this little angel." She said to Bert. "Isn't he the sweetest you ever saw?" She handed him to his Grandpa for a good night kiss, which Little George received hesitantly. He wasn't used to Grandpa just yet. Back to Grandma and Sarah led the way to a crib she had set up in the nursery. "We'll just put him in here for now. I'll take him over to my cabin later. His regular crib is over there, this one I just use for daytime naps, now." Down he went, rolled over and went to sleep after Sarah kissed him.

Talk lasted until late. There was much to catch up on. Finally, Sarah said, "Millie, you and Bert will sleep in the bedroom over there. It has a double bed. George will sleep on the cot in the nursery. I'll be next door with the baby for now. We had to rearrange things so you'd be able to have a room to yourselves." She explained that George usually occupied the cabin and she and the baby had the house to themselves, partly because they needed the extra room. She also explained that she took care of all the meals, so George would have time to be close to his son. Millie just nodded her head and finally said. "I see." She just smiled and said, "Well, I think everything will be fine with us." Sarah excused herself and picked up the baby and went off to her cabin.

CHAPTER EIGHT
Family Time

Thanksgiving was a success. Sarah had done her homework well. The turkey turned out just as it should. Millie watched from the sidelines, but kept her remarks down to a minimum. She could see that Sarah knew what she was doing. Grandma lent a hand wherever needed, but avoided the appearance of interfering. Marney had coached Sarah during the previous week as Sarah had put together the menu and Sarah's memory kept her on track. She brought out the set of serving dishes that were for events like this and loaded them with food. They ate and enjoyed. Finally, Millie said, "I've got to quit. If my doctor could see me now, he'd be the one having a heart attack." Everyone laughed. Bert remarked, "Alright, Mother, I'm gonna save room for some of that mince pie, though." Through the entire dinner, Little George had been in his swing sitting between Sarah and Millie. Sarah had prepared a little turkey and dressing for him by mincing it up fine so he could swallow it, then she set the dish next to Millie so she could feed her grandson. The baby loved all the attention he was getting and his grandmother loved giving it to him.

Once dinner was over, Sarah cleared the table, putting the leftovers in the fridge. The dishes went into the sink and on to the dishwasher. Once things were in order, everyone moved into the living room. The baby fell asleep in Grandma's arms and was put down in the day crib. Talk went on for hours. This was a family gathering and hadn't happened for a long time. Finally, Sarah rose and woke Little George for his bath. "You folks stay put, this won't take long.

True to her word, the baby was back dressed in pajamas and ready for good night kisses and tickles. Sarah bid everyone 'good night' and disappeared for the night.

Sarah had phoned her mother in Sacramento, asking her if she'd like to come for Christmas. Things didn't work out; her mother had to appear in court and wouldn't be able to come. All she would say when Sarah asked her what happened; was that she'd been picked up. Sarah knew what that meant and let the matter drop. She spent several hours in tears trying to get her emotions under control. Life could be bitter, even still.

The days came and went. Millie and Sarah developed a close and casual relationship as they worked together accomplishing the daily chores and getting ready for Christmas. The men took one of the Jeeps and went off into the hills for a small Christmas tree. George set it up on a small table in the living room high enough where Little George couldn't get into it. Sarah brought out the gifts she'd bought for Little George and his father. She kept back the presents she'd gotten for the grandparents, not wishing to spoil the surprise. The week before Christmas, Sarah approached Bert and Millie together. "Will you two take charge of decorating the tree? We've got all kinds of decorations, lights, streamers, stars and everything. Since you're the grandparents, I think you should have the privilege." Millie was grateful of Sarah's thoughtfulness and said so. She gave Sarah a hug, saying. "Thank you. That's nice of you. We appreciate it." Sarah blushed. She'd never been hugged by anyone that way before. It was new experience and she felt honored.

The tree got decorated and presents got wrapped. Little George watched all of this activity with great interest as he sat on the floor and watched. He marveled at the colorful decorations on the front door and in the windows. He was especially taken with the pictures of Santa Claus and his Reindeer. Of course he couldn't say much about it, at least in English, he didn't know that, yet, but his actions and squeals of laughter said all that was necessary. What pleased him even more was the attention he was getting from Grandma and Grandpa. He was used to that, now and delighted in it. It wasn't unusual to see him hold out his arms to be picked up every time the two favored people came by. Most of the time, his entreaty was honored and he wound up in someone's arms.

Christmas was a wonderful time. It centered around the joy of two grandparents and a delightful little eleven months old baby boy. Most of what he got was clothing, but there were several baby toys that he inspected and played with for a few moments, then put aside as interest waned. Attention spans are very short at Little George's age. Sarah had taken the little tyke to a professional studio and had his picture taken the week before Thanksgiving. Now the grandparents opened a framed picture of him as a Christmas gift from her. Millie said that it would be the first in her collection of grandchildren. A second picture went to his father. George didn't know what to say.

After dinner, when things were cleared away, Bert made a request. "Would you mind if I read the Christmas Story from the Bible? It's been a tradition in our family since George was a year old and I'd like to continue it." George looked at Sarah with a question on his face. Sarah said, "I don't mind, I've never heard it before." Bert explained. "Well, you see, there are really two Christmases. The one is for the little children. It has Santa Claus and all that and it comes from traditions in different countries. Santa Claus is a derivative of Saint Nicholas. The tradition is that he went about giving gifts to little children. Of course, as different peoples came to America, they brought their traditions with them. All this has been put together gradually and the celebration we now have has stemmed from that. Now the second Christmas is less changed and is far more serious than that of Santa Claus and reindeer and toys and such. That has to do with the birth of Jesus Christ about two thousand years ago. It is the story of a miraculous birth, one we should always remember and which should be a part of every child's education when he or she becomes old enough to understand its meaning. We read this story every Christmas so that we keep it in mind throughout the year."

Sarah said, "Well, I guess I'd like to hear it. I just don't know anything about it. My mother never took us to church or anything like that." Bert spoke up. "That's alright, Sarah, there's lots of us, nowadays who don't know about Jesus Christ's birth. I brought my Bible because I like to read a little in it every day."

Bert settled down in an easy chair and opened the Bible to the Book of Luke and began. He started with the fifth verse of Chapter one. "There was in the days of Herod, the king of Judaea, a certain priest named Zacharias, of the course of Abia and his wife was of the daughters of Aaron, and her name was Elizabeth." Sarah straightened, "That's my name!" She smiled, and leaned forward, her interest was suddenly focused on the story. Bert went on. "And they were both righteous before God, walking in all the commandments and ordinances of the Lord blameless-------." Bert continued on, but Sarah's interest sharpened as the story continued. "What does this mean? Why is this important?" Bert's reading continued and covered the story. "Did God talk to Mary? And what was the Holy Ghost?" The questions began to multiply. She'd never heard anything about this before. She was more than curious. She wanted to know more. She wanted answers. It was as if a door had opened into another world that she hadn't known existed. Her curiosity had become intense.

Bert finally closed the book and laid it aside. "Sarah, I see questions all over your face. What would you like to know?" She hesitated, then asked. "Where can I get a book like that? I'd like to read more about it." Bert turned to George. "Don't you have one, George?" George stumbled momentarily, then said, "Well, yes, but I don't know what I did with it. Maybe Sarah would be more comfortable if she had her own." Sarah agreed, "I would like to have one, then I could read it any time I have a moment." "Well, ask Marney, I think she knows where you can get one." The matter was dropped for the moment and they went on with other things.

It was two days later that Little George provided the excitement for his grandparents that they'd hoped to see. He walked! He'd been pulling up on the chairs and other furniture for nearly a month, but he wobbled and swayed and refused to let go and take steps. His balance wasn't good enough to suit him. This day, however, he'd pulled up as usual and as everyone watched, Sarah held out her hands and coaxed him to come to her. He forgot himself and let go of the chair. He turned and reached out with his foot. First step! Then the other foot came forward and he slowly wobbled his way toward her. She continued to beckon with her hands and he almost made it. His balance deserted him and he fell into Sarah's arms. Good boy! Sarah picked him up and kissed him. He just squealed and giggled while Millie and Bert cheered. Bert exclaimed, "Do you suppose he could do that again?" He had his camera in his hand, now. Sarah put Little George down by the chair again and went back to her seat. As Little George watched, she beckoned to him as before. Again, he turned and let go. This time, his steps were a little more certain and Bert's camera caught him with one foot lifted to step forward. He made it all the way to Sarah's waiting hands and he got picked up and kissed again, to his delight.

The most delighted ones were his grandparents. They'd seen their first grandchild take his first step! Not only that, they had recorded it on film. The only one that missed it was his father. Poor fellow, he had to work and wasn't around

✻

George took his dad on a tour of the ranch to show him how it was laid out and what they were doing at the various locations. Millie stayed behind. She'd wanted to get closer to Sarah and get to know her better. Little did she know what her curiosity would uncover. Sarah was putting some face cream on her cheeks to combat dry skin when Millie exclaimed, "Sarah, what happened to your face? How did you get all those scars under your chin?" Sarah got a grim expression on her face and admitted, "I got beaten up." Millie was horrified. "How'd that happen?" Sarah just said, "Millie, come sit down. There's something you should know and I beg of you to keep it to yourself" Millie only nodded before she sat down and then she said, "I won't let anything between the two of us get out, not even to Bert if you don't want it to."

Sarah gave a long sigh and then started in. "Millie, before I came here, I was a streetwalker. A customer beat me up and robbed me." Millie gasped. "What happened?" Sarah went on. "Your son saved my life. I was almost attacked by another creep and George was parked just behind him. I ran and jumped into George's car. We got away and lost him. Then, Little George started crying and that was it. I got George to find a quiet place and I took care of Little George and got him quieted down. That all happened after Lois had abandoned him. George was looking for a baby sitter that was willing to start right then. That was me. I came here with him and I've never been so happy in my life." Millie broke in, then, "Well, what about what you were doing before?" "Millie, I'll never go back to that. I hated it. My life right now is Little George. I love that little guy. I wish every day that he were mine."

Millie was quiet for long minutes. She'd gotten more than she'd bargained for. Finally, "Does George know about all this?" "Oh, yes, in fact he insisted on medical tests before we came here. I have the letter from the doctor. I'm clean and it's going to stay that way." More pondering on Millie's part. Finally, she said, "Sarah, I'm sorry life has been what it has for you. I like you. I think you're good for my grandson. You're right. All this is just between us.

Now, I have a burning question. I've watched you take care of the baby, I've seen how you've fixed up the house and

I've seen how you've provided meals for George. My question is: How do you feel about George?" Millie was being frank, now. That question startled Sarah. It involved a question that she had been asking herself for several months. It bothered her. She hadn't been able to answer it up to that moment. She'd not dared to be forward toward George. He knew what she'd been. He'd treated her with respect and had been totally circumspect around her at all times. She related all this to Millie, who said, simply, "I thought as much. You're in love with him, aren't you?" Suddenly the answer was clear to her. Sarah answered, "Yes, I guess I am. I know I love his baby boy with all my heart. I know I love George, too, but I feel it's up to him to tell me how he feels." Millie did the unexpected, then. She arose and came over to Sarah and put her arms around her. "Sarah, he will. He will. Give him time. He's had a bad jar with this business of Lois and all. He wrote and told me how badly he felt when she deserted him and the baby. It'll take time for him to get over that, but I don't think it will be much longer. Just be patient. I think you'll be good for George and I know you are the best thing that could have happened to Little George. Don't give up. I'm on your side on this thing if you want me to be, believe me."

Sarah hugged Millie. "Oh Millie, life can get so mixed up. The ladies here are very good friends, but I can't talk to them about this. It would cause problems. That's one reason why I ask you to not tell anyone about it. Another thing. I've worked hard to improve my education and if I can find a way, I'm going to get my high school diploma. I've learned how to do book keeping. I can help George with his work if he wants me to. I want him to want me because I'm worth having, not just as a baby sitter." Millie broke in. "Look, Sarah, you're doing fine. Just take your time. George sees you every day. Just let him get over this divorce thing. I know my boy. He is a stable character and he won't disappoint you. OK?"

CHAPTER NINE

Birthday and Church

Things went along well after Christmas. The families became house bound because of the heavy snow that came after Christmas. The grandparents weren't in a hurry to leave anyway. After all, their grandson's first birthday was due on January 12th and they decided to stay for that event before going home to Idaho. They phoned their son, Walter and he assured them that the ranch was doing quite well without them. "Makes me want to stay here 'til spring," Millie said. Sarah just smiled.

Little George's big day came with more presents, this time practical ones. He appeared outside in a new red snow suit, courtesy of Grandpa and Grandma. By now, he'd mastered the art of walking and Sarah found that nothing was safe from his prying eyes. She'd put locks on the lower cupboards some months ago, now she had to do the same on the higher ones. He'd learned to move chairs in place so he could climb to raid the higher cupboards. His new mobility outstripped Sarah's ability to keep track of him minute to minute. He drove her to distraction at times.

Finally, the day when Bert and Millie decided that the home ranch was calling and the roads were clear at last. George and Sarah loaded them in the ranch station wagon and took them off to Colorado Springs to catch their flight. There were hand shakes, hugs and a kiss for Little George from Grandma, then they were waved through the departure gate and George and Sarah climbed in the car for their trip home. As they started off, Sarah asked George, "George, could you find me a book store. There's a book I want." "Sure, what is it.? She replied, "A Bible. I want to learn more about Jesus Christ." "Alright, I think I know where there is one." They found what they were looking for and ten minutes, later, Sarah had a Bible she liked.

George was curious now, "Why all the sudden interest in the Bible?" he asked. Sarah's answer was a bit tentative. "I don't really know, I just have a feeling about it. I want to know more about Jesus." She said. "I have a feeling that it's important, somehow."

George got talkative on the subject on the way home. He talked about church and his early life. "We used to go to church every Sunday when I was a boy. I went to Sunday School and when I got older, I was active in youth activities. I was even a scout and got my Eagle Award. Things kind of changed when I got in college. Classes demanded so much study time, I quit going all the time and when I got this job, it was hard to go because it's so far. Lois didn't care for it anyway and I kind of gave up on it."

The subject was dropped for awhile and Sarah left it for later discussion when she knew more about it. She started reading her new Bible after she'd talked to Marney about it. Marney told her that she ought to read about Genesis first, so she would have some idea as to how things all got started, then she could start picking and choosing what might interest her. This continued for a time until she asked George if he'd take her to church one Sunday. "I want to find out what they're like." She said. George asked her. "Which one do you want to go to?" She answered, "Well which one would you go to? I don't know one from another. Why don't you take me to the one you used to go to?" He agreed. "Is next Sunday alright with you?" She agreed. "Alright, we'll go to the one in Canon City. That's closest. Now, you'll want to wear your best dress, the blue one, I think. Also, we'll dress Little George up, too. He's big enough he can wear his long pants." "Won't he make too much noise?" Sarah asked. "Well, we'll just have to take him out if he gets too noisy. Otherwise, it's good for him to learn to behave in church at this age. It saves him trouble later. You'll see. Don't worry, I've been through all this with my sisters."

The next Sunday, they got ready early and made the long drive to Canon City. They arrived, parked the car and found seating in the chapel. Others crowded around, introducing themselves and trying to make them welcome. Sarah was a little intimidated at first, but she realized that they were only trying to be friendly and returned their greetings with a smile. She explained, "I'm Sarah Mills and I live out at Oxbow Ranch. I take care of George's baby." She was accepted and welcomed as was George. They sat through the worship meeting, hearing several talks on different subjects and then adjourning for Sunday School. Since Sarah was unfamiliar with the regular classes, she was invited to go to a special class that taught basics. She began to relate things she'd read about with things the instructor was teaching and she felt that she was getting something out of the class. When the class was over; she was invited to participate in a meeting exclusively for the ladies. She took Little George with her and promptly found herself surrounded by other mothers and their babies, some even younger and some older. She was made welcome and invited to come again.

On the way home, George was curious. "Well, what did you think of that?" Sarah said, "George, it was all so new, but I think I liked it. People seemed to be glad that I was there. I've never experienced that kind of treatment before." "Well, do you want to go back again?" "Oh, could we?" "If you want to. As long as there's nothing going on at the ranch, we can always go. It's probably good for Junior, too. In a couple of years, he'll be big enough to start in the little kid's class. He'll start learning about Jesus on a little kid's level. I'd like that to happen, if it's possible."

CHAPTER TEN
Wedding Bells

This routine took hold and, other than Sundays when George had to work or when he was gone on a business trip, they were in church. Whether this new adventure was the cause or not was never established, but George and Sarah's relationship began to change. New feelings toward each other began to develop. Sarah had become such a close part of George's life that he could no longer ignore it. Likewise, George was a prominent part of Sarah's thoughts much of her waking hours. George seemed to take more and more notice of her each day and she went out of her way to do special things for him. Finally, one evening in August, they were sitting under the poplar trees in the yard, waiting for the daytime temperature to get cooler. George suddenly brought up a subject that had been left alone for over a year. The divorce! He remarked. "You know, Lois has been gone for over a year. It's strange, but I can hardly remember what she looked like. I do remember how badly she treated Little George. Sarah, I have you to thank for how that boy is doing, now. Remember when I said that I decided that I wanted you to be his baby sitter and why I wanted you?" Sarah nodded her head. She thought, "Where is this going?" George soon explained. "Sarah, I was right. That kid thinks you're his mother." At that, Sarah burst into tears. This was a surprise, she hadn't expected it. George was surprised by her tears. He hesitated only a moment, then put his arms around her. "I'm sorry. I didn't mean to hurt your feelings." "You didn't," she sobbed. "I only wish it were true what you said. I'm not his mother and I wish I were." Tears streamed down her face. George pulled her closer and hugged her tightly. "Sarah, I want you to answer one question. I've been thinking and I've hesitated to ask, but I think it only fair to ask you, now. Do you love me?" She couldn't speak, but she nodded her head.. "I thought so. I know how you feel about Little George. Mom told me." Sarah said, hesitantly, "What else did she tell you?" "Nothing. She told me I'd have to ask you." "Ask me what?" "If you'd marry me. Sarah, I love you. I only wish I'd met you long before I met Lois. I've rued the day I married her. She didn't know one thing about love and all that. I'm finding it's an instinct with you." Sarah felt a question rising within her. She had to know the answer before she could answer George's proposal. "George, I have to know one thing. You know what I was before you took me off the streets. Does that make any difference to you, now? Honest answer." His answer was short and instantaneous. "No. That girl doesn't exist any more. You'll never hear one word about it from me, ever." Sarah asked one more questions. "George, did you know that your mom knows about me?" "No, I didn't. Why? Did you tell her?" "Yes, I did. I felt that I had to be honest with her and that she should know, so I told her. She felt that I'd left that behind, also. Now, to answer your question; the answer is yes, I'll marry you. I've wanted you to ask me for a long time, but I knew you had to put Lois out of your mind so she'd never interfere between us. I think all that is past and gone. When do you want us to be married?" George thought for a moment. "Well, I think, for convenience sake, we ought to be married as soon as possible, but I also think that we ought to allow enough time for people we know to be told so they can attend the wedding. Oh, yes, do you want to be married in the church or at a Justice of the Peace's office?" The answer was quick and firm. "Church." "Alright, I'll get on the phone in the morning and make the arrangements. Today is Monday. We need to send out announcements and we need to call Mom and Dad and ask them if they can come. In fact we can do that tonight. How about Saturday after next?" Sarah was excited, now. "George, that's just fine with me. Do you want me in white or is some other color?" George thought for a second. "I'll ask Mom, but white is my choice and I know you'll look super in white. If you want, I'll take you into Pueblo tomorrow and see if we can find you a dress. Who do you want for your bridesmaids?" Sarah exclaimed, "Oh, I've got to run over and ask Marney and Laura if they would do that. I'll do that after we talk to your Mom. They went on for a few moments and then George said, "You know what?" "Know what?" "I haven't kissed you yet. Don't you want me to?" George, I'm waiting and you know where I am." After a long interlude, she said, "Now, I feel engaged. I love you George. Let's go call your Mom."

George made the call and his Mom answered. "Mom, I'm engaged. Sarah says to tell you that you were right. It did take a little time, but it was worth waiting for. Here she is." Sarah just said, "Mom, I want you to come, will you? And bring Bert. You will? Good. Here's George again. Love you Mom." She blew a kiss at George and went out the door to see Marney and Laura.

Her meeting with the two women was a joyous one. "You are! Congratulations." She got more hugs from both and promises that they would be happy to be her bridesmaids. Back to the house, now, she had one more call to make. Hopefully, her mother hadn't gone out yet and she could catch her at home. When she dialed, the phone rang several times and a querulous voice answered. "Mother?" she asked, then spoke,. "This is Sarah." "Sarah? Is that you?" "Yes, Mom, it's me. I have some news for you. I'm getting married Saturday after next. Can you come? I can send you a ticket if you want." There was a long silence, then, "You're getting married?" "Yes Mom, I'm getting married and he's a good man. I've been taking care of his baby for over a year and we've decided that we love each other. Now, can you come?" The answer came slowly "Yes, I think so. Send a ticket and I'll be there. OK?" "Yes, Mom. I'll call you and tell you where to pick up the ticket when I get it arranged. Bye, Mom."

The very next day, George took Sarah and went to Pueblo to see about a wedding dress. Marney and Laura went with them to see about the bridesmaid's dresses, as well. They found a shop that specialized in these garments and Sarah found a dress that suited her. She was fitted and found that very few alterations needed to be made. The lady who attended her said, "We can do these in a couple of hours and you can take the dress and veil with you this afternoon." Likewise, Marney and Laura found dresses that matched and fitted them well enough. They were carefully boxed up and carried away. One more item was needed. Sarah needed a pair of white shoes. These were found and purchased. Mission accomplished.

On the way home, later, a stop was made in Canon City and George talked to the Pastor of the church. Arrangements were made for the wedding and for a reception after the ceremony. He was promised that announcements would be made on the very next Sunday, so that everyone could plan to come. In the short time that they had been attending the church services, they'd become well acquainted and Sarah felt that many would want to come. With that done, they went home with a feeling of accomplishment and progress. Sarah thanked Laura and Marney for taking the time to go with her and help her. They both hugged her and Marney said, "Sarah, we're doing this for you. We love you, dear!"

The next Sunday, the announcements were made from the pulpit and the rest of the day was filled with congratulations and words of encouragement. In all of this, Little George was awed by the activities that were going on around him. He didn't understand them, but everyone seemed so happy, he decided to be on his best behavior and added his approval.

Sarah and George noticed something about Little George that they hadn't been aware of before. He was starting to say things. 'No' was a big part of his vocabulary. The thing that caused a jump in their hearts were two other special words. "Mama and Dada."

Sarah noticed it first and called it to George's attention. They decided to ignore the fact that Sarah was not his mother, because she shortly would be, anyway. They encouraged him. At nineteen months, Little George wasn't really a baby any more, he was a little boy! In a few days, his life was going to change. His family would be truly complete.

On Thursday preceding the wedding, Sarah's mother arrived and Sarah and George made the trip to pick her up at the Colorado Springs airport. Sarah had called the airline and arranged for her ticket and then called her mother to tell her where to pick it up. Her mother seemed apprehensive about coming, but Sarah told her that she especially wanted her to come and that she'd be glad to see her again. "It's been a long time Mother, I've missed you."

When Edith Mills appeared at the baggage claim, Sarah was shocked to see the change in her mother's appearance. She appeared to be ten years older than the forty five years of her actual age. She had been a rather pretty woman when Sarah had last seen her four years before. What had happened? Sarah walked up to her and spoke her name. She turned and Sarah folded her into her arms. Sarah's eyes filled with tears. This was her mother. For all the time that had passed and hardships they'd both been through since they'd last seen each other, this was still her mother. They held this embrace for several minutes, just rocking back and forth. Then Sarah spoke, "Mom, I've missed you!" Her mother moved back a step. "I've missed you, too. My, you're beautiful! My memory's slipping. I don't remember your looking this good when I last saw you." Sarah laughed through her tears. "Mom, a lot has happened. I'll tell you all about it when we get home. Come and meet my husband to be."

"George. This is my Mom. Edith Mills." Her mother stuck out her hand to George. He ignored it and put his arms around her and hugged her. "I'm George. Pleased to meet you. And this little fellow is my son, George. We call him 'Little

George'. He's starting to talk, now, so you'd better tell him what you want him to call you. On Saturday, he'll become your grandson, so get used to him." Edith smiled tentatively. "Well, I never had one, before, so I guess that kind of goes for both of us." Bending down, she said, "Hello, Georgie, I'm Grammy." Little George just eased back against his father's legs. This one was new to him and he'd take his time getting acquainted.

Edith only had a small bag, so it was quickly loaded and they headed for home. Sarah provided most of the conversation as they traveled. "Aren't the mountains beautiful? This is part of the ranch we live on. Mom, there's fish in that creek and it runs right behind my house." On and on she talked, trying to make her mother feel welcome. Little George didn't say much from his car seat. This lady was still a stranger and he was taking his time deciding about her presence. Finally, they drove into Oxbow and up to the house. Sarah told her mother, "Mom, I'm going to put you up with Little George and me for now. Is that OK?" Her mother just nodded for a moment, then said, "Whatever you think. This place is going to take some getting used to. This is almost a little town isn't it?" Sarah laughed. "It used to be, Mom. It's our headquarters, now. This ranch is a big place and all of this is where we run it from. We've got quite a few people that live and work here. Never mind, we'll tell you more about it, later. Right now, let's get you inside and settled. I've got so much to tell you. I'm so glad you could come." Edith hesitantly said, "Well, yes, I've got a lot to tell you, too." That said, she opened the door and got out.

Sarah touched her arm. "Come on inside and I'll show you my house. You'll be proud of me." With that, she led the way inside. She pointed out the different rooms and told how she'd made it the home it was. Her mother was awestruck. Her daughter wasn't the same person she remembered. "What had happened to her that changed her so much?"

"Mom, I'm going to put you in here for now. This is the nursery and Little George has been in here, but I'm going to make some changes anyway, so we'll put him in with us in my room for now. OK?" "Sarah, this is beautiful. How'd you do it? I can't believe all this." She stood, taking it all in. It became obvious that she wasn't used to the neatness and the well appointed place she was standing in. Sarah suddenly got the impression that her mother wasn't well off, physically or financially at all. Seeing Edith's shabby appearance told a lot about her circumstances. It painted a rather ugly picture of abject squalor and Sarah wondered what the true picture was.

George had appeared with Edith's bag and put it in the nursery where Sarah indicated it should go, then turning to her, said, "I'll leave you to get reacquainted with your mom and see you later. I've got all kinds of things I've got to get done. I'll be back for dinner." He kissed her and left. Edith noticed the open affection her daughter had been given and felt a pang in her heart. It had been a long time since she'd received such from anyone. It hurt, more than a little.

The next day was Friday. Sarah attended to her regular routine and took care of a number of details that were needed to get ready for the wedding. Among them was the chore of setting up a small junior bed in her room for Little George. It was time for him to leave his crib behind, perhaps for a brother or sister. She had George take down the crib and store it.

George got a call from his parents early in the morning. They would arrive at three o'clock and could he pick then up? "Coming, Mother!" In the meantime, Sarah and her mother got busy and prepared another vacant cabin for the elder Tolands. This had been anticipated, but they hadn't had time to take care of it. Now, it had to get done and mother and daughter went to work to get it done. Late in the afternoon, George brought Bert and Millie into the yard and there were hugs and kisses all over the place. Sarah showed the two to their cabin and got their luggage put in the closet. It wasn't long before Millie got Sarah aside. Her first words were, "See, Sarah. Didn't I tell you?" Sarah was jubilant to see her. She told her, "I knew exactly what you were going to say. I just knew it! You were right, of course. It just took George a little time. Lois hurt him pretty bad and it took awhile to get completely over it." Millie came right back with, "I know, dear. But let me tell you something. It was you that turned the tide. You've been everything but a bride to him. You've been the mother Little George didn't have with Lois and that's what swayed George. He knows how much you love that little guy. Don't you ever forget how important you are to him. I'm glad to have you as a daughter-in-law and don't you forget that either."

Sarah found time to spend with her mother and talk with her about her life since she and Sarah had separated four years before. Sarah was shocked when she heard the hardships her mother had gone through. Life on the street hadn't been kind to Edith at all. She'd been beaten several times, had been in the hospital and in jail twice. She'd had to live in places that were dumps and had even slept in the streets for months at a time. She'd managed to hold a job as a short order cook in a small restaurant for awhile, but that ended when the owner had suffered a heart attack and the restaurant was no more. She told Sarah she was staying with a friend who had room for an extra bed in a transient hotel. She finally admitted that the things she had in her suitcase were all she had of this world's goods. Her last meal before boarding the airplane had been two days before. As this narrative went on, Sarah succumbed to her emotions. All she could say between sobs was, "Oh Mom, how could this happen to you? You were always looking ahead. You were always on top of things." Her mother's answer was, "Things change when you get older." Finally, Edith said, "I don't know what I'll do when I leave here. The picture isn't pretty." That's all she would say. She told Sarah that she was sorry if she was disappointed in her mother, but that was the way it was. All Sarah could say was, "Mom, we can't let you go back out of here like that!" She stopped. What could she do? The thought printed itself in her mind. What could she do? She didn't know.

Suddenly, it was Saturday and at two O'clock, Sarah Mills would become Sarah Toland. Not only that, she'd become a stepmother to the little boy she loved almost more than life itself. Her heart swelled nearly to bursting in thinking of it. As morning went by, she moved all of George's belongings over from the cabin back into the house where he'd lived with Lois. She moved Edith's meager possessions into the cabin and hung everything up for her. She moved Little George's new trundle bed into the now deserted nursery. He would be comfortable there. He was used to sleeping there and he was familiar with the room if not the new bed. She pressed out the new dress she'd gotten for her mother when they'd picked her up in Colorado Springs on Thursday. Finally, she called her mom and George in for the early lunch she'd fixed and they ate and got ready to drive to Canon City and the church. Everything had been packed in the car since early morning and George had given Fred Sowles the wedding ring that he'd bought for Sarah the week before. As far as they could tell, everything was ready. Even Little George was dressed in his finest. He strutted around the house crowing about his new shoes.

Shortly after noon, the procession started for the church. It would take an hour to get there, but that would allow a little time for her to dress in her wedding dress and veil plus time for a rehearsal and for final primping. All went well and at two o'clock, the chapel was full. The ceremony went forward and finally the magic words, "I pronounce you Husband and Wife." were heard.. George cast aside all inhibitions and firmly kissed his new wife of less than a minute. She kissed him back again without any embarrassment at all. He was hers and she was his. That's all there was to it! It took only a few minutes for Sarah to change into her best dress and to carefully fold and box her wedding dress. Her eyes misted when she thought of what that dress represented to her. She was a happy woman.

The reception lasted for two hours and the reception line moved slowly as each welcomed guest and well wisher congratulated them. Finally, the church cleared and the wedding party gathered up and headed back to the Oxbow. Things were arranged a little differently, however. Edith elected to travel with Fred and Marney Sowles. Little George was on the seat between the bride and groom, however. He belonged there and they were glad he was. It was a comfort to him because his new mom held him and talked to him all the way home.

Sarah and George decided to postpone their honeymoon for several reasons. First, there was Little George to consider and Grammy wasn't in a position to be left to fend for herself, either. She wasn't acquainted enough at the ranch to properly do that, plus, Sarah was worried about her because of her physical condition. Finally, there were problems with George's work that needed attention. Sarah and George agreed that they would take an extended vacation in November when the work has wound down for the season.

CHAPTER ELEVEN

Edith Stays

Things settled down for a few days, Grandpa and Grandma Toland had to go back to Idaho. Sarah took them to the airport and after affectionate hugs and a kiss for Grandpa, sent them on their way. Grammy Mills was still recovering from her semi-starved condition and Sarah cared for her as she began to get her health back.

George came in one evening a couple of weeks later with a problem he was trying to solve and didn't have an immediate fix for. "I've got a sick cook." he complained.. "He apparently bruised or cut himself some way and it got infected. Now, he can't go on. I'm going to take him in to the hospital in Pueblo tonight, but I don't have a cook at Division Five. There're twelve hungry guys out there and not a one of them knows how to burn water."

Sarah turned to her mother and asked, "Mom, didn't you tell me that you worked as a short order cook some months ago?" Edith answered, "Yes, I did, but I don't know if I can cook for a bunch of cowboys. I've never done that, before." George broke in, "Listen, Edith, if you could just fill in for three or four days, that would help us get through this. Maybe we'd at least know if this guy that I'm taking to the hospital is going to be alright by then." Sarah added her voice to the discussion. "Mom, would you at least give it a try?" George added, "We'd pay you what we're paying this man and you'd have a cabin to stay in as part of the deal." Edith wavered and then agreed to give it a try. She said, "Look I don't have any clothes that will stand up to that kind of work. You'll have to bring me some by tomorrow or I'll be wearing gunnie sacks." Sarah said, "What do you need? I'll go into Canon City and get all you want and bring them to you." Edith added, "You better bring me a pair of ankle length leather shoes, too. I only have a pair of tennie runners and they won't stand up to anything. I wear a size six." "Done." Sarah said.

George broke in. "Now that we have that worked out, I'll take Flapjack in to the doctor starting right now. I don't know how long I'll be, so don't look for me until late. I'll call you if I get in trouble. I'll call the minute I know anything about Flapjack's injury. Meantime, can you take Edith up to Division Five and get her started? Tell Hackamore, that foreman we've got up there what we're doing. You know how he frets when things go wrong. Tell him we'll either get Flapjack back up there if possible or we'll find him another cook. Take Little George with you, if you want. He'll like the ride and he can be company for you. It's only eight miles up there, so it shouldn't take too long. OK. Gotta go." With that, he disappeared down the road to Pueblo.

Sarah helped Edith pack her little bag and loaded her and Little George into a jeep. A half hour later, they pulled up at Division Five headquarters and found Hackamore. Sarah explained the arrangements to him and asked him to give Edith a try for at least a few days. She said, "At least, the men will have something to eat, 'til we can get this sorted out." Hackamore nodded and said, "Come on in the kitchen and I'll explain where everything is and what you'll have to do." Sarah picked up her little boy and followed Hackamore and Edith into the cook shack. Once inside, the foreman explained how and when meals were served. He explained to Edith a little about what the men liked for meals. He said, "There's a pot of beans on the stove. All you'll have to do is heat it before you put it on the table. Also, I know that Flapjack was going to fry some steaks for supper and put on a green salad with all that. There's salad dressing in the refrigerator and I'll show you how to run the coffee machine. Think you can make out with that?" Edith nodded her head. "That's not much different than I did before. I think I can do it alright." Hackamore added, "Flapjeck made out a menu for the week three or four days ago, so you can use that to put together meals for each day for awhile. Also, I know he had listed bacon and eggs for breakfast tomorrow. Now, our guys are touchy about their eggs, so ask them what they want and try to see that they get them. If you have trouble with anyone, come see me. OK?"

Hackamore moved off and Sarah asked her mother, "Mom, are you going be alright?" The answer was "Yes." "Do you want me to stay and help out to get started?" Edith said, "No. I need to handle this on my own. If it works out, I'll stay on if they'll let me." Sarah said, "Way to go, Mom. That sounds like the old you. Alright, I gotta go. I'll see you as soon as I can round up the clothes you need. Oh, work with Hackamore and make up a list of supplies you'll need for the next couple of weeks. When you get it together, have Hackamore phone it down to us at Oxbow, so we can order it. I'll explain more about that when I come up tomorrow. Now, you're sure you're going to be alright?" Her mother said , "Yes." kissed her and sent her on her way.

The next morning, George called from Pueblo. Sarah went over everything she'd done at Division Five and told George that she was going into Canon City to get the outfits her mother needed. She asked about Flapjack. George said, "Bad news, there, I'm afraid. The doctor told me that he could go home within three or four days, but the infection wouldn't be healed for over a month. Do you think your mother is going to be able to handle that job up there alright?" Sarah said, "I'll know by this afternoon when I take the clothes she needs up to her." George told her, "Go to it, but, be fair. If she can't handle it, tell me. If she can, we'll leave her there until Flapjack can come back." With that, he gave her a kiss through the phone and hung up.

Sarah made the trip to Canon City and picked up the clothing items her mother had asked for then headed for Division Five. When she got there, she unloaded the items and sought out Edith. "Well, how's it going?" Edith smiled and told her that she'd managed supper just fine. "The boys' liked the beans and steak combination and they said that the coffee was better than they'd been getting. Breakfast was OK, too. I had to work like a beaver to get the egg orders right, but it was just like old times and I did alright. I fixed them some toast and put some jam on the table with it. They took after that like a cat after a squirrel. I think I'm going to like it here. The boys were actually nice to me. I'm not used to that, but I like it." Sarah hugged Edith and said, "See you later." She sought out Hackamore and asked him point blank. "How'd she do?" Hackamore grinned, "Well," he said, "If she keeps on like she did last night and this morning, she can stay on if Flapjack doesn't want to come back. By-the-way, how's he doing?" Sarah frowned, "He's not too good. George said that the doctor told him Flapjack could go home in three or four days, but he won't heal completely for at least a month. I think we'd better hope that Edith pans out. It would save us a lot of trouble. If this works out, I think George will probably put Flapjack to doing something around Oxbow at least until he's healed up. I don't think George will send him back up here until he's ready to go back to cooking." He said, "That's probably a good idea. That stove jockey would probably just sit around here and complain if he came back before he was ready."

Sarah said, "Well, I gotta go. Don't forget to have Edith make out your supply list by Wednesday, so we can get your supplies ordered. Thanks, Hackamore" With that, she put Little George in the car seat and drove home.

CHAPTER TWELVE
Marriage and Family

Back at Oxbow, Sarah stopped at Marney's to visit. Marney asked her, "How's the bride?" Sarah just laughed and remarked. "I think I'm going to like it It's kind of fun. Seriously, though, you know what I'm finding I really like? Little George is getting big enough that I can take him with me and he's not so fragile any more." Marney just laughed.' Sarah; just wait 'til you have two or three little ones around you." Sarah gasped, 'I never thought about that, did I?" Marney got a malicious grin on her face."Look out, girl, it could happen." Sarah grinned right back. "Marney, I hope it does. I've never felt more needed than I do right now and I found out when I first came here that I really love little kids." Marney got serious, then. "You're right. I feel the same way. I've watched you with Junior, there. That kid really got the best of the deal when he got you." All Sarah could say was, "Thanks, Marney. That's nice of you to say that."

Sarah spent the rest of the afternoon putting her house in order. The trundle bed was in the nursery for Junior and all of the wedding fixings including her dress were put away. She did a wash and set the clothes to dry. Finally, she put together a tasty supper for George when he got home. She'd made a Jello salad and mixed in peaches, a favorite of George's. She was ready to set the table when he walked in the door and was attacked by his son, who he promptly picked up and tickled where he liked it the most. Dad was in a good mood.

Supper was on the table and with Junior in his high chair, they enjoyed a tasty if quiet meal. Supper done and dishes washed and put away, Sarah spoke, "George, could I have a special moment?" George got a questioning look. "Sure, what about.?" "Well, come and sit" He sat. She said, "You know that Little George isn't so little any more and I think we need to call him something a little more dignified" George said, "What do you think we should call him? His middle name is Thomas after my mother's maiden name. We could call him Tom or Tommy, I suppose. I don't like Junior, because it seems demeaning somehow. Do you want to try Tommy?" Sarah said, "That's a good name. We can try it and see how he likes it.. Now, that's not exactly what I wanted to talk about. Little George, sorry, Tommy, is getting close to age two. I think it's time we had another baby in the house. What do you think?" George smiled. "That is a different subject, alright! Well, that's a bit of a surprise. Do you want one?" Sarah smiled, "Yes, Sweetheart, I do. Here, she leaned over and kissed him. Tommy needs a brother or sister. I don't think it's a good idea to raise an only child. I was one and I was always lonely. We can afford another one and I've had a wonderful time raising Tommy so far. How do you feel about it?" George was on the spot, now, but, he'd hoped that Sarah wouldn't object to another child. Now she was asking for one. Lois never did that. George got up from his chair and took his wife in his arms. He kissed her and said softly, "I'd like another baby, too. I know you like babies and I think it'd please Mother and Dad. They've been hinting that they'd like to have lots of grandchildren." With that, he held her in his arms and tenderly kissed her.

One evening a day or two later Sarah brought up a subject she'd had on her mind for several days.. "George, I have a question. Now, that we're married, what happens to my salary for taking care of the baby?" She put a grin on her face. "I bet you married me just so you could quit paying my high wages. Come on, admit it." George got a sly look on his face, "Of course, I'd never do a thing like that. You know how honest I am. Tell you what. Suppose I keep on giving you the fifty dollars a day as a household allowance. You can use it to buy whatever you need for the children or clothes for your self, whatever you feel you need. Would that work out?" She pretended to think about it for a moment, then responded. "Well, we can try it. I'll work up a budget, too. I've got a sample one on that bookkeeping program I have on the computer. I'll let you know how I'm doing each month and if we have to adjust, at least we can see what we're doing. How does that sound?" George put his finger on his chin as if he were thinking. "Let's try it. We can always make changes if we have to. Oh, yes, make an allowance for a savings account. I want you to put some by for emergencies and that sort of thing. We can invest some of it and build a nest egg." Sarah got excited at her husbands suggestions. "Oh, Sweetheart. This sounds wonderful. So many people don't do this sort of thing and they never have anything but debts. I don't want that. I've seen too much of it. Look at what's happened to my mom. She's broke and she has nothing." George was pleased at Sarah's practical approach to their family finances.

Sarah took her conversation with George seriously. She talked to Marney about it and Marney simply said, "Sarah, you're on the right track. We went broke once while Fred and I were both in college. We overspent our credit cards and couldn't pay them off at the end of the month. It was the most frightening thing I ever went through. I cried for a week" Her friend told her that putting money away so it could be used in an emergency was the wisest thing she could do. Marney went on and expanded on the subject. "Sarah, don't over spend yourself. Don't ever overspend your credit card. Spend only what you can pay for. Pay your bills on time. You'll never be sorry like we were that time." Sarah spent some time working out a system of saving that would stand her and her family in good stead for years to come. First, she opened a savings account , then gradually built it up as she could. Once it had reached a substantial level, she left it alone and opened an IRA, which she kept building up. She showed George what she was doing and he was surprised, but praised her for it. He learned bit by bit how much she loved him. It seemed that she took every opportunity to strengthen their marriage and he was proud of her.

CHAPTER THIRTEEN

Life on the Oxbow

Flapjack Rawlins spent a week in the hospital while the doctor got control of the infection in his arm. He finally came home from the hospital, weakened but happy to be on the mend. George set him up in one of the cabins and told him to take it easy. He said, "Flapjack, I want you to rest for awhile. I've got a little job you can do if you feel up to it. I do it myself, but its small enough it doesn't take long." Flapjack's interest perked up right away. "OK, George, just what do you want me to do?" George explained, "What I want you to do is take all these supply orders that come in from the divisions and make out the orders we send to the suppliers. It doesn't take long and they only come in once every other week. If you can do that, it would help me keep ahead of some other things I have to do." "Sure, George, I can do that, I think." George went on. "I'll set you up on this desk and you can work there if that's alright with you." Flapjack sat down and said, "I'm ready. What do you have?" George reached out to his desk and picked up several papers. He set them down in front of Flapjack. "OK, here are orders from Divisions, Two, Four and Five. What I want you to do is list all of the articles listed on the general order sheets and pencil in the amounts of each item the divisions order. Now, since we don't have orders from all of the divisions yet, just pencil in the amount each division wants in the square for each division. When you've got all of the orders from each division listed, then you can add up all of the orders for each single item and that's what we'll send to the suppliers. Here, let me show you." He took a general order sheet and said, "Suppose you have an item on Division Two's order sheet, let's say it's potatoes."

George went on to explain the details. He finished with, "When you've got it all together, bring it to me to check, then, I'll give it to Fred Sowles and he'll send in the order. Think you can do that?" Flapjack looked George in the eye and said, "This won't take long. What else do you want me to do?" George just laughed. "Well if you get bored, come see me and I'll find something else for you. I'll just keep you as busy as you feel you want to be. If you get tired, or want to quit, take a rest. That OK with you?" Flapjack's response, "OK, Boss, I can handle it."

Time passed. Flapjack caught on to the various jobs George gave him. His energies began to recover, but he'd decided that he didn't want to go back to cooking. He'd done that for many years and put up with the usual guff that working men on ranches often give cooks. One day, he went to George and asked to discuss the problem. He said, "Look George, that lady you've got cooking up at Division Five is doing better than I ever could. I can tell by her orders, she knows what she's doing. In fact, if I were to go back up there and take her place, they'd probably lynch me. Now, why don't you find something I can do here and leave her up there to keep those hardhead cowpunchers happy?" George was surprised. He'd not realized that Flapjack had caught on as well as he had. "Flapjack?" he asked. "Do you suppose you could keep track of our complete supply budget on a month to month basis? You'd have to know about costs and keep track of how much each division was spending on supplies and what they were spending it on. I noticed that you could see how Mrs. Mills was feeding her men by just looking at what she was ordering. I think we need to know more about what our divisions are doing. One of the things we want to do with the people in each division is to keep them happy. They do better work that way." Flapjack thought for a minute. Finally, he spoke. "I think so, Boss. I'd like to try, anyway."

Flapjack buckled down to learning the job. It was more difficult than he'd anticipated, but Sarah came in and helped him work out ways to get what he was looking for. She taught him how to use the computer to compile data that he needed and it wasn't too long before he'd mastered the job and George found that they'd realized considerable savings in their supply expenses.

Edith Mills suddenly found that the emergency position she'd hesitantly taken was rapidly becoming a full time job that was giving her a new perspective on her life. Within a few month's time, she'd developed an entirely new regard for herself. Her feeling of self worth grew by leaps and bounds. Sarah's visits to Division Five and to her mother made her feel that her mother was recovering her self esteem from the desperate, hopeless level she'd had when she came to Oxbow Ranch.

Sarah had been visiting her mother occasionally ever since she'd become cook for the Fifth Division. Edith was firmly in charge in the kitchen at Fifth Division, now, and the cowboys had developed a staunch respect for her. There was no ribbing or snide remarks about burned food. She had added little goodies that appeared on the table from time to time. She'd even baked several birthday cakes when she could discover the date of the birthday as she had for the foreman, Melvin Hadding, otherwise known as Hackamore. She was careful to only use a cowboys name if he didn't mind her using it. For example, Hackamore would be ready for a fist fight if someone called him by his given name, 'Melvin'. He was sensitive about it and would not tolerate anyone using it. Edith was careful and never did.

Spring was over and summer begun. One day, early in July, Hackamore came by the cook shack and asked Edith a question. "Ever been fishin'?" The answer was "No, why?" "Wanna go?" "Sure if I can be back by five o'clock. Gotta get supper started by then." "Don't worry. Everybody took off for the Fourth.. There's only three of us here to watch the place. "Alright, wait'll I get my hat." They all three piled into the Jeep and started up the creek into a deep shady canyon. After a mile or so, Hackamore stopped the Jeep in the shade of a large poplar tree and climbed out. He picked up a creel off the floor of the Jeep and helped Edith out of the back seat. The other man, Slowpoke by name, picked up a similar creel and started walking up the canyon. Hackamore told Edith, "We've got about a mile walk to get to the good fishing holes. This gets steeper and the Jeep won't go any further."

It didn't take long for Edith to see what he meant. The walls of the canyon closed in and they had to walk over rocks and through bushes and occasionally even in the water to keep going. Finally, they found a broader area where the walls of the canyon pulled back away from the stream. Hackamore set the creel down and pulled out a large knife. He went up to a bushy willow on the creek bank and proceeded to cut two clean branches about eight or nine feet long. He carefully cut away all the twigs and forks, leaving a sturdy fishing pole. He opened the creel and extracted two rolls of fishing line. He carefully tied one end of each roll to one of the fishing poles and then unrolled the line. Once each line was unrolled, Edith could see a small weight and a fish hook fixed to the end of it. Hackamore then brought out a small jar that had some little balls in it. "Fish eggs" he told Edith. He unscrewed the cap and took out a couple of eggs, affixing them to the fish hook. "Now, watch," he said. "Notice, I hold the end of the pole in my hand and hold the hook with the other hand. Be very careful. You can hook yourself in the hand if you catch the line on something." He walked quietly toward the stream bank where there was an opening through to the water. Carefully, he thrust the pole through the hole and released the hook so it swung out over the water, He then gently lowered the bait into the water, allowing it to sink slowly. Suddenly, there was a brown flash in the water and a jerk on the tip of the pole. "Got him" Hackamore said. He carefully lifted the pole as the fish jerked the tip back and forth. He kept easing the pole back away from the stream until the fish was against the bank. Then, he reached down, got his fingers down below the fish. Suddenly, he grabbed the fish and brought it out on the bank away from the water. "There, see how I did that? Now, you try it." He baited the hook again and handed the pole to Edith.

Hackamore coached her on getting the pole into position and dropping the bait into the water. In a few moments, she experienced a jerk on the pole and reacted instinctively. She jerked up and back on the pole. There was a loud splash as the fish left the water, arched up over the willows and flew off the hook back into the bushes. Hackamore started laughing and nearly choked. Finally, he said, still laughing. "Well, ya got 'im. Congratulations." Edith was as surprised as the fish had been. She said, "What did I do wrong.? And what are you laughing at, anyway" Hackamore had gone over to the bushes and had picked up the now wriggling, stranded fish. "Well, you just got a little excited when the fish went after the bait, that's all. Most everbody does that the first time!"

Hackamore then explained what she'd done wrong and what she should do the next time she had a bite. He explained that she only needed a gentle jerk to set the hook and then she could lead the fish over to the bank where they could grab it or catch it in the net that Slowpoke had brought. "Tell you what, why don't you bait your hook and try that open spot over there?" he said, pointing. He watched her bait the hook as he had showed her and followed her down to the creek again. This time, she was careful as the bait went into the water. A fish struck, she did the gentle jerk as she'd been coached and the fish was on. Hackamore talked her along as she slowly led the fish to the bank, where Hackamore used the net to capture Edith's second fish.

Edith was in a hurry to get bait in the water. She put on another fish egg and dropped it into the water. She got the same results after about a five minute wait. Jerk. Set the hook. Work the fish over to the bank. Hackamore was ready with the net again. Number three. Using the same efficient technique, she got two more. Then Hackamore said that was all she was allowed. He baited up his own pole and said. "Why don't you watch me for awhile. You can net the ones I catch if you want to. Oops, Slowpoke's got one. Take the net down to him and maybe he'll let you catch it." She did as he'd suggested and soon had another fish to add to their collection.

The rest of the afternoon, she netted fish as Hackamore and Slowpoke caught them. About four o'clock, they called a halt. Hackamore had four and Slowpoke had three. Hackamore cleaned the fish when they got ready to leave. As he cleaned them, Slowpoke carefully wrapped them in fern leaves and put them in a cloth sack. He then dipped the sack in the cold water to keep them cool. Finally, they took the fish lines off the poles and coiled then up, then put them in the creel. Hackamore retrieved the sackful of fish and the fishing party started back to the Jeep.

As soon as they reached the headquarters, Hackamore told Edith to wash the fish carefully and put them in the refrigerator. They would fry up nicely and make a good treat for the whole crew.

As the summer wore on, Hackamore got in the habit of dropping in on Edith after the evening meal. At first, they talked mostly about how she was doing with the job and what she felt they could do to make meals better. However, as time went on, conversations got more and more personal. Each one explored the other person's likes and dislikes, where they came from, what they'd done as kids and on and on. It wasn't long before Hackamore had found out about Edith's past and she'd discovered that he hadn't been much of a saint either. Hackamore led the way by making it plain that past was past and today is what you are right now. Edith knew a lot about men and she told Hackamore that she wasn't interested in someone's past as long as it stayed past. With that, they started off with a clean slate as far as their regard for each other was concerned. She found out that Hackamore had been married once, but it had ended in a bitter divorce and loss of his daughter. He, in turn found out that Edith got into her difficulties because a ne'er do well husband had disappeared and she'd been forced to support herself and her daughter anyway she could.. They found out from each other just how lonely the other was. Edith had been Division Five's cook about eight months when Hackamore decided that he'd rather be married than lonely. He said as much to Edith one evening and after realizing what he was getting at, she agreed. Taking a day off, they left meals prepared for the crew, went into Canon City and took out a marriage license. The very next Saturday, they appeared before a minister in Canon City and asked him to marry them, producing a marriage license to prove that they were serious about the matter. They came back to Division Five as Hackamore (Melvin) and Edith Hadding. Little was said, but Edith moved out of her quarters and into the foreman's house. When asked, Hackamore simply said, "She's my wife, now." Sarah wouldn't have known about her mother's marriage if Edith hadn't filed a different W-2 form for her pay checks. George spotted it and nearly fell off his chair.

He told Sarah and she decided it was time to pay a visit to her mother. She drove up to the Division Five headquarters in the middle of the day and found Edith sweeping out the foreman's quarters. "Good afternoon, Mrs Hadding," she said with a grin on her face." Her Mother's face turned bright red. "How'd you know?" Edith asked. "You filed a new W-2 form with the office. George looks at all of those" "I guess I should have known." was all that Edith said. "Congratulations, Mother." Sarah told her and hugged and kissed her. "I hope you and Hackamore will be very happy. You deserve it. and Hackamore is a good man. Well, do you need anything or can we send you anything?" "No, not a thing. We're as happy as a couple of clams." Sarah ended the conversation with "Well, I've got to get back. I just came up to congratulate you. Give Hackamore my best." With that, she hugged her mother again and drove home.

When Christmas time came, Hackamore and Edith were invited to come and spend the day with George and Sarah. Tommy was almost three years old, now. He could carry on a reasonable conversation although some words needed some polishing. He'd heard many of the modern songs of the day and could sing some of them. His music was a bit shaky, but his Mom was working on that.

Christmas was a jubilant celebration. Bert and Millie Toland came again as they had the year before. Little George wasn't Little George any more, he was Tommy to distinguish him from his dad. He could talk and he was more aware of what was going on around him than he'd been a year ago. Grandma and Grandpa Toland literally smothered him, they were so glad to see him and evaluate his growth. Grammy Edith was a lot more reserved toward him but he had a place in her heart, too. He planted a kiss upon her cheek when she picked him up and set him on her lap. This was new to her. Oh how life had changed for her! Hackamore delighted in telling him stories all about the 'wild west' of yesteryear. Young Tommy took these in with wide eyed attention. Surely, Grandpa Hack was one of Tommy's special heroes.

CHAPTER FOURTEEN

Family Matters

One day, Sarah came into the office and sat down next to George's desk. Tommy had just passed his second birthday and she had noticed something disturbing. Tommy tripped a lot when he ran. He was 'pigeon toed.' She called it to George's attention and asked, "Isn't there anything that we can do to fix that?" George, thought and said, "I don't know of anything. Why don't we ask the doctor?" Sarah pointed out that Tommy was due for his two year check-up and she'd make an appointment right away. In fact, she'd do it today. She left the office and was gone about twenty minutes. She came back and told George that Tommy was scheduled for his check-up on Wednesday at one o'clock.

Tommy's visit to the doctor went well. His general health reflected the care Sarah had given him throughout his short life. That done and a couple of shots out of the way, Doctor March's attention turned to the problem of tripping. The doctor had seen this problem before and told Sarah that he was going to send Tommy's problem to a Doctor Lane in Denver. She could see Dr. Lane on Tuesday, next at two thirty. He gave her the address and told her the best way to get there. He said that the treatment would involve a special device that the doctor would fit to correct the problem He also told her that it usually took about two years for a child of Tommy's age, but the results were very successful in most cases.

With this information, Sarah went back to Oxbow with mixed emotions. She told George what the doctor had said and told him that it was probably hereditary. George suddenly recalled something from his past. Lois had always walked funny. Her shoes always pointed in! Well, any children he and Sarah had probably would not be afflicted in this way. He then settled down to contemplate the problem as far as Tommy was concerned If it only took two years, he'd be through with it by the time he started school so he wouldn't be subject to the ridicule such things often caused. "Well," he decided, "Best start it as soon as possible, Doctor March said that it went quicker with younger children. Let's get on with it."

The next week, Sarah, George and Tommy climbed into the ranch's airplane and were flown to Denver's Executive Airport. They rented a car and found their way to Doctor Lane's office. An examination with x-rays showed that Tommy was a good candidate for the treatment that Doctor Lane recommended.. He estimated that they might be completely successful as early as eighteen months. He wrote a prescription for the belt and harness that was needed and told them to take it to a maker of such devices. He also told them that they would have to buy a special shoe that the device would be attached to. The object of the treatment was to lightly rotate the foot outward a little at a time. Since the child was growing, the hip joints would reform to allow the foot to turn slowly outward until they were properly positioned.

They went back to Doctor Lane a week later and little Tommy was fitted for the device. He didn't like it at first; in fact, he didn't like it at all. He wasn't used to having his feet turned outward that way. He cried and acted up for a little while, but Sarah calmed him down. He finally accepted the inevitable and things went much better from then on. About every three months, the device was readjusted, turning each foot a little further outward. When they'd been in place for eighteen months, Dr. Lane said, "We've just got a little more

Top of the Mountain

to go and we're done. Another three months should do it." Everyone breathed a sigh of relief. The end was in sight.

Christmas came and went and different ones went different directions. Life had to go on and it did. There were special events that stood out. Tommy's third birthday was one. He had a cake with three candles on it and a party with all the Oxbow kids in his age group present to help him celebrate. His most profound announcement brought laughter from his parents and from friends. "I'm big, now!" He was, too. He weighed twenty seven pounds on the bathroom scales. He'd gotten a set of building blocks with the alphabet on them for Christmas and he'd begun to realize that the letters meant something. "Look Mommy, I can spell my name!" And sure enough, if you asked him he'd hunt out the letters and lay them out so they could be seen. There it was. TOMMY. He was so proud of that! So was his Mom.

In the meantime, about a year after Tommy started wearing the rotators, Sarah kissed George one evening after dinner. "George, I've got something you should know." "Oh, what's that?" "George, you are going to be a father again in about seven months. How do you like that?" George grinned. "I like it fine. When is it supposed to be here?" "Well, I've counted off the months and I suspect mid September should be about right. Oh George, I'm so happy." George stood then, kissed his wife and kissed her again. "I'm happy for you. You've wanted a baby ever since we got married and so have I. I can't imagine anything quite like realizing that we're bringing a new life into the world." Sarah reached up and kissed her husband. "Thank you, George. I love you."

George and Sarah kept her pregnancy secret for another three months and then she told Marney. "Sarah, you've been holding out on us. When?" Sarah smiled. "September, about the fifteenth, I think. Doctor thinks maybe a week or so earlier, maybe" "Oh, my. We have to organize a baby shower for you. We haven't had one around here for a coon's age. Oh, they're such fun. May I give it?" "If you want to." Sarah said. All this was new to Sarah. Her mother had never been involved in such things and was too busy making a living to be a part of such activities.

George had been through this with Little George, (Tommy), but to Sarah, it was all new. The morning sickness, (She had it) The first faint heart beat. (She heard that in the doctor's stethoscope) movement as the baby began to grow and finally the first definite kick. It was all a new experience and she gloried in it. Even from the first day that she realized that she was expecting, she began writing down her feelings and as she began to be notice these signs of motherhood, she wrote them down. She wanted to remember them all.

Marney helped Sarah enjoy her pregnancy. These two along with Laura had become fast friends and what excited or stirred one stirred the other two. The older women had given birth to babies before, now they helped Sarah enjoy her experience as it happened. Some weren't so pleasant, of course. Morning sickness never is. Later on the awkwardness and discomfort wasn't easy, either. But, with her friend's help Sarah made it a great adventure. One of the traditional events of any impending baby arrival is the Baby Shower. Marney, true to her word gave one for Sarah. She invited all of the women that were a part of the Oxbow. She also invited some from the church George and Sarah had been attending. Many couldn't come because of distance, but some did. The baby things that Sarah got reflected how her acquaintances felt about her. She got all kinds of baby clothes and other baby fixings. She remarked that with the things that baby George had outgrown, she wouldn't have to buy much to complete her equipment list.

Finally, September opened. Tommy went to see Doctor Lane and he pronounced Tommy a new boy. He could take the rotators off and enjoy being able to run without tripping. Tommy made the most of it. He ran everywhere. Walking was a waste of time. He had things to do and other boys to play with and "Let's get at it." His Mom was overjoyed. This little boy had been the trigger of her new life three and a half years ago and she loved him. She wondered how she would feel toward the new baby that was about to fill her life as little Tommy had. It wasn't long before the signs began.

It was four in the morning of September tenth. Sarah woke George with, "George, it's time. I've got to go!" George never hesitated. He quickly dressed, got Sarah's robe and helped her into it, called Marney to come get Tommy and explain that Mommy and Daddy were going to get their new baby. He grabbed Sarah's suitcase as they hurried out the door. The trip to Pueblo was two hours long, but they made it in plenty of time. Tiny Susan Mildred wasn't born until 2:43 that afternoon. She was beautiful. Sarah said so! Sarah proudly handed her to George to hold when he came in to see her after the rituals of the baby's arrival were complete. He was tender with his new daughter and kissed his wife three separate times, he was so proud of her.

George made phone calls to his mom and dad, to Hackamore and Edith and to Marney. He figured that Marney would take care of telling everyone at Oxbow of little Susie's arrival. George had taken a room at a local hotel; he couldn't see the need to drive back and forth from the ranch each day to see Sarah and the baby. He spent as much time as the hospital would tolerate just holding his wife's hand and visiting the nursery to see his baby daughter. Mothers and babies don't usually stay in hospitals very long and on the third day after her arrival, little Susie was on her way home with her doctor's blessing. "She's healthy. Home is just the place for her." he remarked.

The question of feeding had come up early in Sarah's pregnancy and Sarah made it clear that she would nurse the baby until it was ready to be weaned. She was going to be the source of nourishment for any baby of hers, period! End of discussion. Before she left the hospital, Doctor March had prescribed a formula for Susie just in case, but he approved Sarah's intent to nurse her.

One of the things that Sarah had not received at her baby shower was a cradle. Yet, when she brought the baby in the front door, there, on the floor sat a cradle with all the blankets and other equipment needed for it. She gasped. "Where did that come from?" Then the real surprise came. Out of the kitchen came Bert, Millie, Hackamore, Edith, Marney and Laura. Bert and Millie had come down from Idaho two days before and Fred Sowles had picked them up and brought them to the Oxbow. They'd taken time to go to a baby shop in Colorado Springs and get the cradle.

Sarah had to sit down. She was completely overcome. These were her friends. They stood behind her and made her life rich with their love for her. Even her mother who hadn't had much of a background in that respect for many years; stood there with tears in her eyes. Sarah slowly rose, gently deposited Susie in the cradle and slowly went around the room hugging each one who was there. Hackamore had a red face when she hugged and kissed him but she wouldn't let him escape. He'd done wonders for her Mom.

❊

Two years went by. Little Susie had grown just as her older brother had. She was the apple of her father's eye and she could talk to him much as any two year old could. Tommy was in first grade by this time, going to school with the other school aged children in the Oxbow headquarters. Some years before, the aged school building that had been built in the late eighteen hundreds had been rebuilt and modernized and an elementary school teacher had been hired to conduct school for the seven school children that lived there. The corporation picked up the tab for her salary because it was cheaper than maintaining transportation to the nearest school in a tiny community sixteen miles away. This arrangement also solved the problem that arose every winter when snow closed the road for days at a time.

CHAPTER FIFTEEN

New Assignment

Corporations are usually formed to produce a product and to make money. Such was the intent of the Oxbow Corporation. It was formed originally in the late 1940's as a cattle ranching venture. The original ranch was successful under the management of old Ben Sears. However, having four sons caused some deep thinking and before long, a corporation had been formed to include other ranches that had been purchased be the sons. Because the ranches were in Wyoming in the neighborhood of the emigrant trail, the name Oxbow was attached to the corporation when it was formed.

When the six ranches in Colorado were purchased and consolidated into one operation and the old cow town was made the headquarters, the name Oxbow was attached to that operation. Several other ranches including one in Montana were also owned by the corporation, although the Oxbow name was not attached to them

The organizational structure of these ranches owned by Oxbow was fairly simple. Each one operated independent of the others. Each one had a manager and assistant manager each of whom reported to corporation headquarters in San Francisco, California. The managers had the latitude to hire and fire personnel in management and supervisory positions, but hiring and firing the cowboys and other bottom level positions was left to the foreman of each ranch or division.

The Oxbow Ranch in Colorado was well organized under manager, Tom Houghton. His Assistant Manager, George Toland was his strong right arm and that organization ran smoothly and made money. However, not all ranches in the Oxbow Corporation produced successfully. The Wind River Ranch in Wyoming was one that was marginal economically.

Wind River was managed by Harold Smith, an older man, who had been hired because of his previous experience in California. However, those who hired him failed to understand that ranching in the moderate climate of California was a long ways from being the same as ranching under the extreme conditions in Wyoming. To compound the error, a young man from Texas A&M University in Texas was assigned to the Wind River operation as assistant manager. It was a mistake. Two factors caused problems immediately and put the operation at a disadvantage almost at once. First, Bill Rankin hadn't had any ranching experience, even in college, yet, he was assigned to Wind River almost immediately after graduation from A&M. Second, Texas didn't get along with California at all. The mix simply wasn't compatible. Disagreements dissolved into arguments and on into shouting matches. Harold and Bill sometimes didn't speak to each other for several days at a time. Morale among the hired help gradually eroded and not much work got done properly.

This situation deteriorated to a point that a ranch that had been showing a modest profit began to go down hill. Upper management watched the profit and loss figures for almost two years. Representatives, sent to look into the situation, were unable to pinpoint the trouble initially. Both Harold and Bill covered it up enough to avoid any blame for their part in the problem. Finally, a ringer or spy was slipped into the crew as a hired cowboy and he carefully psyched out the problems and documented them.

A meeting at Corporate Headquarters produced a decision to correct the problems and to get the ranch back on track. A phone call came to Oxbow one Monday morning. George was called to Corporate Headquarters to report the next morning. He was told to bring Sarah with him. Another phone call came to Oxbow that same morning. Tom Houghton was told that he was losing his assistant manager and that he would have a graduate of Texas A&M, one Bill Rankin to replace him. Tom was told that this man needed some seasoning and that if Tom found that he wasn't management material, he was free to terminate his employment.

Sarah talked to Marney and asked her if she could look after Tommy and Susie for a couple of days while she and George were in San Francisco. Marney said that she was glad to do that and the children were briefed on what they were to do. Once that was accomplished, George and Sarah were flown to Denver and on to San Francisco via United Airlines.

Tuesday morning, they met with executives of the corporation and George was offered the position of manager of Wind River Ranch. He was told that it was in trouble and that the manager was being retired, while the assistant would take George's place at Oxbow. Sarah was called in at that point, the entire plan was explained to her and she was told that she and George had until 4:00 PM to decide to accept or turn down the offer. The two returned to the hotel and sat down over lunch to decide their fate for the future. Did they want this or not? Sarah remembered how a sudden opportunity was offered to her on the streets of this very city and look where it brought her. She decided that, as far as she was concerned, they should go for it. George was a little more conservative toward this sudden opportunity. He discussed the pro's and the con's with Sarah, but ultimately, the answer was the same. They did talk about the need for an assistant manager at Wind River Ranch. George told Sarah that he felt that he needed strong help to make Wind River a success again. Sarah hesitated to interfere with company business, but she finally voiced her opinion. She said, "George, you know who'd be the best choice you could make?" He perked up and asked, "Who would you suggest?" Sarah only hesitated a second. "I'm surprised. He's right under your nose. He keeps his department up to snuff so well, you haven't even noticed." George got a smile on his face. "You're right. Fred Sowles. Am I right?" Sarah responded. "Yes, you are. The only objection I can see is that Tom Houghton will have to break in an assistant manager and a transportation manager at the same time." George got thoughtful. "I see what you mean. However, I think we'll leave that to corporate to figure out. I want Fred and I'm going to ask for him. I think he'll be just the one to make the team complete." He kissed Sarah and told her that he didn't know what he'd do without her.

One other thing bothered both of them. They'd have to uproot the children and Edith would stay at Oxbow. George knew a little about Wind River Ranch and remembered that its headquarters were only a mile outside of the little town of Edgerton, Wyoming. School would not be a serious problem, nor would supply procurement in winter time. Finally, Sarah said a prayer and got a smile on her face. "George, let's go for it. I think you need a chance to show how good you really are and I'll back you up however I can. I love you dear husband of mine and I think this is our big break. Let's do it." George kissed her and said, "I'm with you. Let's go tell them they've got a deal!"

The deal was made; the salary was pegged at 30% more than they were getting at Oxbow with raises within a year if they were successful in turning Wind River Ranch around. Then a question came up. "George, who would you suggest as your assistant manager?" George startled the questioner. His response had been almost instantaneous and it surprised everyone but Sarah.. "I want Fred Sowles. He's transportation and supply manager at Oxbow. He's a graduate of Montana State, so he knows that country and he does a good job at Oxbow. I want him."

Sarah smiled. She knew George's mind and was proud of him. She realized that he'd taken her advice and was willing to act on it. She crossed her fingers and hoped the bosses would approve the request. She wanted Marney to share in their good fortune.

The vice president that was conducting the interview drummed his fingers on the desk as he thought and sorted through the if's and's and but's of this. Finally, he said, "We'll call him in tomorrow and see what he says. We'll let you know. Call me tomorrow afternoon, will you? We want you to stay in town 'til we get this all sorted out. Also, if Fred accepts, we'd like you two to be briefed together as to what to expect at Wind River and what we expect of you. Go on, now and have a little vacation 'til tomorrow. See you later." With that, they were dismissed.

George and Sarah spent the evening and the next morning touring the sights of San Francisco, avoiding areas of Sarah's old haunts. She said that those days are over and gone and "I don't want any reminders." They spent a leisurely hour with lunch at Fisherman's Wharf the next day, then caught a taxi back to the hotel. Promptly at two o'clock, the phone rang and George was asked to come back down to corporate headquarters. Sarah said, "I don't care, I'm going with you. I don't want to wait here for the news. I can sit in the outer office if I have to, but I'm with you." George just laughed. "You've been with me all the way, Sweetheart, even before we were married. You know that." He hugged her and kissed her, then, "Come on, let's go see what they want us to do."

Within ten minutes, George was in the inner office while Sarah sat at the reception station, talking to the receptionist. Fred was sitting on a chair off to one side. As he entered, George looked at him, winked and smiled. "Hello, Fred. Imagine seeing you here." "Yeah, uh, huh!" That's all he could say, but it was obvious that he was nervous. He was surprised at being called to headquarters and he looked as if he was somewhat overwhelmed by whatever the company had offered him.

"Well, George, here's the deal." The executive began. He started in explaining what they wanted him to do as manager of the Wind River Ranch. "It's up to you to organize that place and put it back in the black. We've talked to Fred, here and he's to be your right hand man. He's agreed to give the assistant manager position a try. I think he can do it. If you have to make any changes up there, you have full authority to do whatever you think is necessary. Just remember this: If you can't turn it around, we've already made up our minds to sell the place, but we really don't want to lose it. Understood?" "Yessir! How soon do you want us on the property?" George asked

The answer was, "How soon can you get up there?" George thought for a moment. He owed Tom Houghton at least a couple of days to break in the new assistant. Then he added two days driving time and setting up shop. "I can be on the ground on Monday, next." He said. "How about you, Fred? Can you make that schedule, too?" Fred didn't hesitate. He wanted this job bad. All he said was, "Yes I can. Do we take our wives with us?" George said, "Fred, why don't you come over to the hotel when we leave here and we'll see how we want to work this out?" Fred said, then. "That's a good idea. I've got to check into a hotel anyway. I might just as well stay the night in yours. I'll see you in an hour. What room are you in?" George answered, "Room 1542." Fred turned to the executive. "Sir, do you have anything more for me?" A negative shake of the head, and Fred was gone.

George asked, then, "Well, that about takes care of my questions. Is there anything else?" The executive shook his head and said.. "Not from me. Lots of luck and keep us informed." With that, George followed Fred out only to find that he'd gone downstairs and was on his way to get checked in at the hotel. George put his arm around Sarah and said, "Well, we're in, both Fred and I. I'm lucky to get him, actually. I've found him to be overqualified for the job he was doing at Oxbow. I hope he feels that he can do the job, here. It's going to be hard work for awhile. I've seen some of these run-down ranches and they're no picnic. Come on, let's go. We've still got work to do." Sarah turned to him and asked, "What now?" George's answer made her realize how important to him this opportunity was.. He explained, "Well, it's like this. The company wants us up in Wyoming as soon as possible.

I've got to break in the new assistant for Tom Houghton and from what I hear of the man, that isn't going to be easy. Then Fred and I need to be at Wind River Ranch as soon as possible. I don't know just what we'll have to do to get things turned around until we see just what's going on. Once we get things organized and going again, we can start working out the details of getting you and Marney up there. I don't want you to have to wait too long, either. We'll need to get everything in Oxbow packed to move and we need to get Tommy in school and get a house set up at Wind River. I wish I could be more specific, but I can't until we see what we're up against. I hope you'll trust us to do the best we can."

They'd no more than gotten settled in the room when Fred knocked on the door and was let in. His first words were, "I never expected something like this." George spoke quickly, "Look, Fred. I asked for you. I've watched you work, I know what your education is and I think you're the best man I know of to do what we have to do at Wind River Ranch. I think we need to lay out what our attack is going to be when we show up there on Monday. How do you see this?" Fred stopped for a heartbeat, "You asked for me?" "That's right. And don't think you're getting a cushy job, either. It's not going to be easy. We'll be lucky if the men don't lynch the pair of us. Now, here is what I think we need to do right off the bat. You tell me if you don't agree. We'll work it out."

George went on to explain how they needed to tour the ranch and talk to the crew. He felt that it would probably take at least three days to do that. Then they needed to sit down and prioritize the needs that they saw and start assigning the work to the crew. "One thing we need to be especially aware of is the attitude of the foreman and the other supervisory people. Things have been slack for quite awhile and they may be reluctant to buckle down and do the job." George went on. "Look, I've been thinking about this some more and I've got an idea. Just hear me out and tell me what you think.

Today is Wednesday. We can get an early flight out of here in the morning. We need to meet with Tom Houghton and lay this deal out to him as soon as we get back. Corporate told me that they wouldn't talk to Harold Smith or Bill Rankin until we could be in place on Wind River Ranch. Now, here's what I think we need to do. If we catch a flight out of here tonight instead of tomorrow, we can be at Oxbow by midnight and talk to Tom Houghton in the morning. Can you talk to Tom and tell him what's going on? I'll talk to the vice president and get him to call Rankin and tell him that he is re-assigned to Oxbow and that he's to be picked up and brought down to the Oxbow tomorrow afternoon. I'll go up in the Cessna, pick him up and bring him down. I can have him at Oxbow by tomorrow night. If I brief him on Friday, you and I could be on Wind River Ranch by Saturday evening. All the vice president will have to tell Harold Smith is that Rankin is being re-assigned and that I'll talk to him about the changes when we come up on Saturday."

Fred thought about the plan for a couple of minutes and then expressed his opinion. "George, I think you're rushing things a bit. We told the VP that we'd be in place on Monday. Why don't we do it this way? I'll talk to Tom in the morning while you go after Rankin. That way, you can spend the weekend briefing him and showing him the Oxbow. Then, we can go up to Wind River on Monday morning. If we leave by six in the morning, we can be there a little after ten. Rankin will already be gone and we can break the news of Smith's retirement without a lot of fuss. No matter which way we do it, the final action has to be on Monday anyway. If we do it this way, we'll have more time and won't be so rushed."

George saw the wisdom of Fred's proposal and Sarah nodded her head as Fred finished explaining. George smiled and said, "I think you've got something there. Let's do it that way."

George looked at his watch and reached for the phone. He called the vice president and found that he hadn't left the office as yet. George explained what he and Fred had worked out and asked for the VP's approval. The vice president asked a couple of questions, which George merely said, "Yes, sir, we can do that." Approval came and George hung up. Fred asked, "What was that all about?" George answered. "Well, he was concerned that we be very careful when we talk about retirement with Harold Smith. He's been around for a long time and retirement is kind of sensitive with him."

Within a few minutes, George and Sarah along with Fred Sowles had booked reservations on a five thirty flight on United Airlines and were headed back to Colorado Springs and Oxbow. Arriving home late, they went to bed to rest for tomorrow's activities. George left for Wind River in the Cessna before six o'clock and Fred met with Tom Houghton later in the morning. He explained what was going on. "Tom, we're going to try to be at the Wind River Ranch on Monday. George has gone up there to get your new assistant and bring him down here. He wants to brief him and show him around over the week-end, then we'll leave on Monday morning." Tom wasn't pleased at all with the changes that were being worked out. He'd heard of Rankin's reputation and he wasn't optimistic that he would be able to fill George's shoes. He expressed his opinion in short words. "Well, I'll give him a fair shake, but as far as I'm concerned, he's going to be on a short rope. One crosswise word out of him and he's on his way to Texas."

Later that afternoon, the Cessna landed and George got out with Bill Rankin. It was obvious that they hadn't gotten along too well. George directed Rankin toward one of the cabins and told him that he'd meet him at eight o'clock the next morning to show him around and tell him what was expected of him in his new job. George turned away and saw to it that the airplane was put away in the hangar. That done, he walked down to his home and Sarah. By the way he walked, it was obvious that he wasn't impressed by this new assistant manager.

The next morning, he was in his office early, taking care of some leftover paperwork. The door opened and Bill Rankin stepped in with "You're supposed to tell me all about being assistant manager of this place, let's get started. George turned his chair. "Sit down, I'll be right with you." Bill spoke sharply. "Listen, man. I've got things to do. Let's get on with it." George looked him over for all of thirty seconds, then said, "Bill, you've got two choices. Either you sit down and shut up or go pack your bags and I'll have a car take you up to Colorado Springs. You can pay your own way back to Texas. You've got two seconds to make up your mind." Bill sat. "Now, Bill, let's get started. First, I've got orders to talk to you, but I've also got orders to fire you if I think you aren't assistant material. And believe me, we will see that the details of your termination will go on any recommendation you ask for from us. Now, you've got two choices. You can impress me with your eagerness to please or you can go pack your bags. Am I fully understood?" Bill's quiet "Yes Sir" reflected a quick change in attitude.

George spent the morning taking Bill to all of the divisions to meet the foremen and to get an idea of where each one was and what they did there. Bill made some snide remark about the cook at Division Five. It seems that a lady cook for a male crew wasn't his idea of good management. He said so. George politely told him that the best way to have a revolt at Division Five would be to interfere with their cook. She wasn't just the cook but she was also the foreman's wife. George made an important point then and there. "Bill, as assistant manager, you will be a supervisor. If you abuse that role, you will lose the respect of the crews and in the process, your effectiveness. If you lose that respect, you will probably be warned, or you may be terminated on the spot. Tom Houghton doesn't stand for making crews unhappy and losing their respect. Don't cross him. He won't fool with you. I'll tell you this. If you were to try what you got away with at Wind River Ranch, you'll be fired the second day around Oxbow. Keep that in mind. We know all about Wind River Ranch around here."

By the time George got back to Oxbow with Bill Rankin, Bill was looking at his chances of success through new eyes. His bulldozing days appeared to be over. George had taken all of the division foremen aside and told them to take any mistreatment by the new assistant manager directly to Tom

Houghton. George's final word to Bill Rankin was, "You can be the boss, that's what you're going to be paid to do. But, do everything you can to earn the respect of the people that work for you. It's up to you." With that, he climbed out of the Jeep and walked away.

George reported his morning to Tom Houghton. "Tom, I don't know if he'll make it or not. I scared the bejabbers out of him, let's see if it does any good." Tom smiled, "Thanks George. Gad, I'm going to miss you around here. You've been the best." George just reached out and shook Tom's hand. "Tom, it's been a pleasure to work for you." "Good luck, George. I know you'll need it."

Sunday, George spent the morning showing Rankin the various paper work records and other things he was to be responsible for. He showed him the financial records and explained what was going on with the ranch's finances. There were payrolls, accounts with vendors and a number of other accounts that George kept track of. He showed Rankin all of them and explained how they were kept current.

Rankin listened, but remarked that some of the methods were antique. He kept up a string of criticisms as George ran through them. Finally, George said, "I've shown you everything I did, now, it's up to you. You can do anything you want with this. Just remember I showed you what I've done. I will say that they are up to date and they'll stand an independent audit any time. What you do is up to you."

Later, George reported to Tom Houghton. "Tom. I've shown Bill everything. I've found him to be rather anti-social and critical of almost every thing we've been doing here. I would suggest that you keep a very close eye on the financial accounts. He wants to do them his own way and I'm frankly suspicious of that. I know my work will stand up to an independent audit, I don't know if his will."

"I tell you what I'll do. Give him a chance. If he pans out, fine. If not, I'll keep my eyes open for a replacement if you have to let him go." Tom smiled. "You're alright, George. Thanks. I may just need your help. I'll keep it in mind."

Early Monday morning, the Cessna was rolled out again and three men loaded their gear on board. George and Fred kissed their wives 'goodbye' and climbed in. They were going to the Wind River Ranch and the third man would bring the airplane back to the Oxbow. Their plan was to be on the Wind River Ranch before noon.

The engine started and they taxied away after waving to those left behind. In a few minutes, the airplane lifted off and disappeared to the north. Four hours later, they touched down on the airstrip at the Wyoming ranch. As they taxied in and shutdown, George and Fred climbed out and unloaded their gear. A delegation had walked out to meet them and a pick-up truck came out to haul the suitcases and bags off to their cabins.

They were met by a large man who announced himself as Marty Martin, the Wind River Ranch foreman. George asked where Harold Smith was and was told that he was in the office. "Well, where is that?" George asked. Marty replied, "Follow me and I'll show you." Shortly, they were led to a small white frame building and shown inside. An elderly man was seated behind a desk and as George and Fred were shown in, Marty announced them. "Come in, gentlemen, I'm Harold Smith, the manager here. And you are--?" George held out his hand and said, "I'm George Toland and this is Fred Sowles. May we have a word with you?" Smith gestured toward a couple of chairs. "Please be seated, gentlemen. What can I do for you?

George handed Mr. Smith a letter that he'd been entrusted with by the corporate vice president the previous Wednesday. "Mr. Smith, I tried to meet with you on Thursday when I picked up Bill Rankin to take him down to the Oxbow Ranch. Nobody seemed to know where you were and we were on a tight schedule, so I had to go back down to the Oxbow. What that letter will tell you is that the company is complimenting you for your service as manager of the Wind River Ranch and announcing your retirement with a comfortable retirement for your service. I've been appointed as manager, here, effective immediately. I would appreciate it if I could meet with your supervisory people and get acquainted with them as soon as possible."

Mr. Smith was taken by surprise although he'd been aware that changes in the ranch's management were coming and that he'd be informed as to what those changes would be. Now, he had the official notification in his hands. He sat for a long time without saying a word. Finally, he smiled. "You know, you work hard for years, dreading the day when you'll have to quit, but it's still hard, even though you know its coming. I suppose I ought to be glad to be put out to pasture, but I'm not." He rambled on. "My wife isn't going to like this, either. We've been putting off retirement, now for a couple of years. We should have prepared better, I suppose. Well, gentlemen, is there anything I can do for you to help you get started?"

George replied, "Yes sir, there is. Could we meet your key people and get to know who they are? Then, I'd like for you to give us a thumbnail sketch of everything you've been doing, so we don't have to learn it all from scratch." Harold replied to the request by hollering, "Marty, will you get the lead men in here?" Marty stuck his head in the door and said, "Right away, boss. They'll be here in a minute or two." He pulled his head back out of the door and disappeared. Soon, he was back with two men in tow. They trooped into the office and took off their hats. Harold pointed at first one and then the second one, naming off each one as he went. "That, there is Boots Riskin, and the middle sized one is Charley Hubbell." Those two are the lead men around here. They run the crews in each end of the ranch." George told them that he was the new manager and that Fred Sowles was the new assistant manager. He said, "I hope I can count on you to carry on to keep this ranch producing the way it should. Fred and I are going to be all over the range. Don't mind us. We need to get an idea of how this place runs. Just do your jobs and ignore us. You may see us on horse back or in a jeep, so don't be surprised. Thanks for coming in." George went on, "Could we meet with the book keeper?" Harold got a pained look on his face. "Well, we haven't got one. My wife has sort of been keeping track of that department, but it hasn't been kept too well." George turned to Fred and said, "Would you meet with her and see what you can find out. See how good or bad it is and we'll have to bring it up to date as best we can. Corporate is probably going to send someone up here to audit the books, so try to get them in some kind of shape for that, will you?" Fred winced, then sighed. "Alright, George, I'll see what I can do."

George turned to Harold again. "Mr. Smith, could we talk to Marty and get him to give us a tour of the headquarters, here. We'd like to get an idea of the layout and see what kind of shape it's in." Harold rose, went to the door and hollered, "Marty, could you come in again, please?" When Marty reappeared, Harold repeated George's request. "These gents want a tour of the place. Can you do that?" Marty nodded and said, "Sure boss. Come along, gents."

The tour took over an hour and as they progressed, George and Fred were appalled at the run down state of every part of the facilities they inspected. Corrals, barns sheds, the bunkhouse and the cook shack. Even the yards were neglected with leaves blown up against fences. Vehicles and machinery stood out in the weather instead of being parked in sheds out of the elements. Finally, George stopped Marty and pointing to various signs of neglect, asked him why? Marty's answer was truthful, if not encouraging. He spoke carefully. "Well, sir, it's hard to keep men interested in doing anything when the bosses are fighting all the time. That's the way it's been around here for the last three years. Boots, Charley and I have tried to keep things going but it's hard when one boss tells you to do something and the other one tells you to do something else instead. The fellers are tired of it and I guess we all are."

George just shook his head. He turned to Fred. "I think we need to declare a holiday and clean up this place, first thing. This can't go on like this." Fred agreed. "Let's start at breakfast in the morning. That way, we'll have most of the men in one place and we can get the word out to the most of them at one time." George agreed. "Good thought, Fred."

Both men retired to the cabins they'd been assigned to and George started writing a report of what they'd been shown that afternoon.

Once the report was written, George began reviewing a folder that had been given him in San Francisco. It described the particulars of the Wind River Ranch. The ranch was a big one. It had a little over ten thousand acres of land within its borders; all of which was enclosed in fencing. It was stocked with Hereford cattle of which there were about one thousand head. The land itself was semi-mountainous, part of which was a small mountain range called the Black Hills along its southern border. There were large areas of open land and some timber on the property. It had been the policy of the Oxbow Corporation to leave the land as natural as possible and there had been no timber harvested off the land since Oxbow had purchased the ranch some ten years before. The ranch headquarters lay to the western edge of the property along a small stream that flowed into the Powder River The crew of the ranch numbered about twenty five men during most of the year, however, extra hands were usually brought in at round-up time to handle the additional workload. Supervisory personnel consisted of a foreman and two lead men. This arrangement allowed the work load to be divided between two crews and to be overseen by the foreman. The lead men filled dual roles. They provided leadership for their crews but they also participated in the day to day activities. The work of maintaining the headquarters facilities was divided between the two crews as needed and individual projects were assigned to the lead men by the foreman. Housing consisted of the usual bunkhouse building for the single men and small houses for those who were married. There were eight of these individual dwellings.

Oversight of the land areas was provided for by four line cabins, one in each quadrant of the compass, ie. Northwest, northeast, southeast and southwest. Each was manned by two men during most of the year. These consisted of a one room cabin, a corral and lean-to shelter for the horses, a water source and an outhouse. The line cabin crews were expected to cruise the land in their territories and to keep track of the range conditions, the locations of the cattle and their physical condition. If problems arose additional crew could be called out from the headquarters to deal with them.

Meals for the crew at the headquarters were provided by the usual dining room or cook shack arrangement. A cook presided over the kitchen and did the grocery ordering for the crew kitchen, the management complex and for the line cabins when they were manned. George noticed that the present cook had been hired some six months ago when the previous cook had quit. That matter would bear looking into.

George had reviewed the records of cattle shipment and found that the last two shipments had been smaller than usual. Ordinarily, a set percentage of the stock on a range were shipped to market each year. Usually, shipments contained so many steers, so many heifers and a small percentage of over age animals. He did some arithmetic on the last two shipments and found that over age animals hadn't been shipped at all. Also, the number of steers shipped was lower than in years previous. Why? He'd look into that situation.

George got together with Fred and went over what he'd found. They decided that each one would look into each part of the operation and try to find its deficiencies. When they had a reasonable picture of the state of the operation, they would attack the worst problems first. This would have to include finding out more about the men who did the work and assessing their attitudes toward it. As the two men looked at what apparently needed to be done, they agreed that it was going to be a lot of work on their part. For now, it was bedtime and tomorrow would be handled tomorrow.

CHAPTER SIXTEEN
The Axe Falls

Tomorrow came late. No noticeable activity was heard until after seven o'clock. George thought this unusual for a ranch of this size. Usually there were all kinds of activities going on, at least making ready to get out on the range to take care of the myriad of activities that involved care of cattle. Breakfast should usually be ready by seven and the men on their way to their assignments by eight. George was up and ready for breakfast long before he saw anyone moving towards the cook shack. When he saw movement in that direction, he went over and found a seat at the table. Like everything else, he found neglect. The room needed cleaning, the table cloth was dirty and the dishes left a lot to be desired. Men came in a few at a time. Breakfast appeared after a wait of some twenty minutes and the cook's helper was a slovenly little fellow that didn't seem to care about the condition of the food. He passed it out as if he were dealing cards

George and Fred picked the ends of the table to seat themselves. When the food appeared, George found himself looking at cold, greasy eggs and bacon. He looked around and found no toast or bread on the table. He and Fred picked at their food until they could stand it no longer. They pushed their food away and sat, looking at each other across the table.

As the first cowboy rose to leave the table, George rose also. He announced, "All you guys stay put. We're going to have a 'get acquainted meeting right now." He turned to Marty, who was sitting down the table from him. "Marty, is all the crew here?" Marty answered, after looking around. "No, there're three that are sleeping in it looks like. Also we have two fellas at the northeast line cabin." George pointed at Marty, "Go and get those three sleepers, I don't care if they're in their pajamas. Just get 'em in here." Marty grimaced, "Well, alright, if you say so. They ain't gonna like it, though." He disappeared out the door. Five minutes later the three and Marty were back.

George spoke, then. "For those who I didn't meet yesterday, I'm George Toland. I'm the new manager, here and that ugly one at the other end is Fred Sowles. He's the new assistant. Now, this place hasn't been doing well and you are going to help turn it around. To do that, we're going to have some rules. After the rules, we're going to make this place livable. It's a pig sty right now and we're going to start today to change it. Marty, what do we have going on that has to be done out on the range?" "Nothin', Boss." was the response. "Alright, now, who are the lead men, here? Put up your hands." Two hands went up. OK, who are you?" The first one said, "I'm Boots Riskin." The second one answered, "Charley Hubbell" George pointed at Boots. "Pick out five men. Two of them are to clean up this room. I mean clean it up. The other three go in and start on the kitchen. Boots, you're in charge. I'll come back and check in an hour and see how you're doing. Any questions?" There were none. "Alright, get at it." Boots named off five men and started to assign chores. One man spoke up, "I didn't hire on here to clean up no cook shack." George answered his complaint. "Do you work here?" Grudgingly, "Yeah" "Well, whatever your name is, if you work here, you'll do whatever is necessary to keep this place going no matter what it is. Right now the job is to clean it up. If you don't like it, I have a check book in my house. Marty will tell me your time and I'll write you a check. Sorry, but you'll have to find your own way into town. We can't spare anyone to take you. Understood?" The man scowled. "OK".

"Alright, now to the rules. Where's the cook and his helper? Marty get them out here." Marty turned and walked into the kitchen. A minute later he reappeared trailed by a grizzled old man with handlebar mustaches. "Cookie, from now on, breakfast will be on this table at seven o'clock, no later, and it will be hot and ready to eat. If I see one greasy egg or burned pancake, you're outa here. Do I make myself clear?" The cook pulled his apron off and threw it on the floor. I'm outa here. I run my kitchen the way I see fit." George, said, "Sorry! As of now, you don't have a kitchen to run. You're through. I'll have a check for you by noon. Oh, yes, same goes for you as I told the other guy. You find your own way into town. We don't have time for you." He then spoke to the helper. "I don't know your name, but, when you start work at noon, I want you in clean clothes and a clean apron. If you don't have any of that, we'll get you some. See Fred about that. Now, I'll inspect you before you start. You'll have clean hands and a clean face. Understood? For now, go back in the kitchen and start washing dishes. Use hot water and lots of soap. One dirty dish after you're finished and you're gone. Fair enough?" The helper just nodded his head.

"Boys, this place is going to be cleaned up before we go any further. We're starting here, because your health is important to the ranch. You can't work if you're sick. Marty, I want you to take the rest of the crew and Charley Hubbell out to the bunkhouse and get it cleaned up. I mean scrubbed clean. That includes putting every piece of bedding on a corral fence to air until this afternoon. I want that place swept out, then mopped out. Marty, you and Charley make sure they do it and see that they have everything they need to do it with. I expect this will take most of the day, so, Marty, you start planning what we need to be doing out on the range tomorrow. If there's nothing pressing, we'll start on barns and corrals. That'll probably take a couple of days. After that, we're going to be looking after the horses. Now, are there any questions?

Otherwise I've got a check to write and some phone calls to make. Where's the guy that doesn't want to cook?"

Minutes later he was on his way to his house with the fired cook in trail. He got his company checkbook and headed to the office. Once seated at the desk, he asked the now subdued former cook. "Alright, Cookie, how much time?" The man told him. "What were they paying you?" He mentioned a figure. "Did they take out Social Security and Income tax?" "No." George wrote out the check, signed it and handed it over. He said, "Sorry you're leaving. No hard feelings, I hope." With that, he picked up the phone book and started looking for Employment Agencies. He wrote down several phone numbers and started phoning. He wanted a cook that was willing to live in or close by and that would cook for up to thirty men.

On the third try, he hit pay dirt. The problem was that the candidate was a lady, a widow with three children. He asked if she could be reached or if she could come for an interview. He got a phone number and called. The woman, a Louise Holden lived in Casper. She'd never cooked for a ranch crew before but she furnished several references and asked if she could come and talk to George personally. He agreed. He asked her to be prepared to make lunch for the crew when she arrived and to bring aprons and work clothes. She agreed. She told him that she'd make soup and sandwiches, but she needed the groceries to do that with. He asked her if she knew Edgerton, she said she did. He told her that he'd call the market there and arrange for her to pick up what she needed. She said that she'd plan on a simple vegetable soup, would he see that the order would include the proper ingredients. Finally, everything was in place. George was pleased, this lady seemed to know what she was doing.

George went back out to see what progress was being made. He noted that the corral fence was festooned with blankets, mattresses and pillow cases. He got an idea. He went into the communal washroom and found just what he expected. A washing machine and a drier. He started the machines and noted that they worked. Turning them off, he went back to the cook shack and told Boots to gather up everything that needed washing, aprons, table cloths,. towels, etc. Then, he was to deliver them to the washroom and detail someone who knew how to run the machines to wash everything he sent over. George went to the bunkhouse and found Fred. He told him about the cook and that he might tell Marty that lunch would be a little late, but they'd have it without fail. He also told him about the washing machine and instructed him to see that all the sheets and pillowcases got washed. Each cowboy could put his own through.

George began to get apprehensive about the kitchen so he walked over to the cook shack to see what progress was being made. He ran into Boots and asked him how it was going and would they be done by noon? "Come, take a look Boss Man. I'm proud of it if I do say so myself." George did that. He entered the kitchen to a room full of steam and soap suds. Every where he looked the place glistened and gleamed. A stove that had been covered with greasy encrusted burned food was a shiny black. It had not only been scrubbed down to bare metal and enamel, but the metal parts had been coated with stove black polish. The refrigerator had been moved away from the wall and the space where it had been sitting was clean. A cowboy was brushing the dust off the back side of the refrigerator itself. Once they got started, they really went at it. Boots broke in on George's thoughts. "Boss, we'll be done in here in about thirty minutes. Are we gonna be able to get some lunch purty quick?" George grinned from ear to ear. "Boots, you guys are great. You betcha we're going to have lunch. I've got a cook coming if she doesn't get lost and if she does, I'll take the whole bunch of you to town on me."

Just then an older car drove in and parked. A lady of about thirty years of age got out and asked, "Is this the Wind River Ranch.?" Boots answered, "Yes Ma'am. Wuz you looking for somebody?" She said, "You don't know where I can find George Toland, do you?" George stepped forward. "I'm George Toland.. What can I do for you?" She smiled and offered her hand. "I'm Louise Holden, they call me Lulu. I was told you're looking for a cook." George smiled and said, "You've come to the right place. Boots, would you show the lady to the kitchen and tell her how soon she can have it to get us some lunch?" Boots saluted sharply and said, "Yes sir, Boss Man. C'mon Ma'am, I gotta show you the sharpest kitchen you ever laid eyes on. We just cleaned and polished her up. She's not quite dry yet, but she will be in about ten minutes." Lulu said, "Look, I've got all kinds of bread and stuff in the back of the car. Do you suppose a couple of your helpers could bring it in while I get set up to make soup and sandwiches?" Boots didn't hesitate. "Joker, you and Gimpy get out there and bring in all that stuff for the lady and be quick about it, Hear me!"

Within twenty minutes, sandwiches were coming off Lulu's hands at shotgun speed. One of Boots' helpers started carrying plates of them into the dining room. Another set out clean bowls along with spoons for soup, which was already simmering on the stove. She told Boots, "Boy, you'd better call those hard heads in here, or the soup's going to be cold. Oh, yes, you'd better get some cups on for coffee, too."

A moment later, the call, "Come and get it." rang out and a rush for the cook shack started. Boots met them at the door. "Alright you cow nurses, go wash your hands and faces and comb your hair. We've got a lady puttin' this on and we won't have any disrespect, here."

Lunch that day was an historic event and the mood around the Wind River Ranch began to change from that moment on. Nor did the change stop that day.

In the meantime, George and Fred got together with Marty as soon as lunch was over. George began the discussion. "Marty, I've gone over the numbers of cattle shipped out of here in the last two years and those numbers are way shorter than what's been shipped in years past. How come there weren't more?" Marty took a minute to organize his thoughts. "Well, Boss, we gathered up what we were told and they were shipped. I'll admit, it looked as if the numbers were short, but the manager and that Texas Wonder never could agree on anything, so we didn't say anything about it, we just gathered and shipped."

Fred broke in. "Marty, we could easily be overgrazing if we have too many cows on the range grass." He got a "Yes, I know." From Marty. George, said, "I think we need to do two things as soon as this clean-up is finished. Number one, we need to do a round-up and count everything we've got and second, we'll ship everything that's over the count we should have. We need the money and we need the grass. Third, I think we'd better get out there on the grass and see how good or bad it really is and we need to do it right away, preferably next week."

The clean-up work continued and by the end of the week, the ranch had a new look that hadn't been there before. The men came for breakfast clean and spruced up. This prevailed for every meal as time went on. Charley Hubbell remarked that the crew was beginning to look like a bunch of 'dudes'.

CHAPTER SEVENTEEN
Rebuilding

George and Fred began riding the range. They took the ranch's Jeeps for some of it, but some they had to use horses because the terrain was too steep. George was the victim of some hurrahing, but showed that he was up to doing the work just the same as any other cowboy would be expected to do. He asked Boots to recommend a horse for riding up into the hills. Boots pointed out a sleepy looking buckskin and mentioned that he was the gentlest nag on the place. George bridled him and borrowed a saddle and blanket. Once in place and cinched down, George mounted up and wound up in the dirt. Buckskin didn't waste any time dumping his rider. George arose amid a chorus of snickers from the corral fence. He'd been had by one of the oldest ranch tricks used to hurrah a cowboy.

George was game, however, he grabbed up the reins and mounted up again, this time with his right hand on the saddle horn for support. He got both feet in the stirrups and with reins firmly in hand, he rode out the storm that erupted beneath him as the horse sought to determine who was boss. Things were rough and wild for about two minutes, but, suddenly, Buckskin's heart wasn't in the battle any longer. Quickly, he settled down and blew. He'd had enough. George gently rode him around the corral several rounds and brought him to a halt. He patted his neck and said, "Good horse; I like a little spirit in a horse." With that, he motioned for one of the hands to open the gate and took off at a brisk trot as if nothing had happened.

George and Fred compared notes on the range condition each night and came to the conclusion that they were overgrazing the grass. George called Marty in and told him to put four men in each line cabin and to start rounding up the cattle in each area. He met with Boots, Charley and Marty and told them the plan. "We'll gather the cattle into four herds, Charley, you're in charge of the northwest, Boots, I want you to take the northeast, Marty, you get the southeast and Fred, you bring the southwest together. What I want to do is separate out the steers and count 'em. Once counted, we'll bring them to the home ranch area and get ready to sell and ship them to market. Now, if we don't get enough steers to lower the numbers, we'll go back through and cull out the worst of the heifers and do the same with them. I want to get this done as quick as possible. We're eating too much of our grass and we're going to have to feed more hay than we need to next winter if we don't lower the numbers now. Alright, any questions?" There were none and the next morning, the roundup started.

It took almost a week and a half before the crew got the first herd together, counted and the steers separated out. Once that was done, the steers were held close to the home ranch and, leaving two cowboys to hold the steers, the rest of the crew hazed the herd back into their usual haunts, then went to help the crews in the other three corners of the range.

The process was repeated with the other three herds and finally, the steers were all accounted for. The count showed that some of the heifers would need to go and the process was repeated in the same way except that the best heifers were kept back. This time, the counts showed that they'd reduced the numbers to a point where the remaining cows would have grass enough.

In the meantime, a call to corporate headquarters was made and several buyers were sent to make bids on the steers and heifers. Within a week, the cattle were sold and were on trucks bound for market. George breathed a sigh of relief. The Wind River Ranch could return to raising cattle efficiently, now. All that was left to do was to cull out the aged dry cows later in the year and the herd would be at its efficient best.

The work load slowed down and most of the crew was busy doing maintenance around the ranch. It was about this time that George noticed that cowboys had gotten in the habit of hanging around the cook shack when they weren't busy. He decided to find out what the attraction was. He caught Lulu in a moment when she wasn't occupied.. "Lulu, how come the cowboys all of a sudden find this place so attractive?" Lulu just grinned. "You mean you don't know?" Now, George was curious. "No, I don't. What is it?" Lulu uttered two words. "Bear Sign" George's eyebrows flew up. "Bear Sign? What's that?" Lulu chuckled, "You know, bear sign! Doughnuts!" Then George understood. Cowboys were known to travel as much as twenty miles for a couple of doughnuts. He'd done it himself in his earlier days.

George asked her, "It's none of my business and you don't have to answer if you don't want to, but when I called the employment people, they said that you were a widow. What happened?" Lulu got serious. She told the story. "Merle and I went around together a lot in high school and we got married after graduation. Then, he went to trucking for a gyppo truck company. That's one with only a few trucks. Well, Merle was on his way to Billings one night in a snow storm and the rig got away from him and turned over. They got him out, but he didn't even get to the hospital before he was gone. That was about a year after little Jenny was born, four years ago. I've been managing on my own ever since." George was curious, now. "How old are your kids, Lulu?" "Well, Jenny's five, Mark is six and a half and Bobbie's almost eight." George's interest sharpened. "How are you making out with that many children?" "It's not easy, I can tell you. If the right man came along, I think I'd rather not be single." George felt that he'd pried enough. "Well, I gotta go. We're glad to have you here. Thanks for the doughnut." With that, he moved off to look into other problems.

One of the problems that was looming ever higher was that of getting Sarah and the two children moved before school started. Finally he called Sarah and asked her if she was ready to move. She was! "I miss you." was all she said.. He asked her if she could get everything packed and ready to move by the end of the week." If you can do that, I'll be down and we'll load everything up and bring you up here by next Monday." Sarah's reply was, "I can hardly wait! Hurry, Sweetheart."

George called and booked a seat on a local airline to Colorado Springs and made arrangements for Fred to take him down to Casper Airport. He left Fred in charge until he could get back with Sarah and the children. He said, "I've got to get them here before school starts and I'll talk to Marney and see if we can't get her packed so you can do the same thing as soon as I get back. We need those two families here." Fred agreed. He'd missed Marney and his children just as much as George pined for Sarah and their young ones. They'd been gone nearly two months, now and the separation was beginning to wear on both of them.

The next morning, the two made the run to Casper starting before the sun came up. George's flight was at eight thirty and they wasted no time getting down and getting George checked in. They shook hands as George was about to depart. "Give Marney a hug for me." was all that Fred could say.

Three hours later, George descended from the airplane, made his way to the terminal and grabbed a taxi to a truck rental agency. He rented a moving van, threw in his suitcase and started for the Oxbow. Two hours later, he pulled up in front of his house at the headquarters. Within moments, he was surrounded by Sarah, Susan and Tommy. "Daddy, Daddy." Susie's reedy little voice kept piping up. Sarah and George didn't say anything at all. They were too busy kissing each other. Two months is a long time.

As they finally turned to go inside, George noticed another moving van parked in front of Marney's house. "What's Marney up to?" George asked. The reply was instantaneous. "What do you think? She's going with us! Did you think maybe she didn't miss Fred as much as I've missed you? She's just as anxious to get moved as I am. Don't forget, they've got kids to get in school, too." George had a stricken look on his face. "Why didn't I think of that? I just thought I'd send Fred down here as soon as we got to Edgerton. This'll work even better. Now, are you all packed and ready to load?" Sarah smiled and told her husband that she'd been packed for a week. The only things that hadn't been packed were what they needed to live in the house from day to day. She said. "We can get everything loaded tonight except for the sleeping bags and a few dishes. Those we can take care of in the morning and we can be on our way. Marney's ready to do the same thing. We can be out of here and on the road when the sun comes up tomorrow. Can we get all the way up to Edgerton by tomorrow night?" George thought a moment, "I don't think so. If we did, we'd probably be arriving in the dark and we'd not have time to do much unpacking. We'll see." Sarah just smiled. "Yep, we'll see."

George went to pay his respects to Tom Houghton and to have a word with Bill Rankin, Tom's new assistant. Tom was glad to see him and said so. George's question of, "How's Bill Rankin panning out?" brought a grimace to Tom's face. "George, I don't think he's going to make it. He's got the talent, but he's too bullheaded to use it. He simply can't get along with people. We nearly lost Hackamore and Edith because of him. There have been several other incidents, too. I'm afraid I'm going to have to let him go. The only reason I haven't done it already is that I don't have anyone else that could take his place." George stopped for a moment, an idea germinating in his mind. "Tom, I think I might have a solution. I've got a foreman that knows what he's doing. He's been to school and he's been up there for at least five years, so he knows how Oxbow works on the corporate level. You'd have to work with him a lot at first, but I think he's got the stuff it takes to do the job. If you want to talk to Corporate and see if they'll go for it, I can let you have him right away. I've got a man I can move into the foreman's spot if Marty moves down here. Are you interested? Tom pondered the in's and out's of the maneuver and finally nodded. "Look, I'll get hold of Corporate today and put it up to them. You're leaving tomorrow?" George nodded. "Well, suppose I have them get hold of you day after tomorrow and let us know if they'll approve this change. That alright with you?" George nodded. "Now, Tom, that isn't what I came over for. I need about four or five strong backs to load my truck and Marney's. Could I beg them from you? I think we can get it done before the sun goes down if we start right away." Tom smiled, "My pleasure, I'll get them myself. It's good to see you again, George. Lot's of luck."

George shook Tom's hand. "I owe you a lot, Tom. Thanks." He headed out the door and walked down to Marney's house. A knock on her door brought her oldest youngster. "Just a moment, I'll get Mom." Marney appeared, flung the door open and hugged George tightly. "Am I glad to see you! Come in. How's my runaway husband?" George grinned. He liked this vivacious neighbor of his. He responded with, "He's just as ornery as he ever was, but he's getting lonesome for his wife and kids. Do you think you could do something about that?" Marney laughed. "Just try me." George went on "Are you packed and ready to load that truck out there?" Her response was quick. "You bet!" He said, "Well, get ready. Tom is sending some people down here to get your truck and ours loaded. I think if we work hard and don't waste any time, we can be ready to leave in the morning. Would six o'clock tomorrow be alright?" She was almost dancing by now. She said. "I'd be ready to leave by midnight if that's when you want to leave." George just laughed. "No, six will be just fine. Well here comes our crew. You tell them what you want them to do I'll take half of them over to my house and get them started on that. See you later."

George split the crew and headed for his house. Loading began within a few minutes and before long, the trucks were bulging with household effects. All that was left were the dishes and sleeping bags for the night and breakfast the next morning. Sarah thought about that and then broached an idea. "If we pack all the dishes and kitchen stuff tonight, why can't we leave a little earlier and have breakfast in Canon City or Colorado Springs?" George thoughts only took a second. "Well, why not? Why don't you go see if Marney wants to do that? I know a restaurant in Canon City that'd be just right for that." Sarah said, "I'll be right back." and took off for her friend's house. She was back twenty minutes later. "She's excited with that idea. She says that she'll fix lunch for us to eat at a rest stop, too. That'll save some time while we're on the road."

It was getting late by this time and the little ones were already asleep in their sleeping bags. Marney had come over to be with them and go over their trip the next day. They planned where they would stop for rest and decided that if all went well, they could actually get to the Wind River Ranch on the same day. It would allow them to start unpacking early the next day and both women wanted to be in their new homes as soon as possible. Possibility became reality in their way of thinking. All of them looked around the empty house and remarked, "You know, we've gotten so used to these houses of ours being full of people and our things, they look strange, now." George said, "Get ready, the Wind River houses are going to look like that to you when we get there, too. But it'll be the other way around." Marney slowly said, "Yeah, I guess so. Well, folks I'd better get over to my house and get some sleep." Sarah spoke up, just then. "Listen, Marney, don't think you are going to drive that truck all the way. I want to change off with you so it won't wear you out. Hear?" Marney said with gratitude in her voice, "Thanks, Sarah. You're a brick if I ever saw one. Thanks. See you in the morning." With that she was out the door.

The next morning, it only took a half hour to get children up, washed up and take care of last minute packing. George and Marney were elected to do the first stint of truck driving, while Sarah brought Marney's car. Their own car was going to be left as it was actually a company car and was part of the Oxbow Ranch inventory. Wind River Ranch had a car assigned to its manager and would be available when they arrived. The children were distributed amongst the trucks and the car with promises that they could change around from time to time as the trip went on. They were in Canon City within an hour and spent another hour over breakfast. Everyone's hunger satisfied and other needs taken care of, they headed for Colorado Springs and I-25. Once northbound on I-25, the trip began to take on a monotonous sameness. It was a hassle getting through Denver, but the road was open from there to Cheyenne, Wyoming. They stopped from time to time for brief rests. Lunch was at a rest stop near the Wyoming line. They had made good time and there were hopes that their goal of reaching the ranch that day looked do-able.

On into Wyoming and Cheyenne. A brief stop for fuel took only a half hour and the final distance began to roll by. They'd gotten to Cheyenne by one thirty and out on the road again by two. George estimated that another four or five hours should do it. They bettered the estimate by a half hour and drove into the ranch yard a little after six thirty.

Reunions are sweet and Marney's with Fred was especially dear to both of them. Hugs and kisses began the meeting then more hugs and kisses with the children. Finally the trucks were opened and bedding, food and dishes went into the houses. Children were fed and went to bed. More dishes, cooking utensils and food were unpacked and put away in kitchens for breakfast tomorrow. Fred went to George, then and said, "George, I've got a surprise for everybody in the morning. We're having breakfast over at the cook shack after eight o'clock. Lulu's treating all of us." "Woooo--, You're kidding." "Nope, This is her way of welcoming us here as families. She's been planning this for over a week. She just didn't tell us about it until after you left." George simply remarked, "Bless her heart. I'd give her a raise if I could. I may do that anyway."

The next morning, Sarah started getting ready to cook breakfast, but George stopped her. "Gotta surprise for you. No cooking this morning. Get everybody dressed and I'll show you." Within minutes, everyone was ready and they trooped off to the cook shack. As they entered Sarah looked around and remarked, "Will you look at this place. It's spotless. How'd you get it so clean? Oxbow is well kept, but this is 'something else'." George just smiled. "That's Lulu's doing. She won't have it any other way. The cowboys didn't care about it when we first came, but, now that it's cleaned up, they think it's great." Sarah interrupted. "Now, who's Lulu?" George went over to the kitchen door and opened it. "Lulu, could you come in a minute, please?" Lulu appeared, dressed in white trousers and shirt, with a spotless white apron on over her front. "Lulu, this is my wife, Sarah and that's Tommy and Susan. We call her Susie." Sarah said, "I'm pleased to meet you, Lulu. I'd sure like to know how you got this place so clean. It's wonderful." Lulu just said, "Thanks, I like to work in a clean place. I make the cowboys come in here clean, too. I'm teaching them to have respect for being clean. You ought to see 'em. I do it with doughnuts. They can't resist doughnuts." George burst out laughing. "She even got me with that one. She makes the best doughnuts from here to Casper and our cowboys can't resist. I've had to put on 'doughnut hours' to get any work done around here."

Lulu broke in. "I'm fixing breakfast for you this morning, I got rid of the crew at seven, so they won't be tromping in here again 'til lunch time. Now, can I get you some pancakes and eggs? I've got bacon or ham if you like. What'll it be?" Sarah said, "A couple of pancakes and two eggs over easy with a small piece of ham if you please. I think a couple of pancakes for Tommy and a bowl of oatmeal for Susie". "Comin' right up." Lulu disappeared into the kitchen and after a time, she set the orders in front of Sarah, Tommy and Susie. She set out syrup and honey for the pancakes and sugar and milk for everyone. Then she set two poached eggs on toast in front of George. She said, "There you go Boss. Welcome home!"

CHAPTER EIGHTEEN

Marty, Charley and Lulu

Breakfast over, George started unloading the truck with the help of two of the hands. By ten o'clock the truck was nearly unloaded and most things were in the house. Unfortunately, this house was somewhat smaller than the Oxbow house and they were having to make decisions as to where they would place some of the furniture and fixings. Suddenly, Fred appeared and told George that he had a phone call. It was Tom Houghton.

"Good morning, Tom. What's going on?" "Well, I just got a call from Corporate. They bought your suggestion 100%. The next thing they want to do is bring Marty in and talk to him. They don't know him very well, I suppose and they want to get a better picture of him. Does he know yet, that he's being considered for this position?" George said, "No, I haven't said anything yet.. I didn't want to get his hopes up until there was a reason to. He's a good foreman and something like that going sour could ruin it. I'll call him in, now and talk to him before Corporate gets hold of him. I can coach him and help him get prepared, I think." Tom agreed. "You do that, George. And keep your fingers crossed. I'm going to tie a can to this fellow, Rankin's tail and send him on his way. I'd just like to know that we've got somebody we know to take his place. Let me know if anything goes wrong with your interview. At least, I can be forewarned."

George agreed and hung up. Next, he called Fred and asked him to bring Marty in. Within a few minutes, the two of them appeared at the office door and George beckoned them in. "Shut the door, Fred and sit down, both of you." Marty got a puzzled expression on his face. "What's going on?"

Seated, George turned to Marty. "Marty, we're going to have to let you go!" Marty came up in his chair. "Why? What did I do?" George laughed. "I thought that'd get your attention. Calm down, it's not bad. Marty, how'd you like to be an assistant manager?" Now, Marty was all attention. "What do you mean?" George just continued to smile. "Just what I said, how would you like to be an assistant manager?" Marty eased back a bit in his chair, but was still tense. "Well, I'd like that fine, I guess, but I'd not dreamed that anything like that would come along after what happened here before you came." George assured him that he wasn't to blame for all of that. "It appears that you did your job generally speaking. The only complaint I'd have is that the place was so run down when I got here and I don't think that was entirely your fault. Now, here's the deal." He went on to explain what was happening at Oxbow and that he was the number one choice to replace Bill Rankin. "He just hasn't been able to overcome his problems and they're going to let him go." George said. "That's between you and us. Now, you're going to get a call from Corporate within the hour. They want to interview you, but you'll have my recommendation and that of Tom Houghton. He's the manager at Oxbow. You'll like working for Tom. He's a square shooter. Just remember, we've already told Corporate that we think you can do the job. Just listen to what they ask and answer honestly and you'll be alright. Now, one last thing. If they agree to give you the position, how soon can you be down there? That place will keep you busy and you need to be there as soon as possible."

Marty didn't hesitate. "I can leave here as soon as I get back From San Francisco." George chimed right in. "Look,

If they accept you, you give me a phone call and call your wife and let her know that they've given you the nod. Once I know that, and she does, we'll start packing the moving van and you can take it back down to Colorado with your stuff as soon as you get back here. That way, you'll be on the job, wife, family and all. Now, I've got one more problem. Who do you recommend that I make foreman when you leave?" Marty stopped. This was moving too fast for him. He needed to catch his breath. Marge was going to faint dead away when she found out! He thought for several minutes while George waited. Finally he said one name. "Charley Hubbell." George looked him in the eye. "Why not Boots Riskin?" Marty stood behind his decision. "Boots is a good man. I made him a lead man, and he's a good one. His main fault is that he hasn't the experience that Charley's had and he comes across a little too light headed some of the time. He just needs time to get more experience. Also, he's younger than a lot of the men and he gets along easier as a lead man right now." George was nodding his head long before Marty finished. "That's a good analysis, I think. Alright, as soon as I know that you're going to Oxbow, I'll call Charley in and give him the good news. Lots of luck, Marty. Thanks for coming in. I'll call you when Corporate calls."

Marty left and George turned to Fred. "Boy, this trip sure has turned out wild. I've been with the company, what, almost seven years and I've never seen things move as fast as they have these past two months." Fred's comment was "Neither have I. I hope it settles down a bit for awhile, I need to catch my breath."

Within the hour, the call did come from Corporate Headquarters, asking that Marty Martin report on the following day at ten o'clock in San Francisco. The request was acknowledged by George and a call was made to request a seat on a late flight to San Francisco via a United Airlines flight from Denver and a connecting flight via local airline from Casper. Fred was dispatched to notify Marty of the arrangements and to get him to Casper Airport to catch the local flight.

About two o'clock Mountain Standard Time the next day, George received a phone call from Marty. "I've got the job. I called Marge and told her. I'm booked on a flight that should get me in to Casper about seven PM tonight. Can Fred meet me?" George promptly said, "Congratulations Marty, I knew you could do it. Fred will meet you and we'll get started loading the truck as soon as I hang up." Marty's reply was just, "Thanks, George. I'll see you when I get there." He hung up.

George promptly had Charley Hubbell brought in. "Charley, Marty's going to Oxbow as their new assistant manager as of today. How'd you like to be Wind River Ranch's new foreman?" Charley grinned from ear to ear. "I'd like that fine, Boss. What do you want me to do first?" George laughed and said, "Well your first job will be to get a crew together and go over to Marty's house and start loading the moving van so he can leave for the Oxbow tonight. Bill Rankin didn't make the grade down there and they need Marty right away." Charley stood up and started for the door. "I'll get on it right now," He left the office and started off for Marty's house, then changed direction and went to the cook shack. Five minutes later, George saw his new foreman leave the cook shack and head off to the bunk house. He thought that odd and made a mental note to look into it. Why the cook shack?

The loading of the truck was finished by seven thirty. A half hour later, Fred arrived from Casper with Marty. He came over and shook hands with George and told him he was leaving as soon as he could change clothes and gather up his family. By driving through the night, the Martins could be at the Oxbow by sun-up tomorrow. Marty was eager to be on his way. George's final word was, "Give my best to Tom Houghton."

As things began to settle down after Marty Martin's departure, Charley Hubbell moved into the house that Martin's had vacated. He was a bachelor, thirty three years old. He told George that he felt that as foreman he needed to isolate himself from the working crews. Suddenly, George remembered a statement Lulu had made one day when he asked her about herself and her family. He also remembered that Charley has made a 'beeline' for the cook shack when he'd been told that he was the new foreman. George managed a secret smile to himself. Sometimes, two and two didn't make four. "Well," he thought, "Is this going to be like what happened to Edith Mills and Hackamore?" The more he thought about it, the more he liked the idea. Lulu was a fairly young widow and she had three children to take care of. Charley impressed George as a quiet sort of a man who could hold his own as a supervisor, but who was gentle around horses and cattle. It would be likely that he'd show the same trait around a wife and children. The more George thought about the situation, the more he liked it. If Charley and Lulu married, the kids would have a full time dad and mom, something they lacked now. Lulu would have the support she needed from a husband and could still be the cook the ranch needed to keep its hands happy.

That night George remarked to Sarah that he felt like a match maker. Sarah hadn't gotten to know what was going on as yet and asked George what he meant by that remark. When he explained, she exclaimed, "Not again! We just went through that with my mom. Good Heavens." All George would say was, "Could happen. Frankly, I hope it does."

The next morning, when Fred Sowles came into the office to discuss what was going on, George mentioned that he was pretty sure that Charley Hubbell was sweet on Lulu, their cook. He remarked, "I personally think we're going to see a wedding around here in a month or two." Fred was skeptical. "Naw, I bet it takes him at least six months to pop the question." George said, "Bet?" "Yeah, bet. I'll bet you a dinner in town that it takes at least six months." George promptly told him the dinner had to include the wives, too." Fred eagerly agreed. "Marney loves to eat dinner on somebody else. You just wait. I'm gonna love this."

Three weeks later, George happened in the cook shack and was talking to Lulu about the doughnuts when he noticed an engagement ring on her third finger, left hand. He asked her, "When'd you get that?" She blushed. "Well, we've been kinda keeping it quiet, but Charley gave it to me a week ago. We're going to be married next month. I'm so happy about it. Now my kids can have a full time dad. I've prayed about this for quite awhile, now it's coming true." George reached out and hugged her. "That's from Sarah and me. Congratulations." All Lulu could say was, "Thanks Boss. I appreciate that."

George told Sarah what he'd found out and said that Charley and Lulu deserved to have more than a casual wedding. They were good workers and valuable assets to the welfare of the ranch. He asked, "Can't we do something for them, so they feel that this wedding is important to all of us?" Sarah replied, "I see where you're going with this. We need to show our appreciation for them. Let me get with Marney and see what we can organize. Now, one thing. You need to get their permission for this. It's not right for us to just take this whole affair away from them. They need to feel that we're doing this because we appreciate them." "I understand. I'll talk to Charley about it. No, wait, I'd better talk to both of them, It's their affair and they need to feel that they have a part in it. My stars! This isn't going to be easy. Let me work on it and see what I can come up with." George kept the matter in his mind all day. Finally, he made a decision. He'd discovered that the two were going to be married when he'd seen the engagement ring. Lulu knew that he knew. He'd talk to her and let her work it out with Charley. The best place and time would be in the cook shack during the afternoon.

George made an 'inspection' of the cook shack that afternoon. While discussing the problems of keeping the place clean, he casually asked Lulu what their plans for the wedding were. She colored slightly, then said that they'd talked about going to the Justice of the Peace in Edgerton and being married by him. Then, George asked the important question. He put it to her this way. "Lulu, whether you know it or not, you and Charley are pretty important people around here. Now, we wonder if we could help you put something more than that together to show our appreciation. Something you and your children will always remember as a high point in your lives."

Lulu got a questioning look on her face. "What do you mean?" "Well, we'd like to fix it up so everybody could be there when you're married and have a reception so all of your friends, everybody here at the ranch and everybody you know can all come and wish you well. Would you mind if my wife and Marney Sowles worked out something then let you see what they have in mind. You could tell us if you want to be married in church or out here on the ranch, whatever you'd prefer. We just want to make this something special for you." Lulu had tears in her eyes, now. This was something she'd never experienced before. When she'd been married before, they'd gone to a Justice of the Peace and had been married in a five minute ceremony. She'd always felt that it lacked something. They'd done it alone and it seemed a little hollow. She could see what George was getting at and she liked the idea. She turned to him and said, "I'd like that, but I don't know what Charley would think about it." George said, "Well, why don't you ask him? Tell him how you feel. I'll bet he'll do it just to please you and the kids. I tell you what. Ask him and let me know. Whatever you two want, we'll do." Lulu's emotions got away from her a little. "George, I don't know what to say. I never thought anybody cared that much. I'll talk to Charley. I know he'll go along with most anything I want. Maybe we could even be married in church. I'd like that. Look, I'll talk to him tonight and let you know." George put his arm around her and hugged her. "Go for it, Lulu. Just let me know what you want to do. OK?" With that he left her.

That evening, George told Sarah what he'd done and she got a bright smile on her face. "You did that? What did she say?" George explained. "She's going to talk to Charley and she'll let us know what they decide. If he goes for what I suggested, could you and Marney organize it?" Sarah hooted. "Hah, you just watch us. Marney and I are a team. We can do anything." George cautioned. "Be careful, don't overdo it." "Don't worry, we won't." He spoke again. "Lulu's the key to all this. When she lets me know what Charley will go for, I'll have you get with her to work all of it out. That way, she'll feel like it's her affair and not something we've jut taken over." Sarah agreed. "Don't worry about us. We're experts."

The next morning, Lulu and Charley came into the office together and Lulu laid out what they'd decided. She turned to Charley and smiled. Charley just said, "Whatever Lulu wants is fine with me. I'm not used to this sort of thing, she's been there before. Boss, I just want you to know, we both appreciate what you want to do for us. I never dreamed this place cared that much about anybody." George said, "Charley, I learned something during the years I spent at Oxbow. You take care of your people and they'll take care of you. That's why you're foreman. Marty told me that's the way you work" He turned to Lulu. "I've told Sarah to work with you to plan this out. You just tell her what you want and let her and Marney work it out. They won't do anything you don't want. "Now," he smiled. "Get out of here, you two. We've got a ranch to run." Charley just grinned. "Yes, Boss." and the day began.

A couple of days later, Sarah and Marney invited Lulu to Marney's house to plan the wedding out. They sat down and Marney started it off. "Lulu, what we want to do is plan this the way you want it. So I thought we'd just ask questions and you can tell us if that's OK with you." Lulu was a little hesitant as it was all new to her. Finally, she said, "OK, let's try it that way and see what happens." Marney started off. "Alright, do you want the wedding in church?" Lulu didn't hesitate. "Yes." "OK, where?" She said, "Well, Charley and I have started going to the one here in Edgerton, so I think that's where we want to be married." Sarah said, "Let me know the name of the Pastor and I'll get in touch with him and make the arrangements." Lulu said. "I'll get you his name and phone number." Marney asked, "Second question. You've been married before. It's traditional to wear white for the first one. Do you want to wear white this time?" Lulu hesitated again. "You know, my first husband was in such a hurry the first time, I was wearing a sweater and a pair of jeans. I've never forgotten how embarrassed I was about that. This is different. I'm going to wear white. I want to remember this all my life." Marney glanced at Sarah and Sarah nodded. "White it is." Sarah broke in. "Marney, that means that we have to find her a wedding dress. Lulu, you and I are going to go hunting for one. Could you take tomorrow off right after breakfast and we'll run in to Casper and see what we can find? Marney, could you handle lunch for the men? We'll never get back in time." Marney just nodded her head. The matter was taken care of. The questions went on. "What about a list of people you want to invite?" "I'll get that to you." Finally, Marney posed the hard question. "Lulu, where do you want to go on your honeymoon?" Lulu got a funny look on her face. "Gee, I never thought about it. I didn't have one the first time and I guess it slipped my mind. I'll have to ask Charley about that." Sarah had been making notes as they went along and she said. "One thing we didn't ask about is the reception. Where do you want to have it? It poses a possible problem. This affair is going to be in October and you know what the weather can be like, then. If we have it at the ranch, it would have to be outside. That wouldn't work in a blizzard. Now, maybe we could have it at the church if they have room, but we'd have to make arrangements to bring any food in. Could we prepare it here in the cook shack and take it in to the church?" Lulu started to say, "Sure, I could --------." Sarah and Marney spoke in unison. "No you can't! This is your wedding and we'll take care of everything." Lulu said, meekly. "OK, OK, I hear you. You can fix almost anything in there except to barbecue a side of beef if you want to. I suppose you can fix everything and haul it in to the church. They have a small kitchen there, where you can warm food up if you have to."

Lulu got ready to leave and Sarah brought up another subject. "Lulu, you're going to be concerned about your kids if you go on a honeymoon. Don't. Marney and I will take care of them while you're gone. We've both got kids at home and we can keep yours busy for a week easily. Your two boys are school age and school will be in session then, so that'll work out fine. Just don't let it worry you. OK? Oh, yeah, I think we should find a way to involve your kids in the wedding ceremony, too. Let Marney and I work on that one."

The next morning, Sarah picked Lulu up at the cook shack and they started off for Casper. On the way down, Lulu remarked that she could not see why the ranch was going to so much trouble for her wedding. Sarah smiled and said, "Lulu, you don't know how much you've done for the ranch. You weren't there when my husband walked into the cook shack and looked at the mess it was in that first morning. You didn't see the food the cook was putting on the table. It's a wonder that anyone would even work there, it was so bad. You cleaned up the place and kept it clean. There isn't a cowboy on the place that doesn't go after your doughnuts. You've done as much as anybody to make this place a happy place to work. It's our way of saying 'Thanks'."

Once in Casper, they located a dress shop listing in the phone book and a phone call verified that they did deal in wedding dresses. A visit to the shop put Lulu in a mood of wondrous joy as she tried on dress after dress. Finally, she narrowed it down to two dresses that she liked. The prices were the same and the styles were similar. Finally, it was decided by the flip of a coin. The sales lady told her the alterations would be complete and she could come in for a final fitting in a week. She'd picked out a veil that set off her red hair and that was pinned onto the dress to avoid loss. Over lunch, Sarah reached out and covered Lulu's hand. "Lulu, I want you to know this means almost as much to me as it does to you. I was Tommy's baby sitter for over two years before George married me. Getting ready for my wedding was as precious to me then as this must be to you. I got a husband that I'll never stop loving and I thank the Lord every day that I've been so lucky. It looks to me like you're getting a man that you can love and who will love you. I know what that's like and I congratulate you." Lulu's eyes got shiny with tears. "Thanks, Sarah." Was all she could say.

The very next Monday, Charley was in George's office. "Mr. Toland, could I talk to you for a minute? I've got a problem I don't know what to do with." George spoke, "Sure Charley, What's the problem?" Charley shifted from foot to foot, then blurted out. "Well, sir, it's Lulu. She wants to go on a honeymoon and I don't have that kind of money. I'm wondering if you could work out some way to get her turned off that idea. Maybe you wife could talk to her and tell her that maybe later or something." George hmmm-ed for a moment, then asked a question. "Charley, wasn't Wind River Ranch in a lot of trouble about six months ago?" "Yeah." "And didn't we shift things around and get it all straightened out, finally?" "Yes sir, we did." George turned away and put his finger tips together as he appeared to be thinking. "Charley, suppose I send you to San Francisco to report all this to Corporate Headquarters person to person along with the written report that I need to send in. Do you suppose that you and your wife could stay a night or two and see the sights of San Francisco?" Charley was catching on quickly. "Yes sir, I guess we could do that." George went on. "Suppose I send you on an extended business trip along with that. Would you want to look into a couple of possible hay suppliers in Nevada? There're several big hay ranches over there and I believe that this ranch buys quite a bit of hay for winter feed, don't they?" Charley confirmed the hay purchases, "Well, yes, we do." "Charley, do you suppose we could get a better price if we were to make personal contact with these hay suppliers than we could over the phone?" Charley was getting into the game, now. "You're probably right, Boss. Yes sir, that's probably right." George made one final point, "Now, I know that we've been buying hay from several places down in Colorado in the past, so it would be fair to check with them and see if it would be cheaper to buy from them again, so, if you were to drive your rental car from Nevada through Colorado to Pueblo and check up on those prices, also, it would be kinda' helpful to our hay buying efforts, wouldn't it? Oh, and by the way, you might want to stop off at the Oxbow and see how Marty's doing at the Oxbow

Ranch. Now, if you and Lulu were to stop and see the sights of Denver, I think that might be worthwhile, too. Just one question. Do you suppose you can get all of that done in a week or so?" Charley was grinning by this time. "I think so, Boss." George finished the conversation by telling Charley, "Charley, this is a business trip, you understand. I'll expect notes on your contacts on the hay prices, etc. What you do towards seeing the country with Lulu is your own business. Of course, I'll pick up the tab for your expenses, so keep good records on that. Hotel bills, meal costs, etc. Now, does that solve the problem you brought in awhile ago?" Charley smiled and said, "I think so, Boss. And thanks ever so much."

A few minutes later, Fred came in and asked if Charley had talked to George, to which George replied, "Yes, he did." George went on to explain what he'd assigned Charley to do. He said that he'd noticed that the activities they'd been through in getting the Wind River Ranch back on track had been successful, but that Corporate had not received a full report in person as yet and that Charley was a good choice to make that report. "Charley was concerned that he didn't have enough money for a honeymoon, but by combining business with pleasure, he can do the company's business and have a pretty good honeymoon at the same time. Anyway, he seemed to think that he could. I think it'll give him a broader view of what the company does, too. What do you think?" Fred thought for a moment, then said, "I hadn't thought about that. I suppose you're right. He deserves it, anyway."

Planning went forward and things got done in addition to the routine work around the ranch. The crew hazed the herds into the hills where they could find shelter from winter storms as weather got colder.

Preparations for the marriage of Charley Hubbell and Louise (Lulu) Holden went forward. The dress was picked up and carefully hung with the veil in Sarah's closet, awaiting the big day. Invitations were sent and food was planned for. Finally all was ready and on the early afternoon of October second, Lulu rode to the church with George and Sarah Toland. Marney had taken the children including her own in to run through one more rehearsal of their part in the ceremony. Jenny, the youngest one was to be the flower girl and the boys would hand out programs.

Finally all was in readiness. Lulu was dressed in her wedding dress and her daughter, Jenney, took one look at her and said. "Mama, you're pretty!" Lulu kissed her and said, "I feel pretty, too." Charley and Boots, his best man were waiting with the Pastor when the music began and Lulu started down the aisle on George's arm. He turned her over to the groom and stepped back. When asked "Who gives the bride away?" he answered, "I do.", then sat down next to Sarah on the front row.

The ceremony went forward with the usual "I do's" and the final words, "I pronounce you husband and wife." were heard. The Pastor said, "You may kiss the bride." Lulu answered, then. "I don't know if I want to be kissed in public like that." To this, Charley spoke firmly, "You'd better get used to it, Dear One. We have to set a good example for these love starved cowboys around here. I intend to see that you get kissed in public by me plenty often." With that statement, he kissed her firmly and for long moments accompanied by cheers from the audience.

The reception followed the wedding and most of the well wishers hugged the bride and shook the hand of the groom.. After cutting the traditional cake and dishing out pieces to a few guests, Lulu slipped off and changed into the traveling clothes she'd brought. Within a few minutes, she and Charley disappeared. They were due at the Casper Airport for their flight to San Francisco.

George had alerted the corporate offices that he would be sending the report concerning their efforts to get Wind River Ranch back on track by Charley Hubbell and had gotten an appointment for him the day after his wedding. He waited with bated breath for comments on the report from headquarters. He breathed a sigh of relief when it came. It was brief in its content. It said, "Keep up the good work!" Fred Sowles echoed his boss's sigh.

The hands all waited patiently for their cook to get back. It wasn't voiced abroad, but the opinion was, while Sarah's and Marney's cooking was acceptable, Lulu's was worth waiting for. Lulu's children were another matter. The boys had listened to their mother and accepted her explanation about the honeymoon, but little Jenny wasn't as patient as the older ones and continually asked when Mommy was coming back. Encouraging explanations only lasted a few hours and the question would come again. The little girl wasn't unhappy that her mother was gone, but to her, time passed slowly and her concept of 'several days' had little meaning. Mommy usually came home in the evening and she wasn't there. Finally, after a week, she did return, right on schedule. Jenny was happy again and the only thing she had to get used to was the new house they moved into and the fact that Charley was her Daddy, now.

The day after Charley and Lulu returned, George called Charley in to report the results of his 'business trip'. They went over the details of the visits to the hay ranches in Nevada and in Colorado. George asked Charley for his opinion about the hay, prices and delivery possibilities. Charley explained that the Nevada hay was slightly better quality, but they wanted too much money for it and the delivery costs would be higher. He thought they should stick to the Colorado hay. He said that they could buy enough more hay in Colorado to make up the quality difference for less than they could buy the needed hay in Nevada. The problem was that it was just too far to haul it. George said, "I thought so. By the way, how did you come up with the figures you did?" Charley smirked. "Huh, I just told Lulu what the hay people told me and she had the answers in seconds. You wouldn't believe how fast that gal can figure in her head! I'm pretty good at it myself, but she can out figure me two to one. I asked her how she got so good at it and she told me she always did her arithmetic in school in her head. She never used paper and pencil." George made a mental note to remember Lulu's talent. It might just be useful some time in the future.

George tuned to another subject. "How are things at the Oxbow, Charley?" Charley grinned. "Well, you know, Marty was always a pretty sharp character when it comes to cattle. Right now, he's going through the divisions looking for ways to make them even more efficient than they have been. He told me of several tricks he plans to try out in the next year or so. Tom Houghton is behind him a hundred percent and the crews think he's onto something. I'd say that we need to keep an eye on all he's doing and if we can make use of it. I think we ought to try at least some of it. I looked at what he described and some of it won't work up here, the weather's too cold in the winter, but I think some of his ideas could work for us."

George thought a moment and then instructed Charley to write up a complete report of what he'd run across on the trip paying especial attention to what he'd seen at the Oxbow. "We'll keep it on file and come next spring I want you to start some experiments and we'll see just how good these ideas really are. Do you think Boots could run one or more of experiments like that?" Charley replied, "Well, I'd like to keep my fingers on what he's doing if you want to put him into that. He's a good man, but I'd like to keep an eye on him so he doesn't get too impetuous."

"Good thought, Charley. Well, I want you to take a look at the feed situation and tell me how much hay I need to order. Figure on doing it with the Colorado hay. I want to get it ordered and get it up here where we can put it out when we need it." Charley answered, "Will do, Boss. I think we'd better hurry on that one. I'll have the figures ready for you this afternoon." With that, he headed out of the office and went to talk with Boots Riskin.

CHAPTER NINETEEN

Projects

George went over Charley Hubbell's written report and spent considerable time digesting the section concerning the program that Marty Martin had started forward at Oxbow Ranch. He tried to make sure he understood the procedures that Marty had put together and that Charley had written down in the report. Finally, he called Fred Sowles in and they went over it together. Fred finally stated, "You know, George, if this will work here, we could save as much as ten percent of the normal winter kill every year." George just nodded his head and said, "I think it's worth a try. Let's get Charley back in here and work out a plan to try this. I think we're early enough; we can do it this winter if we start right now."

True to their thoughts, they called Charley and the two lead men in and all sat down and began working out the details. One of the questions that Fred asked was, "Where on the range do we have most of the winter kill?" Boots and the new lead man, Howard Bell spoke almost together. They said the same thing. "Boss, we get most of it out on the open flats. The cattle seem to lose their energy and strength when the wind and the cold spells hit. They quit eating, even when there's hay available. I thing it's primarily the wind that gets 'em." Charley thought for a moment, then said, "I'd agree with that."

Fred asked, "Well, what can we do to minimize that problem?" Boots answered first, "The cattle that stay back in the hills and draws where they have more shelter do a lot better. Howard agreed, then added a different factor. "What Boots says is true, but we can't always keep the critters up there in the hills. They have a tendency to drift down on the flats when the snow gets too deep in the draws. That's when we have trouble." Charley spoke up, then. "How would it be if we put up a number of wind breaks? The wind nearly always comes out of the north in the winter. Why can't we put up some solid fences, say fifty yards long across the wind? We can put hayracks on the backsides where the cattle can feed out of the wind. That would break the wind and the hay would lure them in behind those wind breaks. We know where the cattle usually bunch up out there on the flats, so we already know where to put the wind breaks. All we'd have to do is put down posts in a line and build the wind breaks on them. We could build the hay racks onto the posts and make a pretty solid set up wherever we put 'em."

George spoke, then. "What do we need to do that, Charley?" The answer came promptly. "Well, we've got two tractors with posthole diggers for them. That solves the problem of digging the holes. We've got stacks of posts here at headquarters, all we have to do is haul out the number we need for each windbreak. We'd need twenty posts for each one. Then, we'd need lumber for the rest of it. We've got some of that and we can get more easily enough. We can get a crew together and start putting one of those things together tomorrow if you want." George said, "How many of those things do we want to start with?" Charley's answer was quick. "I think, no more than five. Boots, can you give me five locations that you think we need to put up windbreaks?"

George put the project into motion. "Charley, I want you to start putting up one right away, the weather's still good right now, so that should go pretty fast. Boots, you and Howard help him and see how it goes. Then, when he's got the first one built, each of you get a three man crew together and get cracking on two more each. That'll give us the five. Once you get the windbreaks built, Charley, go back and build a hay rack on each one .Put a roof of some kind over it so the snow doesn't fill up the hay bin." Charley nodded and said, "I'll get right on it, Boss. Come on, Boots, you and Howard come along, let's get this thing organized. Winter isn't going to wait forever." With that, they left.

George turned to Fred. "Look, Fred, I want you to keep track of the statistics of this experiment. Compile the costs of the windbreaks and hay bins. Let's see if we can compare the rate of winter kill on the open range versus the losses we have around these wind breaks. What we want to know is if the normal winter kill costs are higher than the costs of the wind breaks." Fred smiled and said, "That's right up my alley, George. I got an 'A' in statistics in college. How about we keep the numbers on the amount of hay we use and see if we cut down the wastage, too." George thought for a moment. "Good thought, Fred. As a matter of fact, why don't you put this whole thing together as an experiment? Give Oxbow credit for the idea, but document our development of the concept and try to document every aspect of it that may change, you know, like death rates, hay usage, manpower to maintain, etc. Let's see how it all turns out."

The weather held good for a week and the initial parts of the project were completed including the hayracks on the wind breaks. The line shack crews were instructed to haze cattle in their areas into the neighborhoods of the wind breaks and the home crew kept the hay racks full after the first snow. Hay was also put out as it always had been, in open areas where the wind breaks hadn't been installed. The line shack crews were instructed to keep a comparison tally of the cattle that preferred the hay in the open areas versus the cattle that tended to frequent the wind break feeding areas.

It wasn't long before the crews had gotten the procedures down to a daily routine. Fred collected the data from them on a weekly basis and started calculating the results. George kept track of Fred's record keeping and by the time spring had come, it was obvious that the initial expense of the project was paid for out of the savings in cattle mortality rates and the savings in hay wastage costs. Several of the line shack crews remarked that the cows were even sleeping on the leeward sides of the wind breaks.

CHAPTER TWENTY

Motherhood

It was at this time that the manager and the assistant manager both got surprises they hadn't counted on. Sarah announced that she was expecting another baby in October. The real surprise came when Marney announced a week later that her family was due to increase also. Lulu heard about it and chuckled to herself. She'd not told Charley about her own secret as yet. She'd wanted another baby and the death of her first husband had smothered her hopes for a time. Charley loved her children and treated them as if they were his own, but Lulu wanted to present him with another, just theirs. She'd wait a little while before telling him her own secret. She'd calculated her due date as being on or near the first of August, w hile Sarah was due in late October and Marney was due about the first of November. Charley's surprise came during the first week in April when Lulu kissed him one evening and told him he was going to be a father in August. She told him in answer to a remark he'd made that 'Lulu was putting on a little weight, wasn't she?'

When Sarah found out about Lulu's upcoming motherhood, she and Marney assured her that, even though they were expecting a few months later, they would see to it that Lulu had all the help she needed when the baby came and they would take care of doing the cooking for the crew. She told them that she'd see to it that they would be treated likewise when their times came.

There was much going on during the springtime of the year on the ranch. One of the things that kept the crew busy was calving. The cows had been with the bulls at such a time that the calves would be born in the springtime when the weather was getting warmer and the grass was coming on new. It was the cowboy's job to see that everything to do with the birthing went as God intended. Further, there was the occasional cow that didn't want anything to do with her newborn calf. Any problems of these kinds had to be dealt with. A calf was a valuable asset to the ranch because each one was part of the crop and any losses meant reduced revenue when the steers and heifers were sold and shipped to market.

The work didn't slow down when the cows were finished with the calving, Then there was branding and making the male calves into steers. Wolves and their raids on the calves were a constant threat and had to be watched for. Calves were vulnerable to sickness and disease when they were young and small. Because of these multiple threats, cowboys spent long hour in the saddle and others cruised the range in Jeeps wherever the terrain would allow their use. This workload wasn't restricted to the cow hands alone, either. Charley, the foreman, Fred the assistant manager and George all spent hours out on the range seeing to the welfare of the cattle. Because of the constant need to be here, there and the other place, the cook shack had to be open at all hours of the day. Cowboys came in tired and hungry whenever they could take a break. All this meant was that someone had to be at the cook shack to supply the needed meals whenever the men came in.

Lulu did her best, but it was often necessary for someone else to spell her off and give her a break As the springtime melted into summer, Lulu found it harder and harder to keep up, partly due to her advancing motherhood. Finally, George listened to a word of warning from Sarah, one day. She told him that Lulu would have to have help and would have to quit if she didn't. George called the employment agency and had them send several potential helpers out for interviews. They sent four, two men and two women.

George asked Lulu to help him interview the candidates since the cook shack was her department and the helper would be part of her crew. One man decided that he 'wouldn't work for no woman', so he was eliminated early. The second had cooked in a hotel and wasn't used to the plain fare that the cowboys normally ate. He was thanked and told that his specialties weren't quite what they wanted. Finally, it hinged between a short order cook that was trying to decide which job offer she wanted to accept, the ranch job or a restaurant job that paid less but was close to her home in town, or a short, Hispanic girl whose personality had everyone laughing during the short interview. She'd worked in her mother's restaurant until it was forced to close because the building had been condemned. George and Lulu conferred, briefly, "George, I think Carmelita is the one I want. She's got a good sense of humor and I don't think she'll stand for any nonsense from any of the men. I can teach her everything she'll need to know to get along. Let's give her a try." George agreed. "I think you're right. Just the same, I think that every single cowpoke on the ranch is going to be smitten with her. Are you sure you want to handle a ranch full of love sick cowboys?" Lulu just laughed. "Well," she giggled, "maybe one of them will marry her and then we'll have her anytime we need her. Look what happened to me." George chuckled, "Alright, you'll just have to be the one to handle that. Do you think you can teach her how to make doughnuts?" Lulu grinned. "No problem, Boss." Carmelita went to work the next day.

The girl quickly won the hearts of every cowboy in the place. Her bubbly sense of humor often had the men in stitches as she kidded them and told them jokes when they came in for meals and coffee. They quickly learned to respect her, however and any cross or inappropriate word was dealt with by her 'protectors'.

As July came in, Lulu became so uncomfortable that she had to turn the entire work load over to Carmelita. The men were delighted with the change of fare. Carmelita continued the usual menu, but often the supper fare included tacos or enchiladas along with other Mexican favorites.

The first week in August, Lulu and Charley made a hasty trip to the tiny hospital in Edgerton, where Lulu gave birth to an eight pound four ounce baby girl. Marysue was born in the middle of the night which meant that Charley was bushed all the next day. After the usual three day of rest and entertaining visitors and well wishers, mother and new daughter came home to cheers and more visitors. Lulu got so many baby gifts that she said later, "I'm gonna have to have two more just to use up all this stuff!" Charley claimed that he'd have to buy a new hat, his old one was now two sizes too small.

Sarah and Marney helped with Lulu's family while she was recuperating and made sure that she had meals for the children and Charley. For the most part, Carmelita was able to keep the cook shack operation going for the month that Lulu was gaining her strength back Occasionally Sarah and Marney came in and helped with clean up and with supper meals. Everyone was holding their breath to see what was going to happen to Carmelita when Lulu came back full time. As it turned out, a new need cropped up and Carmelita stayed. Fred Sowles had been keeping the data on the wind break experiment the ranch had been running in the winter time. Now, when it came time to use the data to show results, Fred got so busy with other activities that he had to have help with the mathematics of the project. He asked Lulu, "Do you know anything about making mathematical comparisons?" She did. From that time on, she spent most of her time working on the winter project data. George said later "I was afraid we wouldn't be able to justify using Lulu for the statistical data keeping. It seemed like we were making an extra job. But, she's worked into the bookkeeping so well, I don't know how we can do without her, now." Doing the bookkeeping gave Lulu more time to be with her children, also, a problem she'd not been able to solve while she was in charge of the cook shack.

Children were becoming a major factor around the Wind River Ranch. Sarah and George had brought two with them when they moved in from Oxbow, Marney and Fred had two and Lulu and Charley now had four. The children's ages ranged from that of the infant Marysue Hubbell all the way up to eight year old Tommy. That made a total of eight children and would increase to ten when Sarah and Marney gave birth to the two they were expecting.

In the meantime, Little Susan Mildred wasn't so little any more. She was about to turn four years old within a week and she knew everything! At least, she thought she did. Actually, she asked more questions than her mother could answer. "What's this?" and, "How do you do that?" went on all day long. She didn't limit her questioning to her mother, either. Dad and Charley and almost any of the cow hands could find themselves having to answer some query by a petite young lady of four. This little girl was a walking, talking question mark! She wasn't ready for kindergarten just yet, but she was already spelling out four letter words. She could sound out simple words quite well, something that most youngsters her age weren't ready to do. Finally, she was delighted with the idea that she was going to have a baby sister or brother in a couple of months. She'd been allowed to hold tiny Marysue Hubbell and she could hardly wait 'til she could do the same with the new baby when it came.

Tommy, being the oldest in the ranch children was inclined to be a bit bossy at times, but his mother cut him down to size. He gradually began to learn a little humility and respect for others. His father helped Sarah impress Tommy with this attribute. "Tommy, you need to respect others if you want them to respect you." was his theme song. "Son," he would say, "you aren't any better than anyone else. If you make others feel that you're their friend, they will probably be your friend, too." This idea took root, a little at a time and Tommy found that others around him, at home and at school gradually began to look up to him and regard him as a friend and a leader. One to whom this feeling was a deeply rooted feeling was his neighbor, Peggy Ann Sowles. She was his age, but to her, he was a hero.

Tommy was old enough that he was learning to ride horses. When the family had moved to the Wind River Ranch, George had gotten Tommy a pony and all the rigging needed for a boy his size. This included a small saddle and bridle suitable for the pony's size. After a year of riding, Tommy had learned to take care of his animal and it's saddle and other equipment. George insisted that Tommy keep the pony properly fed, groomed and inspected for injuries. Tommy had learned that one did not just throw on the saddle and go for a ride. The animal and the equipment had to be cared for and his owner was responsible to see that it was done. As it turned out, Tommy was fond and proud of the pony he called Sox, and the little critter responded by being a loving pet. The care the pony got, he returned in spades. Whenever Tommy came to the corral or pasture where the pony happened to be, the pony came to the fence nearest where Tommy was and Sox would nicker for him. Tommy always rubbed his nose and sometimes gave him an apple or carrot.

Tommy had completed second grade in the spring and moved on with his schooling in the third grade when school started in September. The boy found that the real, hard learning started now. Reading went beyond 'Dick and Jane, see Dick run, see Jane run'. He was reading about adventures and the history of his country and other more complex subjects. He had to understand what the things he read were all about. Arithmetic began to be more complex. He had to learn skills in simple addition, subtraction, multiplication and division. Fortunately, his Mom was able to help him whenever he got stuck. She had an intuitive skill for figures that opened up the difficulty when he got confused and helped him grasp the concepts. Occasionally, they turned to Lulu when something stumped both of them. She was 'the light at the end of the tunnel', she knew it all. Tommy was also learning a second language. English was a part of schooling, of course, but he was also learning 'cowboy English'. Words like 'gonna' and 'durned' were just a few of his second vocabulary. There were some words that he heard that his Dad and Mom had to put their feet down on. Just not appropriate! "We don't say things like that." He learned that one didn't even say them anywhere, especially around ladies or girls. That was something gentlemen didn't do.

School was a delight to Tommy at the first of the school year. However, things got very difficult for awhile. He got the mumps and was out of school for over a month. He had to stay in a room by himself the whole time as Sarah was trying to protect Susan and her new baby sister, Patricia Carol. He tried to keep up with his school work after he began to feel better, but he was still weak and recovered slowly. Peggy Ann came by everyday with their study assignments, but she couldn't come into the room where he was. She hadn't had the mumps and her Mom told her to stay away from Tommy. She did the best she could; she left the assignments in Sarah's hands at the front door.

When Tommy started back to school again, he was about three weeks behind. Catching up was a strain. There was a mass of arithmetic he had to learn and spelling was behind, too. Peggy Ann tried to help, stopping by and spending time with him when the danger of catching the disease had passed. But she wasn't much help. She'd just learned the lessons herself. Likewise, Sarah was handicapped with the demands of the new baby and Susie. It was a struggle. After about a month and a half of hard work and help from Peggy Ann, his mother and the teacher, he caught up. Tommy learned a valuable lesson, though he didn't realize it until later years. Difficulties could be overcome with dedication and hard work.

CHAPTER TWENTY-ONE

Carmelita and Boots

Things were different in the Toland and Sowles households, now. Little Patricia (Patty) Carol Toland had arrived on the thirteenth of October and Monica (Monnie) Jean Sowles had followed her into the world on the twenty first of that same month. Mothers Sarah Toland and Marney Sowles were busy taking care of little ones for several months following their blessed events. Sarah said, later, "Don't ever have a baby when you've got a four year old in the house and an eight year old with the mumps!" Meeting the demands and needs of each one was a strain for a time. Both mothers were fortunate in that Edith Hadding took a vacation from her job as cook at Oxbow Division Five and came to help out. She'd been on the job steady since the day she went to work there four years before and was due for several weeks' vacation. She stayed for five weeks alternating between Sarah's and Marney's homes. Both mothers were more than grateful for the unexpected assistance.

One morning in November, Charley Hubbell walked into the Wind River Ranch office. He had a complaint. "Boss, we gotta do something about Lulu!" Right away, George could smell a problem. Charley was coming at it from an angle, but he was about to unload. "George, that woman has been all over my case for a week." George could see that his foreman wasn't angry and not visibly upset. "What's she disturbed about, now?" he asked. "Well, it's the kids." George wondered, "Now, what?" Charley went on. "Seems we've got four kids and only two bedrooms for the six of us. Marysue's four months old, now and Lulu wants to put her in a separate bedroom since she sleeps through the night most nights. But, there's no room to put her in. 'Sides, she wants to put our two girls together and the boys are too old to be sharing a bedroom with the girls. The problem is, really, we need a bigger house."

George was suddenly sympathetic with Charley's problem. He had the same problem. Two bedrooms, One boy and two girls. Not only that, Marney had unloaded on him with the same problem the week before. His mind roamed a bit afield and suddenly included another possible couple that might just be bringing up the same problem in two or three years. Carmelita and Boots.

Carmelita had resisted all efforts of the single men to date her. She refused to respond to romantic advances from any of them 'til she saw Boots Riskin. The truth was that she was extremely shy and covered it up with cheerful but casual conversation and a jolly manner. One evening, Boots asked her if he could walk her back to the house that had been assigned to her when she went to work as the cook. He explained to her that they'd seen cougar tracks not far from the ranch buildings and they'd not been able to track it down. Carmelita was frightened and agreed to let Boots see her to her door. He continued this service for a couple of weeks and she came to look forward to his company. One day, the cougar was spotted and the local game warden captured and caged it. From there, it was taken to a new home some seventy five miles further west and then released into a new habitat. It was never seen again.

Now, Boots didn't have an excuse for escorting Carmelita home each night. He did anyway and Carmelita liked his cheerful company. One evening, the temperature was especially cold and she'd forgotten her coat the morning before.

Boots opened his coat and wrapped both of them in it. He wrapped his arm around her to hold the coat closed and Carmelita felt a special warmth that didn't come from the coat. As they walked along across the snow covered yard, she thought about this man. She'd begun to look upon him as her protector. Now, she realized that her feelings were becoming deeper than that. When they arrived at her door, Boots released her and she stepped forward, and turned toward him. Rising on her tiptoes, she reached up and pulled his head down to her five foot one inch level and soundly kissed him long and hard. Then she made a statement that shook Boots to the soles of his polished cowboy boots. She said, "Boots, I need to talk to you about us. Not tonight, Manana!" She'd used a Spanish word that came to her instinctively. Then she turned again and said, "Buenos noches. I'll see you tomorrow." She then opened her door and disappeared inside. Boots suddenly realized this was not the time to press the issue. His thoughts and feelings were in a whirl of confusion. All he could think of was that she'd kissed him. Finally, he bade her "Goodnight, Carmelita." and turned away. That was the last time he called her by her full name. She became 'Lita' from then on."

The next night, after Carmelita had finished cleaning up the kitchen at the cook shack, she and Boots sat at the table. They commented about this and that for a few moments, hesitating to talk about what was really on both of their minds. Finally, Carmelita said, "Boots, I need to know how you feel about me." With that, she'd opened the door and Boots made it plain that his feelings for her were much more than just friendship. He hesitated to come out and say, "I love you." He felt that it was too early for that. But she got the message nevertheless.

From that time on, Boots and Carmelita began spending time together at the cook shack after supper. They talked, some times for an hour or more. Now, the talk was serious, the kind of talk that two people in love and contemplating a lasting relationship usually engage in. They had discovered each other and each one was eager to find out what the other was really like. She was curious about his name, Where'd he get the name 'Boots' He smiled and told her that he'd always kept his boots polished when he was in school, so his friends tagged him with the nickname, 'Boots'. "My real name is Harold, but nobody calls me that any more." Boots in turn asked Carmelita about herself and he was told that she'd been born in Monterrey, Mexico and had lived there until she was seven years old. She said that her father had come to a significant conclusion one day. That was that a job that paid five dollars an hour in the US was a better deal than the same job in Mexico when it only paid fifty cents an hour there. The result was that the father had emigrated to the US and had brought his whole family with him including his mother, Carmelita's grandmother. Once he'd established his status and that of his family, they'd moved to Wyoming where they opened an Hispanic restaurant.

One question had been on Boots' mind for some time and he finally got up courage enough to ask it. "Lita. That night when it was so cold, why did you kiss me? I was so surprised, I never expected that." She giggled momentarily, a little embarrassed, then she got very serious. "Boots, I watch you. You never get mad. I saw a horse buck you off but you never say a word, you just pet him and get right back on. I saw a man get mad at you, but you not get mad. I think, "That man never hurt my children. My father is a gentle man. He never get mad at me, not once. He always talk to me when I got in trouble. Boots, you like him. When the big cat came around, you walk me home. You cared. When I forgot coat, you put your coat around me, keep me warm. I get special feeling when you did that. Now, you understand why I kiss you? I want you to notice me. Remember, I tell you we need to talk? Now, we talk. Now I know you better and I like what I find out. Now you understand?" Boots did understand. His feelings for this slip of a girl grew rapidly.

The more they learned about each other's personalities and became familiar with each other, the more convinced they were that they wanted to make the relationship a permanent one. Finally, Boots asked her to marry him and she kissed him and said "Si, I marry you" Then the questioning began in earnest.

"Do you want children?" "Yes" "How many?" "Lots" "How do we support a big family?" "Work harder" On and on it went. They were happy with what they found in each other and they became firmly committed to the idea of becoming husband and wife.

George had been aware of the developing romance for several weeks and when Carmelita told Lulu that she and Boots were engaged, Lulu told George. He told Sarah and she told Marney. She just said, "Another wedding to plan."

George's problem was not the wedding, it was housing. His house was too small, Fred and Marney's house was too small, Charley and Lulu's house was too small and now another house was about to be challenged. All of these dwellings had been built many years before when people made do with such houses. They were crowded, but people tolerated them.

George contemplated the problem for several days, promising Charley and the others that he would get back to them. The crux of the matter was the fact that a decision had to be made. "Should the existing houses be remodeled with more bedrooms or should they be torn down and replaced with larger ones?" George called a builder in Casper and asked him to give him two estimates, one for remodeling and one for replacement. The results of the study were definite. Replace with new construction. He asked for a bid for a three bedroom house and for a four bedroom model. This time, he asked for bids from three builders. The bids were remarkably similar as were the prices. He wrote a report to corporate headquarters, detailing the problem and included the three written bids that had been submitted. He asked for authorization to proceed, stating that the four homes would be for the supervisory personnel of the ranch.

Boots and Carmelita decided to be married in January. The timing was such that they'd be married and be able to go on their honeymoon before the heavy workload of spring started. Also, the construction of the new homes should be finished by the middle of April and the newlyweds could move into a new houses soon after they'd come back from their honeymoon. It was decided that preparations for this wedding would go forward in a similar manner as they had for Lulu and Charley's wedding two years earlier. Boots and Carmelita were quizzed about their preferences on every aspect of the event. Carmelita had definite ideas about what she wanted and Sarah and Marney set about to work out the details. Everything began to fall into place a couple of weeks before the date the bride and groom to be had set. Because of the delays in building the houses, the wedding kept getting postponed until they had to decide on a firm date. They decided on the last week of February. That would give them just enough time to take a couple of weeks for their honeymoon before coming back to calving time.

When Carmelita went to her church in November and asked about holding the wedding there, she ran into a wall of bigotry. She was asked if Boots was of the same faith that she was and she answered, "No." She was told that her church would not marry them, and further that if she did marry Boots, she would go to 'Hell'. The effect was twofold. She was devastated and she was deeply angered. "Didn't God love her? And didn't God love Boots just the same?" She didn't understand the church's attitude. She appealed to Sarah. Sarah listened a moment and stopped her. She said, "I want Marney to help with this." She went to the phone and called her friend, explaining that Carmelita was at her house in tears. Marney just said, "I'll be right there."

Five minutes, Marney was in, she hadn't even bothered to knock. Sarah explained what Carmelita had told her and Marney didn't hesitate. She took the sobbing girl in her arms and consoled her. "Carmelita, I want you to try something. Sarah and I go to a different church and I know they feel differently about something like this. I want you to come to church with us next Sunday and talk to our Pastor. See what he says. I'm sure something can be worked out. Will you do that?"

Carmelita took several minutes to think the proposal over. She was torn between loyalty to something she'd grown up with and shifting her attention to something she'd been taught to be suspicious of. She voiced her concerns to Sarah and Marney. Sarah spoke out carefully, but Carmelita caught the wisdom of what she said and her deep concern for Carmelita's feelings. She said, simply, "Carmelita, God loves you and He loves Boots. I know he would never tell you that you'd go to Hell for marrying someone you loved. Why don't you come to church with us next Sunday like Marney suggests and see for yourself? If you don't find the love of God and the Savior there, I'll not say another word about it. Will you do that?" Carmelita wiped her eyes and then nodded her head. "I guess it won't hurt to give it a try."

Carmelita did try it and was so impressed that she came on her own the next Sunday and brought Boots with her. When the services were over, she took Boots by the hand and followed the Pastor to his office. There, she broached the subject of their upcoming marriage. "Could we hold the ceremony and the reception here in your church?" The pastor smiled and then he asked a question that caused Carmelita and Boots, both some small fright. "You're not members, are you?" Then he saw the look on Carmelita's face. He backpedaled a little. "Now, don't let that bother you. It's just that we ask people that aren't members but need the use of the church to pay a little something for the use of the building. We can make most any arrangements you need and, yes, we'd be happy to have you be married here." Carmelita smothered him with hugs. Carmelita and Boots continued to come to church each Sunday and they both became convinced that they'd found God's love there. They'd begun attending in November and by the end of December, they both decided to become members, joining the Toland and the Sowles families each Sunday. It wasn't long before almost everyone who came to the church knew about the couples' intentions of getting married and the two became popular members of the younger set in a short time.

In the meantime, wedding preparations went on. Sarah asked the bride about a wedding gown and was told that Carmelita would be wearing the same gown her grandmother had worn when she was married in Mexico forty years earlier. Sarah was delighted with Carmelita's choice of wedding gowns as it added something traditional to the ceremony. The only problem they discovered with this was that Carmelita was about four inches shorter than her grandmother, measuring a bare five feet one inches when backed up to a door frame and measured. Not only that, but she had a more slender figure. They hadn't realized how petite this young bundle of energy really was.

Sarah and Carmelita consulted with the shop that had supplied Lulu's wedding dress and found that the shop could make alterations to the old gown without doing any cutting. This had concerned Carmelita as she didn't want to spoil the gown for her daughter's if she should have them. With Boots' six foot stature, daughters surely would be larger than their mother!

One of the features that Carmelita had insisted on was that they would have dancing and Mexican music for the reception. She had arranged for a quartet that regularly played at a Mexican restaurant in Casper. They were loud, they were lively and the guests loved them. Everyone was delighted when they played for the entire affair.

The ceremony went more or less as Lulu's had. Carmelita got kissed, hugged and welcomed to the Wind River Ranch family just as Lulu and Charley had when they were married. Boots and Carmelita made a delightful couple. Both were cheerful, fun loving people and both had won their way into the hearts of everyone connected with the ranch. Their honeymoon was a mystery. No one ever did find out exactly where they went or what they did. All anyone knew was that they came back with a load of souvenirs from the Southwest US and from Mexico.

The housing project that Charley and Lulu's complaint had triggered had been going ahead after the corporation had approved it and five new homes were going up where their older counterparts had once stood. The project had to go one house at a time as the occupants of the older houses had to have a house to move into when theirs was torn down. Thus it was that Carmelita got the first one and moved in shortly after she and Boots got back from their honeymoon. The project slowed down after that because of the severity of the winter storms and the depth of the resulting snow. Sarah, Marney and Lulu didn't get moved into their new houses until almost mid-summer. It was a 'one at a time' affair. Sarah said later, "I got tired of tripping over cribs and cradles, it was so crowded at our old house." Lulu and Marney were equally vocal about the overcrowding in their old homes, but they managed to be philosophical about it. Anticipation of something better helped a lot.

CHAPTER TWENTY-TWO

Tom Houghton Retires

Life on Wind River Ranch went on as it had for years. The move that the corporation had made in putting the team of Toland and Sowles in place of the previous manager and his hard headed assistant had worked out unusually well. They had turned a losing ranch into one of the jewels in the group. It had started when Charley Hubbell had visited his friend and old boss, Marty Martin when he and Lulu were on their honeymoon. Charley saw that Marty was developing new, more efficient ways to handle cattle. Charley could see that there was a potential for reducing the usual losses that occur in any ranching operation. When he reported what he'd seen to George Toland and Fred Sowles, they latched onto it and among the three of them, they began developing a system for the harsh environment of Wind River Ranch and Wyoming, one that began saving winter losses and reducing wastage in the feed hay. They were so successful in their experiments with wind breaks and other measures they put into place that they began looking for other ways to improve the operation as well. They'd been successful with most of them.

The team consisted of George, Fred and Charley as the heads of their efforts but they depended on several others who supported the various projects. Boots Riskin had mellowed out as a lead man and his approach to things began to be more thoughtful and serious than it had been earlier. He was full of ideas and made several experiments successful when they would have failed or would not have been as fruitful as they'd turned out. Likewise, Lulu had contributed much to the successes. She was the statistician to Fred's record keeping efforts and seemed to have an unusual talent for spotting significant facts when others missed them. George once had laughed when Lulu had surprise them with a fact that had eluded all the rest of them. He remarked, "That woman is like a bloodhound when it comes to seeing things like that!"

Results were the goals the team sought and the team got results. Costs dropped as much as ten percent in some cases and profits increased as well. George paid the entire crew a bonus one year when their profit margin had increased by fifteen percent. He went out on a limb with Corporate to do that, but they couldn't argue with his reasoning. He told Corporate, "They did the work and they deserve the reward." Corporate didn't argue.

Sarah's end of the team moved right along, too. She and Marney had come to Wind River Ranch almost three years before and had participated in virtually everything that had happened since they'd arrived. Sarah remarked at a party one night, "You know, I used to think we were busy at Oxbow. Hah! That's nothing compared to this place."

What she didn't remark on was the fact that she and Marney had been a part of it all. She'd brought two small children with her and had given birth to another one, a baby girl, Patricia Carol, after she came. Marney had matched her with a baby girl of her own. Monica Jean. Nor did either of them remark on the fact that both women were expecting again.

Time moves on and with the movement of time, changes occur. As Tom Houghton was often heard to say, "We don't live forever, thank goodness for that!" George had been manager at Wind River over five years. He had participated in several successful experiments during the time he'd been there, had improved the facilities at the headquarters and had developed the team he had working on the ranch. In the meantime, Tom Houghton had reached the age of sixty five and had decided that it was time to retire. When a manager retired, a movement of personnel began that sometimes took several months to settle down.

The first inkling that George had was when he and Fred received a call from Corporate Headquarters asking them to attend a meeting in San Francisco the following Monday. No reason was given for calling the meeting as Tom Houghton's retirement had not been announced. Sarah and Marney were not invited and would have begged off anyway, since both had small children to care for. Sunday afternoon, they kissed their husbands 'goodbye' and sent them on their way. A flight to Denver and another one to San Francisco landed them in that city in late evening.

The next morning, George and Fred appeared at the Oxbow Corporate offices and were sent to the office of the first vice president. They were shown in and seated after shaking hands with the vice president. Once seated, they were told, "Gentlemen, Tom Houghton, the manager at Oxbow Ranch is retiring and we've called you two in to discuss changes in assignments. We have reviewed both of your records and we've decided to offer an opening to each of you if you want it. To you, George, we would like to offer you the manager's position at Oxbow and to you, Fred, we'd like you to take over at Wind River Ranch. Now, before you give us your answers, let me tell you that there's going to be other movement as well as your own if you accept our offers. Several men are retiring also and those positions will have to be filled.. In turn the positions that the men who fill those open positions will have to be replaced and so on. Do you get the picture?"

George had gotten a little breathless at this point, trying to keep up. The vice president went on. "If you haven't figured it out yet, you two will have to make some of the assignments necessary to fill these open positions. Now, to get the first hurdle out of the way. Do you gentlemen want to accept the positions we're offering you?" He turned to George. "Do you accept the manager's position at Oxbow?"" George nodded. He'd worked for the last twelve years for it and he'd done well in the assignments he'd been given. This was the culmination of all that hard work. He just added, "I do."

The vice president turned to Fred and asked the same question of him. Fred also nodded. His reply was, "Thank you, I'd be glad to." There were tears in his eyes as he thought of how he'd been reached this point and how he owed George so much for offering the assistant position at Wind River. He'd worked hard to do his part in their successes there. He had no illusions about the parts others had played and how hard he'd worked to keep everyone's efforts going forward. It had paid off.

The vice president wound up the meeting by saying, "Gentlemen, I'm going to dismiss you for now. You need to call your wives and tell them what's happened to you. My congratulations. Come back at two this afternoon and we'll give you details of your assignments. Thanks for coming." He shook hands with each one and said, "I'll see you both later." With that, he walked out.

George and Fred sought out an Italian restaurant where they could talk. They sat down, each one reviewing his feelings and trying to decide where they would go from there. They ordered a meal and began to talk. George addressed the moves that would be needed on the Wind River Ranch first. "Fred, you know that ranch as well as I do. You shouldn't have any trouble going on with everything pretty much as we've been doing up to now. The only thing I'd warn you about is that I'm going to try to deal you out of at least one man."

Fred got a surprised look on his face. "Oh, who?" "Boots Riskin, who else? I've looked at the situation at Oxbow Ranch and they're pretty well manned except for the job you used to have there. I'm torn in two directions on that position. The man that took your place is due for an upgrade just as you were. Now, I can try to put Boots in there or I can move Hackamore Hadding in there and put Boots into Division Five as foreman. What I think is going to happen is that Jim

Billings, the fellow that took your job is going to be moved up to that ranch in Montana as assistant manager and that leaves me with an opening that I've got to fill. The only thing I've got to decide is where I want to put Boots, providing I can talk you out of him and providing Carmelita will let him leave Wyoming. Now, what do you think you want to do with your crew? First, if I take Boots, who are you going to put in his place?"

Fred just grinned. "First, who says I want to turn loose of Boots? He's doing a good job right where he's at, now. Why should I want to make a change there? If I let him go, that means I've got to look for another lead man and at the same time think about a replacement for Charley Hubbell. Charley could easily be moved on to an assistant job somewhere else, which means that I'd have to scramble to fill his present spot.

George pointed out a problem that Fred had overlooked in his haste. "Fred, you've got to fill your assistant manager's position, first. Why don't you move Charley Hubbell into that spot and let's talk Hackamore Hadding into taking over the foreman's position at Wind River. He's due for a change, anyway. He's done a good job at Oxbow's division Five, but he needs more of a challenge. It would give him a raise in pay, too. If I give the Division Five job to Boots, that'll give him a start in a well established spot and give him a chance to see how things are run around a bigger organization."

The conversation went on for awhile, first one and then the other making suggestions and between the two of them trying to put together a new personnel structure to run their respective organizations. Finally, it was time to go back to corporate headquarters and hear the briefing that the corporate people would be giving them. They gathered up their notes and briefcases, paid their bill and showed up for the briefing.

The man giving the briefing started their meeting by asking the two if they had discussed organizational plans. They had! Fred made it plain that he didn't want to give up Boots Riskin, but George's explanation of his reasons for requesting him won the day. Fred had an alternate plan in mind and it was approved. The only difference was that corporate would supply him with a new man to fill the foreman's job at Wind River since Fred had asked that Charley Hubbell be upgraded to be his assistant. Corporate named a man that was presently a lead man at a ranch in eastern Oregon and was due for promotion. He came with a solid track record and Fred was glad to get him.

With the details worked out, the meeting went on to spell out the details of the future aims of Wind River Ranch and Oxbow Ranch. Things were changing in the cattle raising industry and Corporate was interested in seeing that these changes were addressed to keep their ranches making money and contributing to the dividends paid to the Oxbow Corporation stockholders. Other, lesser details were covered and after two hours, the meeting was ended. George and Fred were congratulated for their work and their promotions and told to go let their wives know what was going on.

Back at the hotel, phone calls were made and wives were told. Both men had reservations on airline seats to Denver and on to Casper. Within the hour, they were lined up to board their flight and their homecoming. Sarah and Marney had both been admonished to keep the news to themselves as other people were involved and it would be up to the two managers to talk to them personally. They had been asked to meet their husbands at Casper Airport with the promise that they would be told everything on the way home.

When George and Fred were reunited with their spouses, it was a joyous moment. Sarah said it all when she told George, "George, I knew you had it in you when I met you in San Francisco, twelve years ago!" That's all she would say, even when her best friend asked her to explain what she was talking about. As far as she was concerned that was between her and George. Marney's joy was no less jubilant. They'd worked hard for this, too. They would miss George and Sarah, but Fred was a manager, now, and they were more than happy with that knowledge. In the back of Marney's mind, however, she remembered how George's insistence that he wanted Fred as his assistant manager at Wind River Ranch had brought Fred to this point. She was grateful. Fred had filled the position when he got it, but it had been George who'd put him in line.

CHAPTER TWENTY-THREE

Changes

The next morning was a busy time. George and Fred called the affected people into the office and broke the news to each of them as they came in. Boots told George that he wanted to have a little time to think over the decision he was asked to make as to whether he wanted to be facilities manager or foreman of Division Five at Oxbow Ranch. He simply said, "I want to talk this over with Lita and see what she thinks." George asked him to let him know by the end of the day and Boots simply said, "Will do, Boss." Charley was surprised at the offer of the assistant manager's position at Wind River Ranch. His words to Fred were, "I'll take it!" He knew that he'd already been doing much of the same work. He'd be able to make more decisions and would be less involved in the day to day work on the range. Finally, it would mean a raise in pay, which he welcomed.

Sarah's emotions were mixed when she found out that she and George were moving back to Oxbow Ranch. She said, "I've always been fond of Oxbow. It's where the greatest happiness of my life began. I hope we'll be there a long time. It's where my heart has been, where I started my marriage and started raising my kids." She was saddened that she would be separated from her best friend, Marney Sowles. They'd been together for nearly twelve years, had shared the joys and hardships of motherhood together and boosted their husbands' careers together. Their bonds were close and their separation wasn't going to be easy.

Marney's feelings were mixed, also. Some of them were sad because of the impending separation from her close association with Sarah, but she was assuming a new role, too as the wife of Wind River Ranch's manager. She had looked forward to the opportunity ever since it became probable that she would fill it one day. She was determined to fill the position well. She would be a strong support to her husband and would contribute all she could to his success. She made up her mind to be just as supportive to her growing family. She reminded herself that she had five children, now, one just barely a year old and still in diapers. Her life would be full and she looked forward to it.

In late afternoon, just as George was about to close up the office, Boots and Carmelita came in to see him together. Carmelita had tear streaks down her face, but her countenance was a cheerful one. George suggested that they sit down and visit with him. Carmelita went up to him and hugged him before she moved to the chair that George provided for her. All she could say was "Thanks, George." He didn't know if she was thanking him for the chair or for the promotion that he'd offered to Boots. Finally, after George had seated himself, Boots began to speak. "Boss, Lita and I talked this thing over and it's going to be hard for her to leave here. You know that her family lives here and she's very close to them. She's torn between staying here and going to the Oxbow and I've tried to be sensitive to her feelings as much as my own in considering this offer. There's a lot to this. You know that I have a degree in farm and ranch management and this is an opportunity that I've been trained for. Lita knows that and that's what makes it hard for her. We've prayed about this and it took all day to come the decision we've made." George was getting more worried minute by minute. He wanted and needed Boots on his team at

Oxbow and he was getting apprehensive that Boots was going to refuse the offer. Boots finally got to the point. "Boss, Lita and I both feel that we need to accept this offer. We talked about taking the Division Five job, but I think that I can do a better job as Maintenance and Supply manager. I want to be a manager some day but I need the experience I can get being the M and S manager." Carmelita broke in at that point. She said in an excited voice, "George, I tell you another reason for his wanting that job. I'm going to have a baby in a few months and we want to live at the headquarters, not further out. Also, I went to university and I learn to be a teacher. I want to teach the school at Oxbow. My father came to the US fifteen years ago so his children could get the education. we couldn't get in Mexico. Now, I want to pay back for his sacrifice for me."

George breathed a sigh of relief. He'd been tossing names back and forth, trying to find someone to fill the Maintenance and Supply position if Boots should turn it down. Thank goodness, he hadn't. Things could move forward

From that point, the re-organization efforts began. George left the re-organization of the Wind River Ranch strictly to Fred to put into motion and only offered advice when asked. He flew down to the Oxbow Ranch and met with Tom Houghton and Marty Martin to organize the change over there.

Before he left, George arranged for a moving company to pack and pick up his and Boots Riskin's households at the Wind River Ranch and to deliver them to the Oxbow Ranch as soon as possible. Sarah and Carmelita gathered the children into their two cars and started south. Traveling with children took more time and things didn't work out quite as they had planned, so they spent one night in a motel in Cheyenne. They arrived at the Oxbow the next day a little before sundown, tired but jubilant.

George had anticipated their arrival and had prepared a couple of the vacant houses at the Oxbow as temporary quarters. George would move Sarah and their children into the manager's house after Tom and Mrs. Houghton had departed.

Boots moved Carmelita into another house and both families anxiously awaited the arrival of the moving vans.

George called a meeting of the foremen of the divisions and included the heads of the various support organizations including the Maintenance and Supply division. His aim was to state his intended policies and to get re-acquainted with the people he'd worked with before. Most knew what he was like and what he wanted to accomplish. The Maintenance and Supply division's previous head had already been sent to a ranch in eastern Oregon and Boots hadn't been involved in one like the Oxbow had, so George promptly appointed Marty as a committee of one to get Boots up to speed on what his new position entailed.

After the meeting had ended, Hackamore asked to speak to George. His told George that he and Edith wanted to stay at Division Five. They'd talked over the offer that had been made for Hackamore to become the foreman at Wind River Ranch and they both felt that they were close enough to retirement that a change in assignment wasn't particularly attractive. He also said that it wasn't fair to the two children they'd adopted to move them around. Their schooling was part of the problem as well. They'd both started at the Oxbow Ranch School and Edith wanted them to finish their elementary education there. They'd stay where they were until Hackamore retired. George thanked him for telling him. At least, he didn't have to worry about a change in that position.

George met with Marty Martin and had him go over all of the changes that had been made since George had gone to the Wind River Ranch as manager. Marty had been foreman, there, but had been moved to Oxbow shortly after George had taken over as Wind River's manager and he hadn't really gotten familiar with George's ways of doing things. These were things Marty needed to know if they were to work together. They decided that they needed to tour the entire ranch and have a look at everything that was going on. Marty told him that he ought to set aside a day for each division to go through all that was going on. George agreed and scheduled a date that would allow him to get his family settled before they started.

George sat back and reviewed all of the things that were going to involve him in the next little while. First, Tom's retirement and his takeover of the running of Oxbow Ranch had to take place and was scheduled on Saturday, two days hence. He had debated whether he should do the inspection tour with Marty before that happened or after, finally deciding that it would be well to do it after. He needed to take all the time needed to thoroughly digest what Marty had done since he'd left to go to Wind River Ranch. Next, he considered where the industry was going and effect it would have on the economics of the ranch. The market was changing and not for the better. He felt that the survivors would be those that could adjust to the changes in a positive way. Finally, he thought about his family. Tommy was growing up and was nearing high school age. What would he and Sarah have to do to see that the boy could attend high school on a daily basis? That would require considerable thought. Actually, they had five children that would have to go through the same path as they reached the age that Tommy was reaching. Susie would be a fourth grader in the fall, Patricia Carol, (Pattie) was ready for second grade and little Annie would be in Kindergarten come fall.

Three of his children had been born at Wind River Ranch during the seven years they'd been there. Susie was born at Oxbow Ranch, but Patricia Carol, Elizabeth Anne and Andrew Joseph were all born in the little hospital in Edgerton, Wyoming. Little Joe was still not walking. He could crawl and he got into everything that wasn't locked up.

Finally, George put the matter 'in his pocket' for the time being. He'd have to discuss it with Sarah and see where it would go. The other matters were there to be done now, not later, so he needed to plan them out and to go ahead as he always did.

Another possible problem came to mind. Edith had been cook at Division Five for over ten years, now. He thought that he might want to discuss that with her and Hackamore and see if she wanted to continue that. Maybe he ought to talk to Marty about that. That was really Marty's bailiwick and he should handle it. He'd talk to him about it.

George got a phone call from the Executive Vice President of the Oxbow Corporation on Thursday. The gist of the conversation was that the VP was going to be at the Oxbow Ranch on Saturday to make a presentation to Tom Houghton with a present at his retirement. He said that Tom had been one of the company's best managers and the decision had been made to recognize his service as being special. George breathed a sigh of relief. He'd anticipated that he'd have to do the honors and organize the whole affair. Now, the Executive VP would probably have that all worked out and George could sit back and smile. However, a thought of caution nagged at him. Suppose the VP didn't do that and relied on George instead. He made a mental note to talk to Tom about it and if necessary, organize the program anyway, just in case.

Lastly, George thought about Boots Riskin's job as Maintenance and Supply boss. Should he involve himself in breaking Boots in on the job or should he leave that to Marty? If he did it, it would seem that he was usurping Marty's area of responsibility. On the other hand, how well did Marty know that particular function? He'd have to look into that matter also. Maybe he could play an over seeing role and let Marty do his best while he kept an eye on his assistant's efforts. He could always suggest things to Marty without seeming to interfere. Maybe it would be well to review the job description with Marty before he started instructing Boots. He'd talk to Marty this afternoon and see what he could find out.

George sighed a long sigh and put a sign on his desk "Out to lunch. Call me at home if you need me." He then closed his desk and headed for the house and some welcome time with his family.

That afternoon, George went over and talked to Tom Houghton. His intent was to see if Tom knew anything about what the company intended to do toward Tom's retirement ceremony. Tom was home and George sat down with him in his living room to chat. "Tom, have you heard anything from the Corporation about your retirement? I mean, have they said anything about some sort of dinner, or ceremony or anything like that?" Tom smiled and shook his head. "Nope, not a word. Either it's a deep dark secret or they've forgotten all about it." George said, "Well, I can tell you, they haven't forgotten it. The Executive Vice President called me this morning. He apparently has some kind of award or something they plan to give you, but he didn't say how they were going to do it. I thought at first, that I'd just let them do their thing, but, since they didn't outline any program or anything, I've decided that I'd better organize a program so that if they show up, it won't be a surprise and it won't be an embarrassment to them or you."

George went on. "Suppose we organize a dinner for Saturday night. We can invite all of the people that work here and the foremen from the divisions. In other words, we can make it an Oxbow Ranch affair. What I can do is deliberately leave a spot open for the Executive Vice President if he shows up. I'd like you to plan to speak and tell a little of how the ranch got started and what we've accomplished here. This place has been a good training ground for some of the people who are managers and assistant managers on ranches in other places within the company. I think you've had a lot to do with that. I know it helped me get where I am today."

Tom had been listening and nodding his head. "George, I think that's a good idea. I think it's appropriate to make this an Oxbow Ranch affair. Let's do it. Work it up and let me see it tomorrow. If I think it needs any changes, we can fix it then." George nodded his agreement. "I'll have it ready first thing tomorrow and I'll talk to everybody that we'll need to get it ready. Boots can order anything we need and go get it in time if I get the dinner organized by tonight."

George took his leave of Tom Houghton and went back to his office. There he sat down, called Sarah and asked her to come over. Within a few minutes she entered the office and asked him what he wanted. He explained, "Sweetheart, I just talked to Tom about his retirement party and he agrees that it should be an Oxbow Ranch affair. Now, we know that Corporate is going to make some kind of presentation, but they haven't told us what they have in mind, so I'd like us to work up the agenda for the party and just leave a space in it for the Corporate VP to make the presentation. Could you help organize this?"

Sarah was quick to see where George was going with the idea and she agreed. "What kind of a program do you have in mind?" George said, "I think we need to work this around a dinner. I'd like to invite all of our supervisory people, division foremen and wives, department heads, etc. everyone that has worked with Tom directly. I can work up a program easily enough, but I need lots of help with arranging the dinner, sending out invitations, etc. Could you see to that?"

Sarah thought for a moment. "I wish Marney were here. She's so good at things like this. I'll talk to Laura and Barbara and see if they can help. I suppose it would be a good idea to involve Marge Martin, too. Tell you what. Let me work on this for an hour or two and I'll get back to you." George smiled. "Good enough! I'll go to work on the program and I suppose I should call Corporate and tell them what we're doing. That way I can ask them where, in the program, they'd like to make any presentations. I suppose we could even ask the VP to be the keynote speaker. Now, that's a thought." Sarah just kissed him and said, "See you later."

George reached for the phone and called Marty Martin. Fortunately, he found him in his office, a somewhat unusual happening. "Marty, could you come over to my office? I've got a problem and I need your advice." Response, "Be right there." Five minutes later, George was explaining what he was doing and pointed out that he needed a master of ceremonies to get the dinner program going, keep it going and to do the introductions etc. Marty asked a question. "Why can't you do that?" George pointed out that he was the incoming manager and would be one of the speakers. "Oh, I hadn't thought about that. You're right. OK, I'll do it." George went on. "Now, would you see to it that all of the division foremen get invited to attend along with their wives?" "Yep, can do, anything else?" George said, "I've got to see just what events we want to put in this. Let me work on that for awhile and I'll get you to help me lay out the program if you don't mind." Marty said, that he'd be glad to help as soon as he finished a project that he had nearly completed. "See you in a bit." With that, he disappeared.

George called up from memory a number of such dinners he'd been to and finally worked out a program that he thought would be fast moving and hold the interest of the guests. He called the cook that would be in charge of putting the dinner together and then called Sarah. He explained to both of them that he wanted to put together a dinner menu and would they come over and work out what would be appropriate for the event. Within minutes they were in the office. George explained that he thought the dinner theme should be western, possibly a beef barbecue with the appropriate fixings with it. He ended with, "That's just a thought. Why don't you two sit down over there and work out something? I need to call the vice president that I think will be coming, so have at it and let me know when you have something. Remember that I'll need to have Boots send in an order as soon as possible and he can't do that unless he knows what you'll need."

That done, he called San Francisco and asked for the Executive Vice President. In a minute, he had the VP on the line, explained what he was doing; then asked him if he was planning to attend. The answer was "Yes, I talked to you this morning and I thought I'd made that clear." George explained, "Well, yes and no. You said you were coming but we still don't know just what you want to do." All George heard was, "Oh. I guess I didn't make that clear. Now, maybe I should ask just what you are planning as a program." George took a few minutes to explain exactly what they had planned so far and then asked the VP if he would be the keynote speaker. George explained that he thought it would be well to cover Tom Houghton's service to the company and what had been accomplished in his administration, etc. Then, of course, if there were any awards or presentations to be made, they could be accomplished at that time. George finished by saying that as soon as he had a tentative agenda worked up, he'd send a copy to the VP via FAX. The VP seemed happy enough with that promise and told George to go ahead. George's "Thank you, sir." ended the conversation and he hung up.

Just then the cook and Sarah presented him with a dinner menu and he looked hard at it for a moment, then called Boots. "Boots? Can you come over? We've got something that only you can do for us." "OK, see you in a minute." He hung up. He turned and faced the cook. "Can you work this menu up into a list of things you'll need from Pueblo? I'm going to send Boots and Carmelita into Pueblo in the morning to pick up what ever you need. He's coming right now, so you need to get a list ready for him."

The planning went on and the leg work got done. Finally, on Saturday night, the dinner went forward in the Oxbow Ranch dining hall. Virtually everyone that had worked for Tom Houghton while he'd been manager of Oxbow Ranch had been invited and very few failed to show up. Marty Martin took charge of the program and did the announcing as master of ceremonies. Speakers spoke and covered the accomplishments of the ranch and of Tom Houghton. George spoke briefly about his work under Tom and where he thought the ranch would go from that point. He gave Tom a great deal of credit for his own success. Finally the Corporate Vice President arose and explained that Tom Houghton had done much for the success of the Oxbow Corporation as well as the Oxbow Ranch. He lauded Tom as a man of vision, one who saw the potential of the ranch and proceeded develop it At the end, he presented Tom with a gold watch and a complete fishing outfit with an embossed permission to fish on Oxbow on a permanent basis. The dinner had been centered around a barbecued side of beef with all the appropriate trimmings. When the dinner was over and the guests left the table they'd been inspired and well fed. The event was a great success.

CHAPTER TWENTY-FOUR

The Changeover

The change in management of Oxbow Ranch was the beginning of large changes in the workings of the entire enterprise. Cattle prices had gone down when the use of red meat had fallen into disfavor because of the need to reduce cholesterol intake in the American diet. Actually, the need to make changes began to be apparent some time before the retirement of Tom Houghton, but significant changes hadn't begun to be made until that time. Marty Martin had seen the trends when he moved in to replace Bill Rankin. With Tom's blessing he began looking to see what could be done to maintain the ranch's profitability in the face of the changes they could see coming.

The trend was toward a leaner beef on the grocer's shelf and it took awhile to understand how to best obtain this type of beef on the hoof. It was easy to keep the fat off the cow. Just not feed it so much. This wasn't the answer, though. All the producer got was a smaller cow. Research in feeds eventually revealed that a leaner cow could be obtained without sacrificing weight and paying more for exotic feeds. Most of this experimentation took place in the feed lots where the final finishing of the beef is done. In the feed lots, the cattle were fed different mixes of feed, formulated from different varieties of hay mixed with various grains and other supplements. Corn had been one of the most common ingredients fed when fat cattle were favored by the consumer. When fat meat became an undesirable product, other grains began to replace the corn in the prepared feeds. Eventually, feeds were developed that produced lean muscle instead of fat impregnated meat.

All of this experimentation and development took time and research before results began to be realized. Oxbow decided to approach the problem with a twofold program. Up until the time that George Toland replaced Tom Houghton as manager, the range cattle had been sold to feed lot operations in other parts of the country. A conference with the corporate managers, Tom Houghton, George Toland and Marty Martin brought a new approach to the problem. They elected to do their own finishing on a feed lot on the Oxbow Ranch. The object was to save the transportation costs and eliminate a middle man from the process between the range cow and the slaughter cow. When a cow was ready for market, instead of selling it to a buyer who in turn sold it at a profit to a feed lot, the cow was merely moved to the Oxbow feed lot and finished and made ready for slaughtering at the same ranch it grew up on.

This approach required some drastic changes. First, the feed lot had to be located where it would not be undesirable to it's neighbors because of undesirable odors, untreated manure and other wastes. It needed to be accessible either by rail siding or truck loading facilities. Second, there had to be facilities built to process the special feeds the feeder cattle required. All of this conversion took time and money to get set up. Marty Martin was in the middle of this process from its beginning and became the resident expert on the subject. When George became manager of Oxbow, he jumped into the project with both feet. He could see that the changes were needed and became an ardent supporter of the ranch's efforts to get them into operation. It took nearly a year to get everything in place, but even the first cattle that were sold to the slaughter houses were better suited for the lean beef market and had brought better prices to the company.

As the operation went forward, there were other things that emerged as by-products. There was manure, tons and tons of it. The ranch set up the feed lots so that it could easily be removed from the lots and facilities were developed to process it into fertilizer suitable for gardens and farm operations.

George met with his crews and supervisors regularly. The entire operation was monitored to see that the cattle progressed from calf to salable steers and heifers in an efficient manner. Efficiency meant lower costs. Where other ranches were reduced to slim margins of profit, Oxbow maintained a comfortable return for their investment. The changing economy in the beef cattle industry forced Oxbow Corporation to look at the profitability for their other ranches as well as Oxbow Ranch. A careful study of each one showed that the one in Montana was only marginally profitable simply because it cost too much to haul the cattle it produced to the feed lot at Oxbow Ranch and the climate wasn't suitable for developing a feed lot there. It was sold and the funds were re-invested in a ranch in eastern Oregon where the climate was milder.

It was about this time that the corporation began to look at a different problem. Originally, the home office had been on the ranch that the Sears family had owned and was the nucleus of the Oxbow Corporation. As additional ranches had been added to the company, management had opened the main office in San Francisco. However, now the bulk of the ranching operation was east of the Rocky Mountains and any business to be conducted with the home office required people to travel. Management began looking at other options, eventually settling on the Denver area. The ranches that were the farthest from Denver were the two ranches in eastern Oregon. A hard look was taken at that situation, but the decision was made to keep them. They were smaller and were not a problem to administer from Denver. A feed lot operation was set up on one of them that took care of the cattle from both ranches. That situation was manageable.

Finally, It was decided to move the headquarters to Aurora, Colorado just outside of Denver. It was close enough to the International Airport and far enough from the city of Denver that access by car was relatively easy. Compared to San Francisco, the location was much more favorable and the setting was pleasant with the Front Range of mountains being so close in the west. Once the decision had been made, office space was leased and the corporation's officers and supporting staff moved from San Francisco. It took several months to get everything and everyone settled in the new location, but most agreed that it was a favorable move and put headquarters closer to the operating ranches.

The corporation also made another decision that made the move worthwhile. Two more ranches were purchased and made a part of the Oxbow Corporation. Both were located in Oklahoma. Fortunately, the two ranches were adjacent to each other and Marty Martin was advanced into the ranks of managers and given charge of the Wind River Ranch while Fred Sowles and Marney moved onto the new property.. A feed lot operation was set up on this property and took some of the load off the Oxbow by feeding not only the cattle on the two ranches but also took the feeders from the Wind River Ranch operation as well. One of the assistant managers from an eastern Oregon ranch was moved to the Sooner Ranch in Oklahoma and a graduate from Texas A& M was hired and sent to Oregon as his replacement. This candidate was looked at much more closely than Bill Rankin had been and was found to be eager to prove himself.

All of this expansion, relocation and reorganization took nearly three years to complete and George Toland had managed to stabilize the redevelopment at Oxbow Ranch and to perfect the organization that ran it. One of the changes that had to be made was that of Hackamore Hadding. Hackamore and his wife, Edith were reaching retirement age and George had to think about a replacement for him. Between his efforts and Edith's saving ways, they'd amassed a comfortable nest egg which, along with their retirement checks, had allowed them to buy a small acreage near Aurora, Colorado where they were planning to take up the raising of prize winning Hereford cattle.

They'd surprised Edith's daughter, Sarah Toland several years earlier when they adopted two young children shortly after their marriage. There was a four year old boy and a two year old girl. Both of these children were of partial Asian descent and were brother and sister, That didn't matter to Hackamore or Edith one iota. Sarah discovered later that Edith had known their mother in Sacramento. She also knew that they were from a broken family of a drug and alcohol background. Edith managed to rescue them when their mother had died of a drug overdose. Their father had previously disappeared and they were being kept by a friend of the mother. They loved them and the two grew up in a ranching environment and knew beef cattle better than some cowboys. Edith had been content to raise the two children and had worked hard to give them a loving and stable life. They got their schooling at Oxbow and the oldest one, Rob Lee, like Tommy, was nearing high school age. It had meant that Edith had to see that they got to school each morning and required her to get up early to get them ready for school while getting breakfast for the crew at the same time. It paid off as both of them had done well at the Oxbow Ranch School. Rob ultimately would go on to become a doctor and Mai Lin would graduate from the University of Colorado with a degree in accounting. The CPA she would qualify for would be useful at Oxbow Ranch where she would later become the book keeper and accountant.

George Tolands' fortunes had continued to progress after his appointment as manager of the Oxbow Ranch. When Marty Martin was sent to the Wind River Ranch to manage it, Boots Riskin moved up to the assistant manager's position and was replaced as the Maintenance and Supply manager by another new hire from Oregon State University. In the meantime, expansion and retirements had thinned the ranks of the management team at Oxbow Corporation Headquarters in Aurora. The openings had been filled by moving lower management up, but eventually, new blood had to be brought in. George got a phone call from headquarters asking him and Sarah to come to Aurora.

CHAPTER TWENTY-FIVE

Onward and Upward

When George appeared at the home office, he was brought before the Chief Executive Officer himself, one Harold Sears. After preliminary greetings and other small talk, Mr. Sears broached the subject of George's visit. "George, we need a new Operations Manager. That kind of work is pretty much what you've been doing ever since you went to Wind River Ranch ten years ago. You did the same kind of work at the Oxbow Ranch and we've been pleased with you success, there. Now, we'd like to offer you the job of Operations Manager for the whole company. It would be your job to oversee the operations of all the ranches and the other interests of the company. Your home base would be here in Aurora and it would mean that you'd have to move up from Oxbow. We'd like to know your decision right away, so could we talk to you again, uh, say tomorrow morning or at the latest, tomorrow afternoon?" George was a little overwhelmed at the offer. He merely said, "I need to talk to my wife about this, first. I can have an answer by tomorrow morning, alright? I do appreciate your offer and thank you very much." The CEO smiled and said, "Go to it. Give my regards to Sarah. She's a great gal." With that, George picked up his briefcase and took off to talk to Sarah.

George got back to where Sarah waited for him in the corporate outer offices and said, "Sweetheart, I'm going to treat you to whatever lunch you'd like while I tell you what the company is offering us." Sarah's eyebrows shot up. "Offering us? I thought they were probably going to give you the dickens for not doing better at Oxbow or something." George just chuckled. "No, Hon. Nothing like that. Tell you what. I know a really great restaurant down in a little town called Franktown. It's a quiet place and we can talk." Sarah had a mystified look on her face, but she just said, "Suits me."

Twenty minutes later, George pulled into a parking area and helped Sarah out of the car. They went into the restaurant and found a small table at the back where it was quiet. A waiter followed them in and George ordered for both of them. Sarah said, "OK, big shot. What's all this about?" George just smirked. After a moment he asked. "How'd you like to live here?" Sarah exclaimed. "Where? Here?" "Yes, right here. Here in Franktown or a place like it." Sarah was confused, now. "Why? What's going on?" Then George explained the offer he'd been given. He said that it was a wonderful opportunity and one he'd been looking forward to for a long time. It would give him control over what all of the ranches were doing and would allow him to recommend who managed each ranch. "No more Wind River Ranch fiasco's." Sarah was nearly flabbergasted. "But George, what about Oxbow Ranch? Who's going to run that?"

"Well, Sarah, that's the burning question. There are two men that I consider qualified for the job. They've both shown their ability and they've both worked for me as assistants. I think it's about a toss up at any rate. I want to think on it a little longer. In my mind, however, it's Fred and Marty all the way on that one. I don't have to decide until tomorrow.

Now, the real question is "Do we want to accept this position or not? What do you think? Remember, it means that we'll have to move again and we just settled into Oxbow less than three years ago." Sarah mulled the problem over in her mind for a minute and then a bright look came on her face.

"George, this solves a problem we've been worried about ever since Tommy turned thirteen. How are we going to put him in high school and have him live at home? Living at Oxbow, the only solution would be for me to rent a house in Canon City or Pueblo and keep the children there for the school years until all five of them graduate from high school. If you take this position, we can live here and send them from home. I think you need to take the job if for no other reason than that."

George grinned. "Honey, I never thought about that! You've made the decision for me. That's the answer to my prayer. It's the answer to another problem that Hackamore brought to me last Sunday. He told me that Edith doesn't like the idea of living in Canon City in the winter so Rob can go to high school." He looked at Sarah questioning? She looked right back. "You mean could we take them in for the winter and send them to school? You're asking me to watch out for seven children, ages two to thirteen. Five of them are school age and two aren't even in school yet. Both of Mom's kids are in school. Rob Lee is in the seventh grade and May Lin is a fifth grader."

George smiled and asked, "If I got you a helper, could you do it?" She was mystified. "What do you mean?" He said, "Suppose we hire a full time helper for you. Someone that can take care of the household chores and allow you to spend more time with the youngsters?" She said, "Mmmm. Might work." George went on. "I've a person in mind that I think would fill the bill fairly well. She's a forty year old widow that you've seen at Church. She's at loose ends, she doesn't have any family at home. Her only daughter is married and lives up here in Denver. I think we should talk to her and see if she'd be interested in helping us keep our family organized. What do you think?" Sarah got a bright look on her face. "I like the idea. Let's talk to her if this deal goes through."

They talked about it during their lunch. At last, they rose, paid the bill and walked out to their car. As they slid onto the front seat, George turned to Sarah and asked. "Well, what shall I tell them?" Sarah hesitated only a moment, then gave her answer in a couple of strong words. "Do it, George. I love you and I'll stand behind you." George reached over and kissed her. "Alright, Sweetheart. We'll give it our best shot."

The two went to a realtor's office and asked them if they had any listings that would be suitable for a company executive and a family with seven children, all of whom were school age or below. "We'd prefer something in a semi-isolated area if possible. We'd even consider a small residential farm if one is available." Having made their wants known, they visited several other realtors and left their same message with each one.

The couple bedded down for the night at a motel and got a good night's sleep. Next morning, both got up, said their prayers for the day and made their way to a restaurant for breakfast. By nine o'clock, they were ushered into the CEO's office and offered chairs. Mr. Sears got the preliminaries out of the way and got down to business. "Well George, what do you think about our offer? Does it offer enough challenge for you?" George smiled at that attempt at humor and then told the CEO that he was definitely interested in the position. "Further," he went on, "I think I can make the operations more efficient than they are now. I learned some things managing the Wind River Ranch that I think will save us some money in the long run. At any rate, I'd like to give it a try."

Sears said briefly, "Alright, you've got the job. Now, there are several loose ends we need to take care of. I'd like your thoughts on a replacement for the manager's position at Oxbow Ranch. Now, if we pull in a manager from another ranch to do that, we need a name to fill that vacancy. You see where we're going with this. As Operations Manager, we expect you to have some definite ideas about keeping the different manager's positions filled. The managers keep the ranches going, you know that. We don't want them to fall open for more that a day or two at the most. " "I agree, Mr. Sears and I've already spent some time working on a program for each ranch to maintain its efficiency, I'll be getting out to talk all of the managers within the next two or three weeks. I'll have to take a few days off to get moved as soon as we find a suitable place."

Sears rose, shook George's hand." Thanks for coming. George, keep me informed and let us know how you're getting along. Oh, yes, your office will be just down the hall. You'll have a secretary and an office assistant to take care of the routine matters."

With that, the interview was over and George and Sarah drove away to make the rounds of the realtors to see if they'd found anything that fit the specifications they'd left the day before. Sarah told George that she needed to go back to Oxbow Ranch and start getting ready to move. She'd left the children in the care of Laura and Marge Martin and she didn't want to wear out her welcome.

As soon as Sarah arrived home, she made a trip up to Division Five to visit her mother and Hackamore. She told them what she and George had talked about for Rob Lee and Mai Lynn. She suggested that Edith might plan on frequent visits to see the children, during the school year and that they could spend the summers on Division Five with their adoptive parents. Edith and Hack just laughed. "Sarah, we're miles ahead of you. We're retiring. Hack just bought 80 acres up near Aurora and we're going to raise registered Hereford cattle. The kids will be going to school in Aurora and they'll be home every night. If you find a place close to us, they'll be able to be around your kids if they want to." Suddenly, Sarah had a feeling of joy that she'd not had in a long time. She'd been separated from her mother since she'd been in San Francisco and even when Edith had become cook at Division Five, they'd not been able to see each other often. Sarah had longed for a closer association with her mother for a long time, now she could see the possibility that it could happen. She felt that this was important considering the hard lives they'd both lived for a time.. Sarah returned to the ranch headquarters satisfied that she'd done all she could until they could get established somewhere around Aurora. Everything depended on the realtors, now.

A week went by and, finally, Sarah heard from one of the major realtors of Aurora. They had two small ranch locations they wanted to show if they could make an appointment with her. She made arrangements to be flown up to Aurora and to use a company car to visit with the realtor. She tried to contact George only to find that he was on an extended trip to the ranches in Oregon and wouldn't be back for the next three days. Time was of the essence and the opening of the school year was only a month away; she decided to make the trip and hope that any choices she made would meet with George's approval.

She arrived at the realtor's office in mid- morning and was taken to the first listing. She wasn't impressed as it was run down and the house was marginal for a family of Sarah's size. The second location was more promising. The house had been built for a large family, but they badly wanted to sell out because of financial reverses. It showed signs of being empty for several months. Sarah asked how much the rent would be and was told that, while it was for rent, the owners actually wanted badly to sell the property. She asked how much land was with the property and was told that there was roughly forty five acres. There was a barn where they could keep a cow or horse if they wished. She asked about water, electrical service and access to schools and the city, She got answers for her questions, then asked to see the inside of the house. The more she found out, the more promising the property appeared.

The minute she stepped inside, she fell in love with the house. It was well built and well arranged. There were enough bedrooms to house the children and a master bedroom with bath for herself and George. The kitchen pleased her. It was all electric and efficiently arranged." With easy access to the dining area. Everything she saw pleased her. and after a half hour of exploration, she told the realtor that she'd seen enough, "Let's go back to the office." Within an hour, she'd made a deal. She was told a price and offered seventy five percent of the asking price. To bind the deal, she paid down earnest money to secure her offer. She crossed her fingers, hoping George would approve of what she'd done. All she could do now was go home and wait for George to get home so she could explain what she had done.

George did come home. He stayed for three days. During that time, he spent time with his family and in conference with the leaders of the Oxbow Ranch. His elevation to the position of Operations Manager for the Oxbow Corporation had left a vacancy in the position of manager for the ranch and it was up to the assistant manager and his department heads to keep things moving until a manager was appointed and in place. That hadn't happened yet.

Finally, George met with Boots Riskin and talked the matter over. In the case of the Oxbow Ranch, not only had the position of manager had been vacated, but the position of assistant manager was vacant, too. Marty Martin had been appointed as manager of Wind River Ranch four months earlier and a new assistant manager hadn't been appointed to replace him at Oxbow. George talked long and hard with Boots and finally convinced him to accept the position as assistant manager. This essentially put Boots in direct charge of the entire Oxbow Ranch operation, since the manager's position hadn't been filled yet. George decided that he would continue to fill the position himself on an advisory basis, since he was up to his ears getting the corporation Operations Manager department organized as well. He promised Boots that he'd get the manager's position filled as soon as possible. All Boots would say was "OK, Boss, but make it quick, will yah?"

CHAPTER TWENTY-SIX

A New Home

George turned his attention to the matter of the home that Sarah had started the process of buying. First, he asked her, "Why in the world did you decide to buy it instead of renting it?" She stood her ground. "George, I never had a home that was truly mine. You know where I came from and what people like that have. Second, it's a beautiful place for our family and if we were to rent it, and it were to be sold, we could be forced to find another place. I found out that the family that owned it are in desperate financial difficulties, so they are really anxious about selling it. I made an offer that's even less than they were asking and that's where we are now. They've only a couple more days to answer my offer, so we should hear about it by the end of the week."

She went on and explained that she'd talked to a bank in Aurora and made a preliminary application for a loan. She said, "I've got all the papers here and I need for you to sign several of them if you agree with what I've done so far. I looked at our finances and I feel comfortable in putting down 25% of the offer I made. That should make our paying on the loan easy enough." As George listened to what Sarah was explaining, he got more and more humble. Could this be the girl that had jumped into his car in San Francisco so many years ago? She didn't even have a high school diploma, then. Now she was talking about high finance as if she were his banker! How far she had come! He realized that his own success had hinged many times on actions she had taken on her own. Her budget, savings, and investment programs had been a strong example of what she'd accomplished."Sweetheart, never mind my questioning. If the owners accept your offer, that's where we're going to live. I just hope it fulfills your dreams." He then took her in his arms and kissed her. Sarah knew from experience that George had just given her the greatest complement he was capable of. She wiped the tears off her face and kissed him back. "Thanks, George," was all she said.

George signed the necessary papers and left the next morning to talk to Fred Sowles and Marty Martin. He had to fill the manager's position at Oxbow Ranch and fill the vacancy that it would leave on another ranch. Two days later, he got an appointment with President Sears and told him that he was recommending Fred Sowles as manager at Oxbow Ranch and that he wanted Marty Martin to fill the vacancy at Sooner Ranch in Oklahoma. The CEO asked, what do you want to do about filling the manager; spot at Wind River? George replied, "I've got to talk to the two managers in Oregon and try and decide which one of them I want to go to Edgerton, then I've got to move an assistant manager up from one of those ranches. Sears just nodded his head. He said, "I like what you're doing. All of these changes have got my head spinning. Just keep me informed. Thanks George."

George smiled and said, "I've got to clean up a little paperwork, then I've got to go see a house Sarah's set on and a banker about a loan. After that, I'm on my way to Oregon. I'll see you later." He walked down the hall to his own office and set to work to catch up on the details of his department. Within an hour, he called his secretary and his assistant in and laid out the work he'd done. He gave them instructions as to what he wanted done with it while he was gone, then told his secretary he was going to see a banker.

Before he went to the bank George went out and looked at the property that Sarah had involve them in and saw it for the first time. It didn't take him long to realize that his wife knew what she was doing when she chose this one to buy. He could see that it had considerable potential and was worth much more than the asking price and even more than the offered price that Sarah had submitted to the realtor. He stopped at the real estate office and asked if the owners had decided to accept or refuse the offer Sarah had made. The real estate sales person he talked to, opened the folder they'd made up on the transaction, looked up and said, "Mr. Toland, the owners sent us their acceptance just this morning. You've got yourself a deal if you can finance it. You've got fifteen days to arrange the financing and we can close right after that." George just grinned. "I'll see you later. I've got to talk to a banker." With that, he headed for the bank

George walked into the bank Sarah had visited and asked to see a loan officer. When Ben Thompson approached him, George introduced himself and asked to talk about the loan that Sarah had begun the application for. In a few minutes, he was seated at Mr. Thompson's desk and George told him what the status of the real estate transaction was.

Question, "How much money do you need?" George gave him the figure. "How soon do you need it?" He was told, "As soon as possible." Mr. Thompson said, "Well, if we get the paperwork done now, the loan committee will review you application and make a decision by the end of the week. I don't see any reason why you'd be turned down from the paperwork I have here. I'd say that you can tell the realtor that you can go to closing by next Tuesday. That will give us time to verify everything and allow the realtors time to get ready as well. How does that suit you, Mr. Toland?" George allowed as how that sounded 'just fine'. He shook hands with Mr. Thompson and hurried back to his office.

Once seated at his desk, he called Sarah at the Oxbow Ranch and asked her if she could be ready to move by the following Wednesday. "Oh George, they accepted?" "Yes, and the loan is in the works." George could hear her laughing and crying all at the same time. "Oh, George, I'm so happy. My prayers have been answered." George broke into her laughter. "Honey, I'll call a moving company right now and have them show up down there on Tuesday morning. Talk to Boots and have him put someone on getting everything packed and then I'll need you up here to sign the papers on Tuesday, next. I've already called the realtors and they've agreed to close that day. Can you do that?" Sarah just said, "Just try to stop me. I want to get moved into my new house. I fought for it and I want to live in it!"

The minute that George hung up, Sarah called her mother at Division Five. It took a few minutes to locate her, but eventually she picked up the phone. Sarah said, "Mom, could I come and talk to you?'. "Well alright. When do you want to come?" Sarah's answer was, "I'll come right after I get my bunch fed their lunch at noon. Is that OK?" Edith just said. "Fine, I'll be here." and hung up.

Sarah decided to take her two smallest children with her. They hadn't seen their grandmother for awhile and they liked her. After lunch, Sarah drove up to the Fifth Division headquarters and let her daughter out of the car. "Go tell Grammy we're here," she said. She picked up Little Joe and followed Annie into the house. She found Edith busy knitting a sweater for Hackamore, but put it aside when Sarah appeared.

"Well, daughter, what are you up to?" Sarah smiled. "Mom, we're moving to Aurora. George's office is up there and we found a farm that has a big house on it. We've even got a barn and a lot of land. George thinks that he wants a horse. This place we've bought is about a mile from the one you and Hackamore got, so we'll be neighbors."

"Mom, how soon are you and Hackamore going to move to Aurora?" Edith fumbled with that for a couple of moments, then said, "Well, we haven't made up our minds just yet. Actually, Hackamore's got another year he could work before his Social Security will pay full dividend. Why are you asking?" Sarah explained her interest. "Rob's ready to start high school isn't he?" Edith nodded, "Yes, he is." "Well, what are you going to do about it? He can't get there from Division Five or from Oxbow Ranch either, for that matter." Sarah said. Edith explained what she'd thought about doing up to that point. "I'm going to have to rent a house in Canon City and put the two of them in school there, I guess. It's either that or move down to the place out of Aurora and live there while Hackamore stays here. I don't like either option and neither does Hackamore but that's the best we've been able to come up with." Sarah piped up, "Mom, why don't you put them with us at our new place in Aurora 'til you retire? We've got plenty of room. They'd have rooms of their own if they want. We can send them to school with our kids. You could come and stay with us from time to time so Rob and Mai aren't lost to you. There will be trips coming to Aurora from Oxbow fairly often, too, so you could come and go fairly frequently. Another advantage might be that they would be with kids they know well. I think it would be worthwhile to try the scheme and see if it won't be better than what you have in mind. Besides, it would give me a chance to see you more often."

Edith thought about it for a minute, asking finally, "Are you sure you want to do something like that?" Sarah replied, "Mom, yes, I do. I think those two kids of yours deserve the best we can give them." Edith thought it over a few minutes, then, "Alright, I'll talk to Hackamore about it tonight and let you know. Actually, it would give me a little more time at home, here if we do it that way, I think. I think he'll buy it for that reason."

Hackamore did buy the idea and just before school started, Rob Lee and Mai Lin moved into the house just outside of Aurora with George and Sarah's family. The Tolands' had moved into their new home two weeks before and things were getting organized pretty well by the time the two adoptive kids arrived. Edith came with them to get them settled and take care of the paperwork associated with their changing schools.

CHAPTER TWENTY-SEVEN

School and Home

Rob Lee was starting his freshman year of high school and Mai Lin was a seventh grader in middle school. Problems arose almost immediately. Rob had been well established at Oxbow Ranch School and had been near the top of his classes. Beginning a new school where he wasn't known put him at a disadvantage. The school wasn't overly large and most of his new classmates knew each other which made him an outsider. His part Asian ancestry was the subject of jokes with some and made him feel that he was different, something that he wasn't used to. He came home at the end of the first week angry, disgusted and discouraged. Mai Lin had a slightly different problem. She was smaller in stature than most of her age group and took some ribbing because of it. Since she was new in her class, she too felt like an outsider. Sarah's daughter, Susan was the only one Mai Lin knew and this was some help, but she needed to be accepted by more than that to feel comfortable in her surroundings. She too came home somewhat discouraged. The start in their new school surroundings wasn't the greatest for awhile.

Tommy (Tom) was a new student at the high school in Aurora and a freshman as Rob was. He was well established in his study habits and knew where he was headed academically. He let others come to him rather than seeking others out. He wasn't spectacular in what he did, but he did what was expected of him and did it well. It wasn't long before he'd won the respect of his teachers and his classmates.

Sarah and Edith got together and looked at the problems trying to find solutions. Nothing looked very promising until the school year had progressed a couple of weeks. The Tolands had joined the local congregation of the same Church they'd belonged to in Canon City and Edgerton as soon as they'd moved in. When Rob and Mai Lin came, they attended Church with the Toland family. It wasn't long before they'd joined in their age groups and began to become acquainted with members of each group. Mai Lin got to be close friends with two of the girls and, with Sarah's permission, invited them out to the house one Saturday afternoon. It was a success and when school started on Monday, the girls found that they had some classes together. Other girls got to know Mai Lin and her problems disappeared. In fact, she became fairly popular.

Rob's problems weren't solved so easily. He'd developed an angry attitude that wasn't easy to penetrate. Tom tried to pal with him, but Rob had built a shell around himself and wasn't letting others in. However, one of the boys in his church group, one Ken Miller made a special effort to be friendly. He found out that Rob liked photography, a special interest and hobby of his. One morning, he brought in several photos that he'd taken and showed them around. He made sure that Rob saw them, then asked if he knew anything about photography. Rob responded reluctantly, but he showed interest. Ken invited him over to see his camera and his collection of photos he'd taken in the mountains. Rob went and was interested. Gradually, the friendship grew. Others became acquainted and Rob softened up. His anger diminished and his grades began to improve. Finally, because the secretary of Rob's age group in Church had a birthday and went into another group, Rob was made secretary in his place. He began to feel that he belonged somewhere and he started to enjoy things again.

Sarah and George were enjoying their new home and the semi rural environment gave the children room to do a lot of things their counterparts in town could not. They had horses. The older children had learned to ride at Oxbow Ranch, so they were able to continue riding when they had time. Sarah decided to have a garden, and was disappointed that it was autumn and would have to wait for spring, so she could begin to enjoy the delights of learning to garden and raise her own vegetables. As cooler weather came she enlisted the children in the work of preparing for winter. The trees shed their leaves and many of the flower beds were banked to protect the dormant plants from the coming freezing cold of winter. The farm was turning into a blessing as it gave the children things to do that were useful and kept the farm looking prosperous. George even promised to have a few acres plowed and planted to oats. That would provide feed for the horses and straw for their bedding.

Edith went back to Oxbow Ranch and Hackamore after her two youngsters had settled in. The children protested their mom's leaving, but she put them off by saying, "You kids need to stay here and go to school. I've got to make sure that your dad's getting along alright, too. I'll be back in three weeks and see that you're alright. In the mean time, you mind your Aunt Sarah and don't give her any trouble." They agreed reluctantly, but took it in stride. Sarah treated Rob and Mai Lin as near as she could to the way that she treated her own family. They had chores to do, they got the same privileges that the other kids did and got hugs and kind words wherever possible. Breaches of discipline were handled firmly, but with love as she did with the others. There were 'blow ups' occasionally, but, then she had the same problems with Tom, Susan and the others. They all got the same treatment, then, too. She was extremely careful to treat each one fairly in every case and to do so with love and affection. It worked.

One thing began to surface that Sarah hadn't expected. Mai Lin began regarding Tom as her hero. He could do no wrong in her eyes. He played freshman football and she loved the sport. She was after Sarah and George to let her go to every game that was played at home. George had to put his foot down on that one. He insisted that they all go together. Sarah agreed with him on that score. "We'll go as a family or we don't go." It was a little hard, sometimes to convince some of the other children to go so that Mai Lin could go. She occasionally stamped her foot when the family didn't want to attend a game. However, her generally good nature rescued her from serious consequences when she let her anger show.

Little did George and Sarah know where this hero worship would lead in later years. Tom paid little notice to this small, part Asian girl, three years his junior, until he had graduated from UC Davis as his dad had twenty four years earlier. Like his dad, he had a degree in farm and ranch management and applied for an assistant manager's position at an Oxbow Corporation ranch in Burns, Oregon. He got the job and after a year moved to the Oxbow Ranch as the Maintenance and Supply manager. His visits to his mom and dad brought him in contact with Mai Lin and he did notice her. Within weeks, they were engaged and after her graduation from the University of Colorado, the two were married and she went to work as the book keeper at Oxbow. Her Asian background mattered not to Tom, he'd fallen head over heels in love with her and that was enough for him. It pleased his mom and his Grammy immensely.

CHAPTER TWENTY-EIGHT
Top of the Mountain

George's tenure as Operations Manager at the Oxbow Corporation had been one of considerable success for the company. George put his experience and that of Fred Sowles and Marty Martin to good use. Working with these two associates on the ranches they were managing, he developed more efficient systems for raising beef cattle from the time they were calves until they were ready for the slaughter market. Harold Sears, as CEO of the company had a vision for cattle ranching and before his retirement, he'd added four more ranches to the Oxbow company inventory. George worked with each one and brought new systems and procedures into their operations, making them highly efficient and profitable. Mr. Sears retirement brought George into the upper management circle as the new CEO, a position George held for five years to the time of his own retirement. He explained his early retirement this way.

"I've reached the top of the heap in this business and I've contributed a great deal to making this company efficient for the time it was passing through. Now, it's time to pass it on to younger folks and let them struggle with the modern problems the company faces. For me? I'm looking for new worlds to conquer." With that, he turned his desk over to Fred Sowles who'd followed George's career in support roles ever since they'd started at Oxbow Ranch thirty one years earlier.

During the time that George had been Operations Manager and later CEO of the Oxbow Corporation, Sarah had gotten into activities that were women oriented. She worked with the young people of her Church, from tiny tots to teenagers. She was appointed president of her women's group several times, first in Canon City and then in Edgerton, Wyoming. The activity that inspired her the most happened when she was involved in groups that her own children belonged to. She got special warm feelings as she watched her young ones achieve and grow. God had made her for motherhood and she'd found her niche. Mostly, her children responded to her love and concerns although there were plenty of rough spots as the youngsters ran into the same problems she'd had to deal with when she was younger. Their advantage was that their dad was always there, right behind their mother. They never had to wonder if they could trust or depend on their parents. They were always supportive and pointed the way when the kids got confused.

Tommy followed in his father's footsteps in Boy Scouts. With his father's support, he rose all the way to his Eagle rank, obtaining it after they'd moved to Aurora. His father had made efforts of his own to promote scouting by arranging for the local scout organizations in Pueblo, Colorado and Casper, Wyoming to use Oxbow Corporation land for scout camporees. George was an Eagle Scout, himself and had never forgotten his own devotion to the Boy Scout programs.

Sarah's daughters weren't unusually pretty or talented in spectacular ways. Sarah was glad that they weren't. She taught them to do their best in anything they did and to be happy if they did their best. Occasionally, Pattie had trouble with being in the 'middle'. She felt that she was sometimes neglected. Sarah's wisdom and George's tender feelings saved a number of situations where tears were shed because Pattie felt inadequate. George got her started in 4H in Wyoming and Pattie's rabbits won prizes several times. She learned to excel in something all her own. Susan was a whiz with a sewing machine and won several prizes at county fairs when she displayed aprons and bonnets at each fair.

Elizabeth Anne, (Annie) was a loner. She lived in her own little world in many ways. More often than not, Sarah would find her in her room playing by herself, completely involved in her dolls or building block towers with her brother's alphabet blocks. She never complained of being left out of anything although she played games with the older ones when they asked her to. As she grew up, she followed the same line until it came to her marriage. In her marriage and as a mother she didn't hesitate, she was totally involved just as her mother had been with her.

Beginning with Tommy and all through the lives of the family, Sarah and George continually taught family, family, family. Each one was a member of the family. They were taught family loyalty and to look out for other family members when difficulties arose. Annie was, perhaps the fiercest defender of the family. When Joseph, (Little Joe) was picked on, Annie was a whirlwind of arms and feet in his defense. Because of her concerns for him, he was closer to her than to any other family member except his mother.

When it came to Mom, She was the 'Mother Goose' to all of the goslings, including Tommy. She had special feelings for each one and especially for Tom. He had turned her life in a different direction before he was even old enough to know about it. He just knew he could trust her and he told her so even before he could speak a word.

Sarah Elizabeth Toland looked back one day. She wondered how she'd come so far after being so low. As she reviewed all that had happened to her, since that fateful day in San Francisco, when she'd responded to the cries of a tiny baby and ignored the dangers that had just threatened her, she realized that God had wanted her for the job she'd done and she had done what she felt was right. Now, she had a husband that loved her unconditionally and five children that made her feel proud to be the mother she'd turned out to be. She'd enjoyed the loving friendship of other women who she associated with, Marney Sowles and Laura Thompson being the closest. She'd been instrumental in rescuing her own mother from a sordid and losing life and made it possible for the woman she loved to build a new life of her own. She was respected and loved by her husband's family and they'd been her mentors when she was discouraged and needed support. Life had been good for her.

***

George Toland had been involved in scouting on and off since he'd been old enough to join Cub Scouts. He'd gone on and earned each successive rank until he got his Eagle Badge. His interest in scouting had never gone away and his interest became active again when Tommy was old enough to join Cub Scouts. As time went on and his boys grew up, they participated and had been active in scouting when they had lived in Wyoming at Wind River Ranch. The local Scout Council had asked if troops could hold campouts on the ranch property if they didn't disturb the cattle. George had cleared the activity with corporate headquarters in San Francisco and some of the local camporees had become annual affairs there. When they'd moved back to Oxbow Ranch, the corporation had made a deal with the local scout council in Pueblo to hold their camporees on Oxbow property as well. These, too, were successful and became annual activities. George was often asked to speak at fund raisers and other executive events involving scouting.

Tom had gotten involved in scouting in Wyoming and had attained the rank of Life Scout by the time they moved back to Oxbow. George made special efforts to see that the boy had the opportunity to finish his work to become an Eagle Scout and he got it within the year after they had moved into their new home in Aurora, Colorado.

Upon retirement, George started looking around for challenges to tackle. He'd kept his older brother's heroic rescue and subsequent death in the back of his mind ever since it had happened and he'd dreamed of finding some way of honoring his brother's heroism. He found one.

The Oxbow Corporation had sold a ranch they'd owned in Montana shortly after George had become manager at Wind River Ranch in Wyoming. Unfortunately the new owners couldn't make a go of it either. It passed through several hands, but none of the successive owners could find ways to make it reasonably profitable. George began looking at the defunct cattle ranch through new eyes. "OK, so it won't raise cattle why won't it produce successful Boy Scouts?" He took a week to survey the ranch. It had nothing for cattle. Too much timber, too many rocky hills and not enough grass. But, it had a small lake, several streams, lots of timber and hills plus a central headquarters complex. Most of the facilities were run down and needed attention, but they were there and had potential. The more George looked, the more enthusiastic he became. Yes! It could raise Boy Scouts! Now, the trick was to find ways to purchase and develop it for that purpose. George went back to Aurora and started from there. First, he talked to the Regional Boy Scouts of America office in Denver. Would they be interested in using such a facility for scout purposes? The answer was a guarded "Yes." He talked to several adjacent regional offices. Same answer. George formed a non-profit corporation dedicated to purchasing and developing a regional Boy Scout Ranch. He then embarked on a campaign to get corporations interested in supporting the effort. He started with the Oxbow Corporation. It took several meetings and a field trip to convince Fred Sowles that it would work and that the corporation should support it. George went after companies in Colorado, Wyoming, Montana, Idaho and Oregon. Before he was done, he had pledges from twenty one companies to fund the effort. Time to go forward!

The cattle ranch was up for sale again and the non-profit Twenty One Corporation that George had formed moved in and bought it up. The price was favorable because it was a known loser as a cattle ranch. Once title to the property was gained, crews moved in and began converting the headquarters into an administrative complex where the activities of the Twenty One Ranch as it came to be called, could be coordinated with the needs of the various regional scout offices. A number of satellite scout camps were built and developed in various locations around the ranch. In that way scout councils could set up camporees for their councils and bring in several troops at a time for all kinds of scouting from basic scouting activities to merit badge work and adult leadership training schools. Much of the work was performed on a volunteer basis by the companies that did it. There was a special spirit that took hold as the facility neared completion. A special organization was formed with a membership of representatives from all the involved scout councils. This organization moved in to run the place.

It took two years to complete everything, but on a late June day, the gates were opened and the ranch was dedicated. At the dedication, a special plaque was placed in the entry hall of the administration building. It portrayed a relief of a Boy Scout in full uniform. Under the plaque were the words. "In Memory of Scout Russell H. Toland. Boy Scout Troop 431 His Heroism Will Always be Remembered. He Risked His Life For Another" George's dream was fulfilled and complete.

About the Author

Andrew Johnson was born on a sheep ranch west of Red Bluff California November 3, 1927, It was his mother's birthday! Andrew grew up there until he was fourteen years old. Tn 1942, his family moved to Yuba City where he finished high school in 1945. He entered college that fall in Marysvtlle, California, then joined the US Navy in December, 1945,

Andrew went to Bikini Atoll for the atomic bomb tests in the summer of 1946, went to China in 1947 and spent the rest of his time in the navy at San Diego, California. He was discharged from the navy in December of 1948 and went back to college. He graduated from Yuba College in the spring of 1949.

Andrew went to work for a crop duster in 1952 and became a licensed mechanic and pilot. In 1.955 he became a flight engineer for Trans World Airlines. While there, he traveled to many places in the world. He left the company and went to the Boeing Company as a flight engineer instructor. He traveled to many countries on assignment by Boeing. He retired from the company in 1981.

Andrew developed a strong love for literature early in life and has been widely read, having a special interest in science fiction, historical fiction and world and US history. He has small library which contains a broad variety of fiction and technical works. As a flight engineer instructor, he learned to write technical manuals and other technical documents. He has written for a technical magazine about aviation subjects. He has recently written a small number of fiction works, mostly set in the Western United States, none of which have yet been published. Top of the Mountain is his first attempt at entering the published author's world.

Printed in the United States
126531LV00001B/52-99/P